THE LONELY FURROW

The collapse of the City of Glasgow Bank brings disaster to the Drummond family. They lose their business and place in society. Nathan's dream of an engineering career is ended, along with the betrothal to his beloved Isobel. When an unexpected inheritance saves the day, the Drummonds must leave their comfortable Glasgow home for a run-down farm in Shropshire. Chrissie, the maid, proves a godsend during difficult times, despite her secret love for Nathan. Can the family keep the shame of their past hidden? Will Nathan manage the farm and recognize love for the girl who keeps his family together?

Books by Pamela Kavanagh
Published by The House of Ulverscroft:

ACROSS THE SANDS OF TIME

PAMELA KAVANAGH

THE LONELY FURROW

Complete and Unabridged

ULVERSCROFT
Leicester

First published in Great Britain in 2012 by
Robert Hale Limited
London

First Large Print Edition
published 2013
by arrangement with
Robert Hale Limited
London

A catalogue record for this book is available
from the British Library.

ISBN 978–1–4448–1535–1

Published by
F. A. Thorpe (Publishing)
Anstey, Leicestershire

Set by Words & Graphics Ltd.
Anstey, Leicestershire
Printed and bound in Great Britain by
T. J. International Ltd., Padstow, Cornwall

1

Nathan Drummond strode down the drive of the big square house on Langsdale Avenue, silver-topped cane swinging jauntily in the autumn sunshine. A broad-shouldered, fresh-faced young man, impeccably dressed in snowy linen and a suit of best grey worsted, the sun glinted on the burnished brown curls showing beneath his tall top hat.

A smile played around his features. Tonight he would be reunited with Isobel, his fiancée, who was due back from a short stay in the country. Next year he would enter Glasgow University to read for his degree in engineering, thence to embark on a career in Glasgow's booming shipping industry. In time, there would be a home of his own, his beloved Isobel at his side. Life was good.

For the present — Nathan quirked his lips wryly — he was undertaking what his father called 'a good grounding for life' in the family business.

He cut through the leafy avenues of Queen's Park towards town. He quickened his pace, bound for the Drummond Grocery Store on Argyle Street, the first of the three shops Balfour Drummond, his father, had founded some thirty years earlier.

As he neared the store, the cry of a street corner newsboy rose above the familiar din of the bustling Glasgow streets.

'City bank collapse! Read all about it!'

The smile fled Nathan's face. His father had substantial investments there. He hurried to buy a paper. The headlines glared up at him. *Collapse Of City Of Glasgow Bank. Ruin For Many*. Nathan held on to his hat and ran, dodging people and traffic, arriving dishevelled and breathless at the shop.

The doorbell jangled loudly as he barged in, causing customers to turn and stare. It was busy despite the early hour, but Nathan barely noticed. Behind the counter, an assistant was weighing sugar.

'My father! Where is he?'

'He'll be up in the office, Master Nathan.'

Nathan took the wooden stairs at the back of the shop two at a time and entered Balfour Drummond's office at a run. His father was standing motionless by the window, his shrewd blue eyes seemingly taking in the swarming street below.

'Father, have you heard the news?' Nathan cried.

Balfour turned. He was a heavily built man

with a square, craggy face and bushy red beard and hair.

'Yes, I've heard. Calm yourself, Nathan, and close the door. Do you want the entire shop to hear you?'

The slight tremor of Balfour's hand as he took the newspaper Nathan thrust at him betrayed his feelings. Returning to his desk, he sat down to read the report. Pausing a moment, he briefly drew his hand over the embossed leather cover of the family Bible, in its place beside the blotter, as if drawing sustenance from what lay within.

Nathan knew a flash of irritation. It would take more than the good book to help them now.

'It's bad, isn't it?' he said.

'Yes, Nathan. I'm afraid it is.'

Nathan's face twisted.

'It was Macnair who got you into this. Without his persuasion you wouldn't have made those investments.'

'Macnair wasn't to know. He'll be up to his neck in it, as well, I warrant. And we'll not be the only ones.' Balfour sighed.

'Father, what now?' Nathan said, swallowing.

Balfour reached out and rested his hand on his Bible.

'We pray, Nathan. Whatever it takes, we

will meet our responsibilities and God willing, we will come through. But we will have to sell all we own.'

The words fell like doom on Nathan's ears. He stared at the dust motes dancing in a golden shaft of sunlight through the tall sash window, and wondered how it was that the sun could shine with such brightness when all else was so black.

★ ★ ★

The pink blooms of the late Juranville roses tapped against the nursery window. Aileen Drummond, a crisp white pinafore over her day gown of flocked muslin, manoeuvred her way past the wooden crates of crockery and pots and pans that were lined up against the walls. She took a pillowcase from the pile of linen on the scuffed old table and inspected it.

Following his sister into the room, Nathan watched her rapid progress through her tasks. At seventeen she was slender and quick, with their father's keen blue gaze and, to her chagrin, his hasty temper.

'What God has to do with it I shall never understand,' Nathan grumbled. 'It's Father's decision to sell and move out. Everything's always Father's decision. Why

4

can't we have a say for a change?'

'Because Father's like that. He's always been the same and he's not likely to change now,' Aileen replied.

As a devout member of the Free Church, their father's principles were unfailingly rigid. She could find it in her to admire him for his faith, but Nathan was not of the same mind. She pushed back an errant strand of tawny hair.

'Nathan, you must be patient with Father. He's a good man. He loves us. He's always tried to do his best by us.'

'Like selling the shops and the house from under our feet? Is that God's will, too?'

'It's what Father thinks is right. Imagine what it must be like for him. How would you feel to be losing everything you'd worked for?'

'That's exactly how I do feel,' he complained. 'The university — how shall I get there now? I know it's selfish but my engineering degree means a lot to me. But I'll get there somehow.'

'Oh, listen to you!' Aileen cried, her control breaking. 'How can you be so blind? You never were intended to go to the university. You're the eldest son, for goodness' sake! Father always meant you to take over the business. What do you think you've been doing these past months?'

'What?' Nathan stared at her, perplexed. 'But . . . Father promised.'

'I doubt it. Dear Father. He'll have fobbed you off with words to that effect. He'd never deliberately have made a promise he knew he would not keep.'

'You mean . . . it's all been in vain? All my hopes . . . ?' Nathan's face hardened. 'What a fool I've been!'

'Not really. Father can be very convincing when it suits. Funny, isn't it? I'd have loved to have learned the trade and here I've been, stuck at home with Mama, waiting for the right suitor to come along. Don't suppose he ever will now!'

'It's just as bad for you, isn't it? I was thinking only of myself. I'm sorry, Aileen.'

'No matter. What of Isobel? Have you seen her yet?'

'No. I was going to the house on the day the news broke, but her father extended her stay in the country and the evening was cancelled. Understandable, considering.'

'Yes. Mr Macnair had investments, too, I believe. I wonder how they have fared.'

'Better than us, I hope. I shall know tomorrow. Isobel is back, so I'm going to see her in the morning.'

He smiled, his spirits lifting.

Aileen returned her brother's smile affectionately and turned back to her task.

'Oh, well, I'd better get on with this.'

'What are you doing?' Nathan asked.

'Sorting out the linen. The auctioneer's men are due next week. Mama doesn't want people picking over our mended sheets and tablecloths. Things are hard enough without that indignity.'

Shaking his head hopelessly, Nathan left the room. As he descended the long, curved staircase, he heard his mother's voice issue from the study.

'I've done as you asked, Balfour, and sorted out the household goods for the auctioneer's men. Obviously, I need to hold some items back for our own use, but it's difficult to know what when I have no idea where we are going — if anywhere!'

The sharp ring to his mother's tone was not lost on Nathan. Balfour's response, when it came, was predictable.

'God will provide, Florence, my love. Or, rather, God has provided. Do you recall our first home?'

'Of course I do. That little terraced cottage we rented on North Street, near the shop — what of it?'

'It's vacant. I've seen the agent and I collect the keys in the morning.'

7

'Balfour!' Florence sounded scandalised. 'We're never going back there. It's so near to the station. Think of the noise — and the smuts from the trains!'

'We were happy there, weren't we? Take heart, Florence. All may seem lost, but it isn't, not while I have my health and strength. I've pulled myself up once and will do so again — with God's good grace.'

Nathan hurried on down the stairs, arriving in the hallway as Chrissie Ross, the little Highland maid, came bustling across with an armful of flowers from the garden. He cannoned into her, stifling an oath as the blooms went scattering in all directions.

'Clumsy of me! Here, let me help.'

'Thank you, Master Nathan. I ken I shouldnae be bothering wi' them, things being as they are. But I minded how fond the mistress is of her garden and I thought a bowl of roses might cheer her up.'

'Quite right. Splendid idea.'

A stray bloom lay unnoticed under the polished mahogany table. Nathan rescued it, presenting it with a small bow.

'For you, Chrissie!'

'Why, thank you, sir.'

Quick to enter into the spirit of things, she dipped him a blushing curtsey before continuing on her way.

Not for the first time it struck Nathan how fetching she was, with her soft light-brown hair and expressive green eyes. He continued to the coach-house, where a slipping brake on the brougham destined for the coming auction awaited his attention.

* * *

Sunday stillness lay over the streets as Nathan made his way to the Macnair house at Kelvingrove. Arriving at the house, a mature residence of generous proportions, Nathan's summons was answered promptly. The familiar manservant took his hat and cane in a manner polite, yet puzzlingly distant. In the hall, the housekeeper was equally offhand, sending him a nod and sweeping on her way.

The gleaming surfaces and fierce order suggested all was well in the Macnair household. Nathan's sense of unease deepened. He was shown into the drawing-room, a sombre chamber with a view of the square.

'I'll tell Miss Isobel you are here, sir,' the manservant intoned, as if to a stranger.

Nathan moved to the window, wondering about his odd reception. The sound of the door opening made his heart leap.

'Isobel! At last! How good to see you again!'

'Nathan. How are you?'

Isobel Macnair's appearance portrayed the gently reared delicacy of her background.

'Forgive me,' Isobel began, seating herself on one of the room's crimson sofas, 'but it quite slipped my mind you were coming. I am going out with Mama and Papa so I mustn't be long.'

'I see,' Nathan said, though he didn't at all. Certain aspects, however, were becoming clearer and he framed his words with care.

'Isobel, you will have heard about the financial crisis in the city?'

'Indeed, yes. Fortunately Papa had sold his investments before it happened.'

'Oh?' Nathan looked at her sharply. 'Mr Macnair had warning of the collapse? Why did he not say something to my father?'

'Really, Nathan, I cannot comment. Being absent all these weeks, I am not wholly conversant with the situation.'

'Nevertheless, we must discuss it,' Nathan insisted. 'You do realise we are ruined? The shops, our home — all has to go.'

The violet eyes widened.

'So what will you do?'

'Father plans to rent somewhere for us to live and start afresh. He believes what has been achieved once can be done again.'

Isobel gave her head a tiny shake of

disbelief and slid a covert glance towards the door, as if anxious to be gone.

Dismay caught at Nathan's throat. Her attitude was so unfeeling, so . . . cold.

'Sweetheart, hear me out,' he blundered on, moving to sit beside her. He took her cool hands in his over-warm ones. 'I have a plan. There's a fellow I know in New York who is doing splendidly. He says there is always an opening there for an enterprising young man.'

'New York? Dear me. Such a distance. And so overcrowded, by all account.'

'Ah, but I don't intend to stay in the city long. Isobel, the separation will be hard but I swear it will be worth it in the end . . . '

Nathan realised with dismay that she had withdrawn her hands from his.

'Maybe . . . maybe I'm assuming too much.' He heard his voice as though from a long way off. 'It could be years. Perhaps I am wrong to expect you to wait for me . . .

'Isobel, would you rather I released you from our engagement?'

And from realms that were equally distant, he heard her answer.

'Indeed, that might be best. I am sorry.' Taking his ring from her finger, Isobel handed it back to him and rose to her feet.

'I think I heard the carriage. Goodbye, Nathan. Jennings will show you out.'

She left the room, closing the door softly behind her.

Nathan could only stand and stare at the space where Isobel had been. How had it come to this? His Isobel, so chilly and distant!

Even as he stood there, bewildered and uncomprehending, a tiny spark of pride and ambition flamed within him. He'd show her! He'd show the lot of them! He would book his passage to America right away.

Dropping the gleaming diamond ring into his waistcoat pocket, Nathan headed for the door. He did not wait to be shown out.

★   ★   ★

'Ah, there you are, my dear. I was about to ring for you.'

Balfour stood in the doorway of his upstairs study, watching as Florence ascended the staircase with a letter in her hands.

He still admired the way her tall figure, though thickened with childbearing, had retained the upright carriage and vigour of the young girl who had stolen his heart.

'Did you hear the postboy?' She waved the envelope, her grey eyes alight. 'He's brought a letter from Africa. It's been so long since we heard from Davina, I was beginning to worry.'

The Drummonds' eldest daughter had accompanied her missionary husband to Barotse. Two daughters had been born to the couple since they had been in Africa.

Florence agonised about her infant granddaughters being raised in so harsh an environment, but Davina had her father's single-mindedness when it came to matters that were dear to her. And, admittedly, Finbar Lennox, for all he had whisked her daughter away, could not be faulted as a husband.

'Word from Davina, you say? That's good news for a change.' Balfour's ravaged face broke into a semblance of a smile. All his children were dear to him and none more so than his firstborn.

'Come into the study and let me read what she says. Are they all well?'

'Apparently so. Davina complains about the heat. And the flies. Annabel grows apace and baby Catherine has cut her front teeth. Oh, Balfour, how I would love to see them.'

'I know, my love.' Balfour skimmed the closely written sheets. 'Davina mentions a growing congregation at the church. That's good to hear. No mention of our predicament.'

'Not a word. My letter could not have reached her yet. Well, when you consider how far Africa is, it's a miracle the post reaches her at all.'

'The good Lord looks after his own,' Balfour murmured.

Florence's lips tightened. The good Lord had apparently been occupied elsewhere during the past weeks, since she had seen little divine help in their quarter.

Balfour folded the letter and handed it back to his wife.

'Come over to the desk, my dear. There's something I need you to sign.'

She blinked in astonishment.

'What is it, Balfour?'

'It's for the sale of the Shropshire property you inherited some time ago: Glebe Farm. Come, Florence. You cannot have forgotten.'

No, she had not forgotten. Her chin lifting, Florence met the sharp blue gaze squarely. As a rule, she was compliant, the loyal wife. But enough was enough.

A memory of her childhood home, the Shropshire village set in green fields and spreading woodland, came to her so vividly that she caught her breath . . . Hadnall. The Glebe. Her eyes suddenly stung.

'No.'

'I beg your pardon?' Balfour frowned. 'You disobey me, Florence?'

'On this occasion, yes, I do.' The steady

14

grey eyes took on a steely glint. 'My uncle Reeve could have bequeathed the farm to my sister. He'd have been justified, with Dorcas being the elder. But he didn't. He left it to me in trust because he knew it was dearer to me.'

Balfour's frown deepened. He made no secret of the fact that he considered Florence's sister everything a woman should not be. Sharp-tongued and fiercely independent, on the few occasions they had met she had scared him witless.

Florence waited, bracing herself.

'Dorcas!' Balfour spluttered. 'What would a spinster like your sister do with a farm? What would you do with it, come to that?'

'I'd live in it!' she declared. 'Farm the land, rear the stock, make the butter and cheese for which the Glebe is famous.'

Balfour sat down in his chair with a thump.

'Lord save us, woman! Have you taken leave of your senses?'

'On the contrary, Balfour. I think I've just retrieved them!'

Florence pulled up a high-backed chair, sat down beside her husband and did her best to temper her tone.

'My love, consider. We were unable to decide what to do about the farm before. Now it offers us our chance to start again. I know how dreadful this has all been for you.

I've done my utmost to support you. But it hasn't been easy for me, either. People I looked upon as our friends, customers of long standing . . . they can barely find it in them to pass the time of day any more.'

'Huh, take no heed. It'll pass.'

'You've no idea what it's like. The gossip, the snide glances, as if somehow we brought this misfortune on ourselves. Even Jamie has suffered. He's being bullied at school. Six years old, and goodness knows what insults he has to endure.

'I didn't want to worry you before, but the time has come for some straight talking. If we move to Hadnall we leave all this behind.'

'But you're asking me to run away.'

'No! To start afresh.'

'I'm a grocer, Florence, not a farmer.' Balfour sagged in his seat, looking suddenly weary. 'What you say is madness.'

'It's as sane as can be. I'll not be swayed.'

She placed a hand on his arm. The move was gentle, but the look in her eye brooked no argument.

At fifty-five Balfour could not be expected to establish a business single-handed the way he had at twenty-five. She looked at the dark smudges under his eyes and the deep furrows on his brow and knew a stab of dread that she might lose him.

16

'Balfour, please. What about Nathan? He means what he says about New York.'

'I know. I've had a serious talk with him. Tried to dissuade him. He wouldn't listen.

'Florence, he's thinking of us, too. We'll be crowded in that house on North Street. As he said, it would be one less mouth to feed. To think I've come to this. Unable to support my own family.'

'Now you're getting maudlin.'

'Well, what d'you expect? I started up before Thomas Lipton and look at him — shops all over the place. I didn't want that. You can get too big. I was happy to do my trading here, in the town where I was born.'

'Even with Lipton's opening up in competition?'

'Thomas Lipton wasn't fool enough to put his money where he shouldn't.'

'Well, anyway,' Florence said, getting back on track, 'Nathan isn't going to America and that's final. It's bad enough having Davina overseas without our boy doing the same.'

'You think to make a farmer out of him? You haven't a hope, woman!'

'I think you're wrong. Farming has been in my family for generations, remember. Oh, I grant you, Papa wouldn't have left the manor for anything. But my uncle Reeve took over Glebe Farm as a very young man and a great

17

success he made of it.'

'So what has this to do with Nathan?'

'I see a lot of the Webbs in him. Think how good he is with a horse. He handles them as if born to it. Remember that school friend of his? The farmer's son, Donald Blaine? Nathan spent a lot of time helping with the harvests.'

'But he was only a boy, whiling away the summer months.'

'And the winter ones. He was up there for the lambing that time Farmer Blaine broke his leg. They couldn't speak too highly of him.'

Florence narrowed her eyes.

'Did Nathan tell you why he was going to America?'

'He said something about a friend in New York.'

'That's right. This friend's brother has staked a plot of land out at Wisconsin and Nathan has a fancy to do the same. Wisconsin! There's land in Shropshire, three hundred good acres of it, and a farmhouse big enough for us all to live in.

'You can forget North Street, Balfour, because we're not going there.'

Florence stood up, her chair scraping on the uncarpeted floor.

'I shall go and tell Nathan what I have in

mind. He won't let us down. The house will have stood empty since my uncle died and goodness knows what state the land will be in. Nathan can go on ahead and see what needs to be done. I'll take those papers for safe keeping, shall I?' Scooping the papers to her, Florence went to the door and opened it. She turned.

'We're going to Shropshire, Balfour, and that's my last word!'

* * *

'Don't want to go!' Jamie protested as Chrissie hustled him along the road. 'Why must I?'

'You ken why, Master Jamie. You have to learn your lessons. You wouldnae want to end up like me, would you? At a loss to sort out the post because I cannae read the envelopes? They look to me as if a spider's run over them wi' inky feet!'

'The other boys say Father's going to prison, Chrissie. It's not true, is it?'

'Tsk! Of course it isn't, laddie. That's a wicked lie, and if I could get my hands on those boys they'd be sorry! Your father's done the noble thing and is selling all he owns to pay . . . och, but you're too young for that.'

'I know we're moving away. I don't want to

leave you, Chrissie. Who'll look after me?'

They had stopped to cross the road. Chrissie did not answer immediately. They had barely gained the opposite pavement when a brewer's dray thundered by with a clamour of iron-shod hoofs and rattle of wheels. The driver cracked his whip in their direction, hollering abuse.

Jamie blanched.

'That's Archie Muir. His missus gets flour and stuff from our shop — I mean, she did. He never used to shout like that. Chrissie, will it be the same when we get to the farm?'

'Farm? What farm?'

'Mama told me last night. She said we're going to live on a farm where she comes from in England. There'll be pigs and cows and a dog. I'd like a dog. Nathan's gone to get it ready for us.'

Taken aback, Chrissie barely heard what Jamie was saying.

'Will I get bullied at my new school?' he prattled on.

'No, no! The very idea! You'll be a farmer's laddie, and the other children will look up to you. I grew up on a croft myself. It's a guid life, Master Jamie . . .'

Chrissie felt choked. She'd had to seek work in the city after her granny died. When she had first come to Glasgow she had missed the space and the great silences of her Highland home.

But life at the Drummond house had been busy and fulfilling — and there was Master Nathan. She'd kept the rose he had given her. Its pink petals lay preserved between the pages of the prayer book the master issued to all his staff, whether they could read or not.

Chrissie had never owned a book before. It had been her greatest treasure and had now taken on a deeper significance.

Glancing down, Chrissie saw Jamie brush away a tear and her heart welled with love and compassion for him.

'Dinna greet,' she murmured, squeezing his hand. 'Here we are. Go in like a good boy, and when you come out later Chrissie'll have a treat for you. What'll it be? A twist of barley sugar off the market?'

His small face brightened.

'You will be here?'

'I promise,' Chrissie said.

She stood in full view of the playing children until the school bell clanged for them to get into line. None of those imps would dare lay a hand on Master Jamie with her around!

* * *

Heading back for the house on Queen's Park, Chrissie's mind churned. Cook had said that after the sale of the house and effects they were all to be given a week's wages and a reference. Where would she go?

The Drummonds had been good to her. She had come to regard them almost as a second family.

Again, she tried to picture the master in a country setting and failed. Miss Aileen, now, had something of her mama about her and might knuckle down to it. And Master Jamie would relish the life once he was settled. As for Master Nathan . . .

Thinking about it, he was probably the type who could turn a hand to most things if the spirit so moved him. But he had a lot to learn. Who would show him?

The answer was obvious. Chrissie took to her heels and ran, dodging the hurrying throngs, darting across the road, bonnet strings flying.

Reaching the house, Chrissie heard voices in the dining-room. She stormed straight in without knocking.

At the big oval table Florence and Aileen were poring over lists. They looked up in astonishment at the intrusion. Bonnet askew and hair all over the place, Chrissie looked like a wild woman.

'Chrissie? What's amiss? Is it Master Jamie — ?'

'The laddie's fine.' Chrissie gasped. 'Mistress, is it true you're taking on a farm in England?'

'Yes, quite true, Chrissie,' Florence said. 'Rest assured, I shall make sure you are well placed.'

Pink-cheeked and indignant, Chrissie faced her mistress.

'But I'd go with you to the farm! What do you ken about farming, mistress? Or you, Miss Aileen? The master won't know. It'll be up to Master Nathan, and who's going to tell him when to plough and what grains to sow? Well, I can.

'I know about kine and sheep and fowl. I know how to make butter and cheese, and I can spin and weave, too. And there's Master Jamie. Who's to look after him?'

'Chrissie,' Florence said mildly. 'Are you saying you'd prefer to come with us?'

'I am, mistress. You won't regret it.'

'You know we cannot pay you wages?'

'Och, no matter!' Chrissie said airily. 'Time I knew how to read and write a bit. Master Jamie can show me. That'll be wages enough for me to be going on wi'.'

Mother and daughter exchanged a glance. Their lips twitched. It seemed Chrissie's mind was set, and who were they to argue?

Nathan clambered aboard the cart and flapped the reins at the horse. Aged but willing, the animal ambled out of the farmyard, the wheels of the rickety vehicle grating over the weed-covered cobblestones.

He recalled his own arrival at the farm a month ago. He had found the house shuttered and silent, the rooms laced with dust and ancient cobwebs, the walls patched with damp. A quick foray into the dairy and outbuildings had revealed the same depressing state of affairs.

The stable had been thick with dried dung. Over the manger was a name — *Captain*. Nathan had come across the old grey horse in the tangled orchard and found it a friendly beast.

Rolling up his sleeves, Nathan had fetched fork and barrow from the barn and set to, not stopping until the stable was thoroughly cleared out. In the loft above he had found hay and a small sack of oats — surprisingly fresh — as well as some bales of leftover straw. After forking down a good thick bed of the latter, he had brought the horse in and given him the best feed he had probably had in months.

A little stray cat had come yowling round

Nathan's feet. Collecting some wood from an old store, Nathan had chivvied the kitchen range into life. He shared with Puss his first meal at Glebe Farm, a supper of cold fat bacon and potatoes provided by Cook when he had set off that same morning.

Refreshed, he had sketched out a plan for restoring some sort of order to the chaos. With his mother's insistence on cleanliness in mind, Nathan had begun with the house.

On his first morning, he had walked the two miles to Hadnall village, where he invested some of the meagre allocation of money from his father in a besom, some lye soap, whitewash, tar, brushes and candles.

He had singled out the raftered and flag-floored kitchen and four bedchambers for attention and closed his mind to the rest. What furniture was moveable he had dragged out into the yard, and taking up the besom, he began to sweep. Never before had Nathan worked so hard. Each night when he lay down to sleep — wrapped in his overcoat on the kitchen floor by the range — his bones ached from sheer exhaustion.

Now, driving along the pot-holed road that wound through tall beech trees, Nathan had the satisfaction of knowing that the main rooms of the house were presentable: floors scrubbed, walls whitened, beams tarred against the worm — though whether they would meet his mother's exacting standards remained to be seen.

Although it had been Florence's idea to come, Nathan worried for her. She'd be leaving behind the two small graves he knew she tended. How would she feel, coming away from the infant brother and sister who had never drawn breath? He berated himself for the thought. His mother was a strong woman, and she knew where her priorities lay.

Reaching the small country station, Nathan secured Captain to the iron tethering ring in the wall and went on to the platform to wait for the train.

It had been a fine September day, with lavender skies and the tang of autumn in the air. Evening was now approaching and a faint mist rose over the surrounding fields and woods.

The signal changed and soon the train came chugging into the station. Nathan spotted Jamie hanging out of a carriage window, waving his hand and hollering in excitement.

'Nathan! It's us! We're here! Guess who's come with us!'

The train screeched to a stop. Nathan stepped forward to open the door and Jamie, still talking nineteen to the dozen, came rocketing out.

'Chrissie's here! She lived on a croft so she knows about farms. It's taken ages to get here. Is there a dog?'

'Not yet.' Nathan ruffled his small brother's wild red mop affectionately. 'Well, then, laddie. How've you been?'

'All right. Father isn't, though. He's grumpy.'

Chrissie Ross and Aileen were helping Balfour down on to the platform. Nathan was shocked to see the change in him. The trials of the past weeks had told sorely on the once proud merchant. Balfour Drummond looked an old man, his face pinched, his figure somehow shrunken.

'Father, welcome to Hadnall. Hello, Aileen. Are you well?'

'Not bad. What about you? You look thinner.'

'It's a few guid square meals he needs, isn't it, Master Nathan?' Chrissie said, chirpy as ever.

Nathan greeted her and turned his attention to Florence, struggling to alight with an armful of packages.

'Mama! Here, let me take those.'

As Nathan bent to kiss his mother he was relieved to see that she had come through the storm better than her husband. Her smile was wide, if a little strained about the eyes, as she looked about her and breathed in the clean air.

'Hadnall! I never thought to see it again. If I were blindfold I'd know where I was. That woodsmoke smell of autumn — it could only be here.'

'Gets nippy at night, just like back home.'

'I remember. It's a fair step to Glebe Farm, I recall, and your father . . .'

'Never fear, Mama. There's a conveyance waiting. Um . . . it isn't what you're used to.'

Florence made no comment as she was handed on to the decrepit farm cart, over which Nathan had spread sacking as a token gesture of comfort.

Silence fell amongst the tired company as the cart swayed slowly along the deep-rutted lane. Jamie stared wide-eyed about him, taking in the sights and sounds of his new surroundings. En route they passed neighbouring Twelve Trees Farm, which was owned by successful landowner Stanton Hayles.

'The household baggage arrived yesterday,' Nathan said. 'There didn't seem much.'

'There isn't,' his mother replied dryly. 'I hope the house is adequately furnished.'

'It is. I've done what I can, but there's still need for improvement.'

'Dinna fret, Master Nathan. That's what

28

I'm here for,' Chrissie called from behind.

Thinking she would have her work cut out, Nathan threw her a wry glance over his shoulder. Between Chrissie and Aileen, his father sat subdued and morose.

'Father seems not himself,' he said in a low voice to Florence.

'No. This trouble has hit him badly. And there is the move. It will all be very different for him. We must be patient.' Florence broke off as the cart lurched over a particularly deep rut.

'Dear me,' she gasped, clutching the side rail. 'At this rate 'twill be a miracle if we arrive all in one piece. Your letters seemed guarded, Nathan. Was everywhere in a very bad state?'

'You could say that . . . ah, here we are.'

The old farmhouse came into sight, low and rambling, with many deep-set windows, tall chimneys and steeply sloping roofs of dark, weathered slate. It was not until they drew up in the main yard that the sense of neglect became obvious.

Doors to barns and byre were rotted and peeling, and hung crazily on rusted hinges. Weeds flourished between the sunken cobbles of the yard and the central pump, once a feature with gabled roof and bucket, lay overturned and unusable.

Florence, who had nurtured an image of Glebe Farm as it had once been, gasped in dismay. Before them, the house in the gathering gloom looked dark and dreary. She stared aghast, her stoic mask slipping.

'What a dear little cat,' Aileen cried, spotting Puss by the back step. 'I like tabbies.'

'Wish there was a dog,' Jamie muttered. 'When can we get one?'

'All in good time, laddie,' Nathan said, jumping down. He shot a glad glance at one of the chimneys, where a plume of smoke huffed healthily. 'Range is lit. I'll see to the horse.

'Go inside, all of you, and get warm. There's water in the kettle. You'll want to wash. I'll get more from the pump in the stackyard, this one's out of action. Oh, there's eggs and some rashers for a meal.'

'I don't think . . . ' Florence began shakily.

Chrissie stepped in.

'Come along, mistress. You can leave all this to me. Jamie, help your brother with the horse. I've a tin of tea in my basket. Let's get that kettle boiling. We'll all feel better for a cup.'

Nathan came in to find his family seated in the odd assortment of wooden chairs around the range which someone — Chrissie, probably — had stoked to a fine blaze. She

30

had donned a large apron and was pouring tea — hot, sweet and strong.

'Look what you've brought us to, woman!' Balfour had evidently found his tongue. He threw a sweeping gesture around the kitchen which, despite Nathan's best efforts, still showed the neglect of years.

The big deal table was thick with accumulated grease and grime, as was the dresser that stretched the whole length of one wall. Splodges of damp around the uncurtained windows were already showing through the thin screed of whitewash. It was a far cry from the elegant house they had left.

'You can't blame me for this, Florence. It's your doing and yours alone. What a ramshackle hole! The Lord only knows what's through there. Larder, is it? Rat-ridden, I shouldn't wonder. I'd best go and look.'

'Your tea's here, master. Why not have it first?' Chrissie said, but Balfour waved her aside and stalked through to the range of lobbies and stores beyond the kitchen.

There was a moment of heavy silence, then a loud crash as the irate man collapsed in a heap on the cold stone floor.

2

'Balfour! He's collapsed! Balfour, dearest, speak to me!'

Florence crouched beside her husband's inert form, her eyes anguished. Sinking down next to her mistress on the cold stone flags of the floor, Chrissie sought Balfour's pulse.

'There's a beat! The master's still with us! Quick, Master Nathan, ride for the doctor! Miss Aileen, find some blankets — he's like ice. Master Jamie, d'ye ken the hencote in the orchard? You should find some feathers there. Bring me a handful. Scoot!'

Jamie went.

Nathan went for the horse and was soon heard galloping down the lane. Jamie came panting back into the house bearing a handful of grimy feathers, which he presented jubilantly to Chrissie.

'Got some! There's mice in there, Chrissie. Is Father dead?'

'Tch! Of course he isn't!' Chrissie took the feathers and turned to Florence. 'There, mistress. I'll away and singe these.'

Aileen returned with her finds. Tenderly she and Florence tucked two heavy woollen

32

blankets around Balfour and slipped a bolster under his head.

Chrissie lifted the smouldering feathers. The acrid stench brought a gasp from Balfour's throat.

'Thank God!' Florence sobbed. 'Balfour, it's all right. Nathan's fetching the doctor. Pray he'll soon be here.'

'Amen to that,' Aileen murmured. Here in the lobby the air was bitter. 'Father must be frozen, Mama. Should we try to move him by the fire?'

'Not yet, Miss Aileen,' Chrissie said. 'Wait for the doctor. I nursed my granny through something like this. I was told then that moving a patient could possibly bring on another attack.'

The maid's practical attitude brought Florence to her senses. She got to her feet.

'There's brandy in the trunk,' she said. 'I'll fetch it. We could try Balfour with a drop.'

Dark had fallen. Chrissie bustled about, lighting a lamp, putting a flame to the tallow candles on the mantelpiece, adding more fuel to the fire. She brewed tea and stood over her mistress while she drank it, hot and sweet and laced with brandy. She was relieved to see a little colour returning to Florence's cheeks.

Jamie appeared before her, his eyes big and round in his small face.

'I'm hungry, Chrissie. I want my supper.'

'Wheesht now, Master Jamie,' Chrissie said. 'Be a big boy and look in my basket. There's bread and cheese in a cloth.'

Cutting the bread Jamie brought, she speared a slice with the toasting fork that hung by the hearth.

'There now. Hold this to the flame and mind you dinna burn your fingers. I'll do some more, then you can make me some, as well.'

Jamie fell to the task willingly, while the others slid their eyes towards the window and prayed for help to arrive.

It seemed an age before the welcome beat of hoofs and rattle of wheels announced the approach of the doctor's cart. Nathan, following on his weary, lathered horse, slid stiffly to the ground.

He found Chrissie at his elbow, taking the horse, telling him to get away inside. Grateful, he pushed open the door and gestured the doctor into the house.

Dr William Merrick, middle-aged and portly, immediately inspired trust. After examining the patient, he turned to Florence, his expression grave.

'Your husband has suffered a seizure, ma'am. The next twenty-four hours will be crucial. Some patients recover reasonably well. Others do not — and there is always the possibility of a further attack.'

Florence let out a sob, her hands flying to her face.

'This is all my fault. I insisted on coming here. I should never have done it.'

'Oh, come now, ma'am.' The doctor was kindly. 'Let's have none of this. We must concentrate on making Mr Drummond comfortable. He would be better down here; it makes for easier nursing. Is there a room that could be made over to his use?'

'There's the small front parlour,' Nathan said. 'We'll need to get the bed down from upstairs.'

'I'll help you,' Aileen said.

'And I shall light a fire in the grate,' Chrissie said, having just appeared from the stable. 'The wee room at the end of the passageway?'

'That's the one,' Nathan said. 'I had thought Mama might like to sit in there . . . '

His voice tailed away, his eyes going to the helpless form of his father on the floor.

'And so she will,' Chrissie said robustly, heading off.

Jamie, his face scarlet from the heat of the fire, pushed a platter of very well-done toast before her.

'I've done it, Chrissie. I toasted it all. Try

some. You don't have to eat the burnt bits.'

Finding him a smile, Chrissie accepted a blackened offering and went to prepare the sickroom for her master.

* * *

The following days were fraught. Undertaking, for the first time, tasks that used to be done by servants at her Glasgow home, Aileen was not finding things easy.

'We would never have managed without Chrissie,' she said to Nathan one morning as they breakfasted in the kitchen. 'She's a wonderful nurse. She knows instinctively what Father wants.'

Nathan attacked his dish of fat bacon and fried potatoes with relish. That morning he had been out at daybreak, tarring the rafters in the barn, and hunger gnawed at him.

'She certainly knows how to put a decent meal on the table,' he said, reaching for a wedge of bread to mop up his plate.

'If it is the breakfast you are referring to, brother dear, you have me to thank,' Aileen said.

'Goodness me! I didn't know you knew how.'

'It isn't too difficult. Chrissie showed me.'

'I should have guessed! She was asking

earlier about getting some kine for the house. It seems we use a lot of milk and it has to be bought in.'

Aileen pushed aside her plate with a sigh.

'We're floundering here, aren't we, Nathan? What are we going to do?'

'I don't know. Take things a step at a time, for now.'

Aileen glanced around.

'No Jamie. I wonder where he is?'

'I saw him set off to Twelve Trees for the milk.'

'Is that the farm I can see from my window?'

'That's it. Stanton Hayles is the owner — a staunch chapel man, I'm told.'

'He should get on with Father, then!' Aileen bit her lip. 'I mean . . . once Father recovers.'

'I understand.' Nathan smiled warmly.

'I'd better stir myself. I need to visit the smith. The horse has cast a shoe.'

'More expense! Our funds cannot last indefinitely, Nathan. How shall we manage then?'

'Sell something, I suppose. Until the farm is back on its feet, all we have is Mama's allowance from her family. It's something, at least. We shan't starve.'

'There's the gold chain Father gave me for my birthday — '

'No!' Nathan reached across and squeezed his sister's hand. 'We have enough to see us through the winter, providing we're careful.'

Aileen hesitated.

'Nathan, shall you like it here?'

'I don't allow myself to think about it. We had no option but to come — according to Mama . . . '

'Mama only acted for the best.' Aileen started gathering up the dirty dishes. 'I suppose I had better see to these. Ah, me! My hands are so sore with always being in water. And I must think about supper. There's the fat bacon, only we must all be tired of that.'

'It's food. It's fine.'

'Remember the veal and ham pies we sold at the shop? Father had the recipe from Cook at Langsdale Avenue. I wonder if Chrissie has it?'

'You could ask,' Nathan said.

'Yes. You know, I don't mind cooking, though I detest housework. Have you seen the pears in the orchard? Chrissie says we should get them in before the wasps beat us to it. She mentioned bottling them. Of course, we'd need extra sugar.'

'There's a whole cake of sugar in the larder. If it's not enough, I'll call at the stores on my way to the forge and ask them to deliver more.'

'Thank you.'

The door opened to admit Chrissie. She carried an armful of dirty laundry and a bowl of used water, which she took outside and flung on the yard.

'There,' she declared.

'That's the master spruced up. He's a lot brighter this morning. He grumbled at me for not trimming his beard properly. That's a good sign.' She looked at Nathan.

'Master Nathan, is there enough wood for me to light the copper in the laundry? If I don't get some washing done while it's fine we shall run out of clean sheets.'

'I'll see to it, Chrissie.' Nathan rose abruptly.

'Oh, and could you string some washing lines across the orchard? As many as you can, please.'

'Will do.'

Nathan picked up the jacket he had flung on the settle and went out.

Aileen took the opportunity to ask Chrissie about the recipe for pies.

'Veal and ham? Aye, I can show you,' Chrissie said cheerfully. 'There won't be any veal, but I noticed a fine crop of mushrooms in the field. Why don't we do ham and mushroom instead? Do you know how to make pastry, Miss Aileen?'

Aileen shook her head.

'I can show you that, too, miss. It isn't difficult.'

Chrissie went through to the lobby with the dirty laundry. When she came back, Aileen was still sitting at the table.

'Miss Aileen, these pots are not going to wash themselves! Can I leave them to you while I get the fire going under the copper?'

Aileen sighed, taking a woeful glance at her reddened hands.

'Tch! I can't be in two places at once!'

Stung by the unusual sharpness in the maid's tone, Aileen looked up.

'Is everything all right, Chrissie?'

'I wouldn't mind a little more help. I'll do the washing, but a hand with pegging it out would be nice.'

'Me, you mean?'

'Well, I can't see anybody else sitting there!' Chrissie found a smile. 'Come on, miss. There's a good breeze today. Those sheets will be dry in no time.'

* * *

Much later, the washing blowing on the lines, the mushrooms gathered, Aileen was being given a lesson in pastry-making when the outer door burst open and Jamie marched in, all smiles. In his arms was a lanky, half-grown sheepdog puppy.

'Aileen! Chrissie! Look what they gave me at Twelve Trees!'

'Oh, Jamie!' Aileen slapped the flour from her hands and went to stroke the pup's fuzzy black and white head. 'Isn't he sweet?'

'It's a she an' she's called Bess. I met the others, too. There's Moss an' Fly an' Lass. Lass is Bess's mother. Jim said this pup was the runt of the litter — '

'Who's Jim?' Aileen asked.

'The man at the farm, the one who does all the work. She was going to be put down but Jim wouldn't do it,' Jamie continued, scarcely pausing for breath. 'An' now she's growed up as good as the others, so he was right.'

'Grown up,' Aileen corrected.

'Master Jamie, did you remember the eggs and the milk?' Chrissie put in.

'They're outside on the step. Jim fastened some twine round Bess's neck so I could lead her.' He broke off. 'I can keep her, can't I?'

'Of course you can,' Florence replied from the doorway. Her face was grey with fatigue but her smile was wide as she came forward. 'Let me have a proper look at her, Jamie.'

He put the puppy down and she promptly began exploring her surroundings.

'Out of my kitchen!' Chrissie cried,

41

abandoning the pastry to shoo the pup outside. 'Master Jamie, if that dog's to live in the house it must be trained — and that'll be your responsibility.'

'All right, Chrissie. Jim's told me 'xactly what to do. An' when she's growed . . . grown . . . Jim's teaching me how to train her for the sheep. We are having sheep, Mama?'

'Maybe,' Florence said.

'That's good, 'cause I'm going to be a farmer like Jim when I'm big. An' d'you know what? We're both called James. Only Jim gets Jim an' I get Jamie. Funny, that.'

'It's no' the only thing that's funny round here,' Chrissie said, lips twitching.

'I'm going to show Nathan my puppy.'

The three women watched as the boy ran off, the puppy loping at his heels.

'Well, someone has settled in,' Florence remarked. She heaved a sigh.

Chrissie, her face tightening, returned to her pastry.

'How was the master, mistress?'

'Sleeping. I thought I'd take a breath of air. I never was much good with sickness. My sister was different. Dorcas was wonderful with our parents. She nursed both of them to the end.'

'Since you mention it, Mama,' Aileen said, fiddling with her rolling pin, 'we have not been to visit Aunt Dorcas yet. She must be wondering about us.'

'Yes, I suppose we should go while the weather holds.'

Aileen looked eagerly at her mother.

'Do let's, Mama. Captain's being shod today so he should be fit for the journey.'

'We'll go tomorrow, then. Chrissie, will you look after the master while we're gone?'

'Aye, mistress, if I must.'

She scooped up more dough and tossed it down in front of Aileen.

'Miss Aileen, if you're still wanting to know how to make that pie, this is how we do it . . .'

* * *

Autumn sunshine bathed the field as mother and daughter set off next morning, the old horse stepping out gamely, his ears pricked at the prospect of an outing. Aileen glanced about her.

'What pretty countryside. All those rolling hills and woods. It's so green.'

'Yes, I never tired of it as a girl,' Florence replied, her hands light on the reins.

'Tell me about the manor, Mama,' Aileen said. 'I can't wait to see where you grew up.'

'Well, it was my grandfather who bought

Wollerton Manor. Grandfather Webb was a humble potter's son who made good. Very good indeed.

'My papa thought I was marrying beneath me when I chose your father, but I've never regretted it. Dear Balfour! Our troubles were none of his doing . . . ' Florence finished in a low voice.

She turned Captain smartly into a narrow lane that dropped steeply into a small valley. And there, nestling in a fold of the slopes, was her childhood home.

A little gasp of delight escaped Aileen's lips.

'Oh, Mama! It's lovely. Look at the chimneys. Why, they remind me of the halfpenny twists of barley sugar we sold at the shop! So pretty!'

The manor house was square and graciously proportioned. Walls ablaze with russet and crimson paid tribute to the autumn day, and every latticed window twinkled a welcome.

Late-flowering roses wafted their heavy scent as they clattered up the winding drive. Florence guided Captain beneath a stone-built clock arch and pulled up in the courtyard beyond.

Almost immediately, a studded side door was flung open and a spry figure emerged and hastened to greet them.

Dorcas Webb never had been one to stand on ceremony. Today she wore a workaday smock over her blue serge gown, her frizzy fair hair scooped up in an untidy knot on the top of her head.

'Florence! I knew it the moment I heard the hoofs. What a darling horse!'

'This is my niece?' The sharp, grey Webb gaze fell on Aileen, widening in surprise. 'Child, how you've grown!'

'Dorcas, how well you look.' Florence embraced her sister warmly. 'It is lovely to be here.'

'Come, both of you, and let us go inside.' Dorcas ushered her guests into the house.

They passed down a long corridor to the hall, where two enormous hounds and a silken-coated spaniel raised their heads sleepily and thumped their tails. They continued to the library, where a fire burned cheerfully despite the warmth of the day. Under the window was a carved oak desk: a scattering of papers across its surface spoke of recent industry.

'Sit down, do. I was just running through the household accounts before going out to dead-head the roses — let me ring for that tea.' Dorcas activated the bell-pull, and then turned back to her guests, scrutinising them closely.

'Hmm. I vow you are quite pinched, Florence. Is something amiss?'

'It's Balfour,' Florence said. 'We had barely arrived when he was taken ill. The doctor says it's a seizure. That's why we have not called sooner.'

'Oh, my dears!' Dorcas clucked in sympathy and raised her eyes in silent thanks that matrimony and all its woes had passed her by. 'Such trouble you have had. Ah, the tea!'

A housekeeper in rustling black bustled in with a tray on which sat a silver teapot, several pieces of the famous Webb rosebud china and a large plum cake.

'Thank you, Mason.'

The woman dipped a curtsey and left, and Dorcas turned her attention to the refreshments.

'What of Nathan?' Dorcas enquired after hearing a full account of the Drummonds' travails. 'Was he agreeable to coming here?'

'My son knows where his duty lies,' Florence replied.

'Duty!' Dorcas made a wry face. 'Has he the makings of a farmer, do you suppose?'

'You know, I think he has,' Florence said. She forced herself to relax. She was home. This was her sister sitting opposite her. She could unburden herself here, at least.

'Our problem is getting started. Dorcas,

have you seen the state of the Glebe land?'

'Not recently, though I can hazard a guess. When our uncle Reeve was taken ill, the staff dwindled. He was left in the end with only the two hands who lived in the cottages. When he died they had to leave.'

'Yes. The cottages are both empty. Have you any idea what happened to the farm hands?'

'I believe some were taken on at Twelve Trees, though I don't know how many remain there. Most were hired as casuals, I think . . .

'And what of my other nephew?' Dorcas's mind never stayed in one place long. 'How does young Jamie fare?'

Florence put down her cup and saucer, her face breaking into a smile.

'Jamie is very taken with everything and now that he has a dog — '

'Dog? That sounds like a Webb! What breed and where did he get it?'

'From Twelve Trees,' Aileen answered. 'Bess is a sheepdog. She's only a puppy. She has a lot to learn.'

'Like not to eat the house!' Dorcas snorted a laugh. 'Remember the one we had as girls, Florence? He'd chewed every table leg from here to the attic before he was three months old. How are you for money?'

'What?' Florence stared. Her sister's knack

47

of jumping from one subject to another in the same breath was disconcerting. 'I mean, I beg your pardon?'

'Money,' Dorcas repeated. 'D'you need any?'

'Oh . . . ' Florence paused. There was Balfour. Doctor's bills. Medicines. A family to feed and clothe. A farm to set up. Her allowance would only stretch so far.

'Don't answer now,' Dorcas said. 'If you need help, you only have to say the word.'

'Thank you, sister. But I was wondering . . . it may be wiser to sell the Glebe and invest in a property more . . . suitable.'

'Don't be ridiculous!' Dorcas said. 'You're here now. The decision is made. Isn't that right, Aileen?'

'Indeed, aunt. Mama already knows my opinion on the matter.'

'That's the Webb spirit! A girl with sense!' She stood up. 'Come, niece. Let's show you round . . . '

They spent the greater part of the day at the manor and shadows were long-drawn across the lawns when they took their leave.

In the courtyard, a surprise awaited. The old farm cart stood stacked to the hilt with goods. They gazed in amazement at the baskets of fruit and vegetables gleaned from the kitchen gardens. There were several wicker crates holding a dozen clucking Leghorn pullets and a fine young cockerel.

'The chickens should come on lay soon,' Dorcas said. 'You must set the youngster on there. He'll like that. There's nothing like collecting your own eggs!'

They looked further. There was a sack of best white flour from the mill, a cask of cider, sugar in snowy blocks, salt, spices, a hard red cheese, jars of new season chutneys and conserves, little tarts, gingerbread, a light sponge for Balfour . . . There seemed no end to it.

'Sister, do you have anything left in your larder?' Florence exclaimed faintly.

'Don't be absurd! We always did stock up for siege at Wollerton. Do call again, my dears. Better still, I shall call on you. Tell my nephew I shall be sending a man to help with the heavy work on the place. You'll need to have that wilderness under plough while this weather lasts.'

'Thank you, Dorcas. You are most generous.'

'Stuff and nonsense! Only too glad to have you back. Farewell for now, Florence, my love. I hope your man continues to improve.'

Florence took up the reins.

'Goodbye, aunt. Thank you so much,' Aileen said.

'My pleasure, niece. You must come yourself and see me. Can't have you tramping the roads like a gypsy, though. There's a nice little mare in the stables that might suit you . . . '

Dorcas Webb's strident tones followed them down the drive, growing fainter. As they passed between the pillared gateposts on to the lane, mother and daughter were smiling.

'I adore Aunt Dorcas,' Aileen enthused. 'Papa thinks her a dragon but she's more like a fairy godmother.'

'I trust you are right, Aileen. Something tells me we are going to need a little magic if we are to survive.'

★   ★   ★

Nathan was up a ladder, putting the finishing touches to the worm-eaten hammer beam that ran the length of the barn, when a footfall made him glance down. Standing in the doorway was a sturdily built man, not young, but fit-looking. A man of the soil, by his leather breeches, tough boots and the tweed cap clutched between his big red fists.

'Good morning,' Nathan called. He shinned down the ladder.

'Morning, mester,' the caller said with quiet dignity. 'I'm Jim Merridew. Man and

50

boy I've worked here at the Glebe. I was laid off when the old gaffer took badly. Word's got around that the place was occupied again. I were wondering if I could have my old job back.'

'Your old job?' The request took Nathan unawares. 'But there's nothing here, man. No stock, no crops, nothing.'

'I knows that, mester. The old place has got a bit rundown, unna it? A farm can be brought round again and there's not much I dunna know about the Glebe. I could show you the ropes.'

Nathan ran his tar-stained hand over his rumpled hair.

'It isn't that simple. I'll be honest with you, Merridew. At present I couldn't afford to pay you.'

'That's all right, mester,' the man said. 'I'll have my old cottage back if that's agreeable to you? We can forget the rest for now.'

Nathan knew there were two tied cottages at the Glebe. He had not inspected them yet, but he didn't hold out much hope of either being habitable.

'You might want to take a look first,' he said darkly. He had taken to this quiet-mannered man. Puss was weaving round the fellow's legs. Animals always seemed to know who they could trust. 'Which cottage was yours?'

'The timbered and thatched billet by the spinney. Shepherd Turney had the other. It's bigger and he has a son, whereas I've no kin.

'The place will have got in a state, being stood empty all this time. That wunna bother me. I'll soon have it shipshape again.'

The two men regarded one another for a moment. Then Nathan extended a hand.

'Welcome back, Merridew. I'm Nathan Drummond. My father is incapacitated at the moment and I'm acting in his place. I don't pretend to know much about farming so any advice will be gladly received.'

'Pleased to be of service, gaffer,' Jim Merridew said.

Gaffer. That brought a glimmer of a smile to Nathan's face.

'Jim Merridew . . . Have we you to thank for providing my small brother with a pup?'

'Aye.' The smile was returned. 'Twelve Trees unna run like the Glebe. The old gaffer always gave an animal a chance. Let's say that pup was surplus to requirements.'

'I understand.'

''Twas me got in a bite of fodder for the horse. Nobody bid for him at the sale, so he got turned out to fend for himself. Couldn't see him go hungry, and winter coming on.'

'Good of you, man. You must let me reimburse you.'

'No need. Being back here is payment enough.' Jim Merridew glanced at the barn. 'You've not done a bad job here.'

'Oh, I had a friend who lived on a farm. His father would set us on with some tarring to keep us out of mischief. Tell me, Merridew — or do you prefer Jim?'

'That'll do.'

'Tell me, Jim, what was your status here when Reeve Webb was master?'

'Cowman. But I can turn a hand to most things . . . '

Hoofbeats heralded the return of the womenfolk, interrupting the discussion. Florence, alighting from the cart, let out a glad cry.

'Why, it's Jim Merridew! I did wonder when Jamie mentioned your name — Aileen, I told you about Jim who used to put me up on the horses?'

'Yes, Mama.'

'Fancy you remembering that,' Jim said. 'Little Miss Florence. And here you are with a grown-up family.'

'Jim's come to work at the Glebe, Mama,' Nathan said.

'Welcome back!' Florence's smile said all.

'Seems I'd best fetch my tack and get down to the cottage,' Jim said. 'It's good to be home again.'

Later, as Nathan unloaded the brimming cart, a distant hammering from the direction of the cottage spoke of occupancy. He was smiling as he left Jamie playing with Bess in the yard. He entered the kitchen with the final basket of items from Wollerton, which he left by the larder for Chrissie to unpack.

His mother and sister were sitting by the fire enjoying a cup of tea. The hearth was stacked with logs that someone — Chrissie, probably — had chopped that afternoon. In the background was the homely clatter of Chrissie setting the table for supper.

'Chrissie, you might see if the master would like some tea,' Florence said. 'I'd take him one myself, but I feel quite exhausted after our excursion.'

'Me, too, Mama. Wasn't it wonderful at the manor? Such comfort!'

There was a clatter as the cutlery in Chrissie's hand crashed down on to the table. The maid stood, hands on hips, her cheeks burning, eyes bright as a cat's.

'Give the master his tea, mistress? Anything else while I'm at it? And I'm sorry, Miss Aileen, if there's no' enough comfort for you here, but it seems to me that life is much the same for you as it ever was, thanks to a certain body.'

Florence gasped.

'Why, Chrissie, this is not like you. Is something amiss?'

'Aye, you could say that, mistress. It mightn't be my place, but now I've started I may as well finish.

'What's wrong with how you live here, Miss Aileen? Three lines of washing to your one I pegged out yesterday! And another thing — your dirty pots have to be washed, not left for someone else to see to!'

Guilty colour flooded Aileen's face.

'I'm sorry, Chrissie. It was my hands. They're chapped with being in water all the time.'

'Aye, they will be. But you get used to it.

'And, mistress, the master was asking for you earlier. It wouldn't cost much to take in his tea yourself and see he's comfortable. Nursing's no' so bad if you love the person, surely?'

Florence and Aileen exchanged a look of incredulity.

'Dinna stare at me like that!' Chrissie stamped a foot in frustration. 'Oh, I've had enough!'

She spun round and slammed out.

Nathan hurried after her into the gathering twilight.

He found her in the stable, weeping bitterly into Captain's mane.

'It's no' fair, Master Nathan,' she sobbed. 'I work my fingers to the bone and it's never enough. It's not the work — I'm used to that. What I do mind is being taken for granted'

'Oh, Chrissie!' Gently taking her by the shoulders, Nathan drew the maid to him.

'Chrissie, I can't tell you how sorry I am. We do appreciate what you do for us. I was telling my sister so only yesterday. Or was it the day before? Time rushes by so fast I scarcely know where we're at!'

'I ken the feeling, Master Nathan,' Chrissie said soberly.

'Ah. D'you suppose we could drop the 'master' now? Just call me by my name. Our circumstances are hardly the same as in Glasgow, are they?'

'Now dinna you start — '

'I wouldn't dream of it,' Nathan said, hastily. 'It's up to you, Chrissie. Call me whatever you feel happiest with. And about those wages — I know you wanted to learn to read and write. Why don't I teach you?'

Chrissie managed a smile of response.

'We'd be lost without you, Chrissie, truly.'

She frowned.

'I was terrible lacking in manners back at the house. Will the mistress be cross?'

'I shall have a word with Mama. Aileen, too. There'll be changes from now on. Now, why don't you stay and tell Captain a bedtime story while I put things straight inside?'

'Bedtime stories? For a horse?'

But she was laughing as he left. Striding back across the yard, it occurred to Nathan how slight and warm Chrissie had felt in his arms. Her hair had been soft against his chin and she smelled deliciously of lavender . . .

Reaching the kitchen door, he drew a sustaining breath and went inside.

* * *

That day marked a turning point for the Drummonds. A chastened Florence set her qualms aside and concentrated on nursing her husband.

Aileen, contrite, gritted her teeth and did her share in the house.

With the help of the man sent by Dorcas, she began overhauling the Glebe's overgrown kitchen garden. To her surprise and delight, it was a task that gave Aileen tremendous satisfaction and joy.

She felt her young body grow strong and lean. And though her hands did not regain their former whiteness, she ceased somehow to worry about it.

Chrissie, cheered by the changes, continued to work as hard as ever. But now her heart was in it.

Things were slowly shaping up at Glebe Farm.

★   ★   ★

One Saturday afternoon, a smart high-wheeled gig and gleaming cob pulled into the farmyard. The driver, a stout, florid-faced man with bushy side-whiskers, was attired in the garb of the gentleman farmer. The shine on his boots made Nathan ashamed of his own work-worn appearance.

'Good-day to you,' the man said. 'I want a word with the man in charge. Tell him it's Stanton Hayles of Twelve Trees.'

'Good-day, sir,' Nathan replied. 'Nathan Drummond, at your disposal. How can I help you?'

For several moments, Stanton Hayles regarded him from his elevated seat.

'I want to know when something is going to be done about the seeds blowing over on to my fields. Glebe Farm land is nothing but dandelion and thistle! It won't do, sir, and so I make leave to tell you!

'Your fences are so rotted I can scarce keep my cattle and sheep from roaming, same goes for your hedges and walls. Boundary fences are shared. It should not fall to me every time to mend a wall that is collapsing.'

He glowered down at Nathan, angry, uncompromising.

'What I want to know is — what are you going to do about it? Eh?'

3

'Shall we go into the office, sir?' Nathan said. 'We can talk in private there.' With a great deal of huffing, the farmer clambered down from his vehicle. He handed the reins to Jamie, who had been playing with Bess nearby. With a brusque caution not to let the collie pup get under the horse's hoofs, he allowed himself to be shown up a flight of worn stone steps to the garret above the stables which served Nathan as an office.

Stanton Hayles shot a curious look about him.

'The Glebe was a fine farm in its day. Not an easy task, pulling it round again.'

'No, indeed.' Nathan went to lean against the old oak desk. 'I must beg your pardon, too, for not having made your acquaintance before now, sir. You may have heard that my father was taken ill soon after coming here. My mother and sister have had much to do.'

'Yes, it had come to my notice. I am sorry. It was not the best of starts for you.'

Stanton Hayles was now looking slightly disquieted and Nathan hid a smile. Let the man squirm a little, coming here throwing his weight about!

'Farmer Hayles,' he said. 'Just now you referred to the sorry state of my land and I can only agree with you. It is in shocking bad order. Rest assured, we have the matter in hand.'

'Really? Well, sir, I'm glad to hear it. Confounded thistle and dandelion!'

'I understand. You have my word that the first fields to go under the plough will be those bordering yours. My man will see to it.'

'Your man? Merridew, you mean?' Hayles leaned forward. 'Dammit, Drummond! You filched the fellow from under my nose!'

'Jim Merridew had been part of the Glebe staff all his life. It was he who approached me. As I understand it, come winter he would have been laid off anyway.'

'Not necessarily. I know a good hand and Merridew was one of the best. I'd have kept him on, more than likely. Hutch and Turner, the other two Glebe hands in my employ, are expendable. I shan't need their services much longer.'

'Then mayhap we'll see a few more Glebe men back here in due course.' Nathan made an effort to lighten his tone, but the farmer's eyes narrowed.

'Is that what you're planning, Drummond?'

'It is surely up to the men where they choose to work.'

'Aye,' the farmer said, shrugging. 'Where they can find it, eh?'

He barked a laugh, and Nathan inclined his head in acknowledgement of the jest.

'Farmer Hayles,' he went on, 'I see you run a flock of Clun Forest on your high ground. I was thinking of purchasing some sheep to clear my rough grass. Are they a hardy breed, would you say?'

'Oh, none better. Self-lambing, too. We've always run Clun Forest at Twelve Trees. You're going the right way about it there.' Consulting his pocket watch, Stanton Hayles stood up.

'Well, Drummond, I shan't hold you up any longer. I've done what I came for. No offence intended.'

'None taken, sir.'

'Your ladies must visit once they are free to do so. Sadly, my dear wife is no longer with us, but my daughter will be glad to receive them.'

'Thank you. I shall pass on your message,' Nathan said.

Nathan followed the visitor down to the farmyard, where Jamie stood patiently holding the black cob's bridle. Stanton Hayles dipped into his top pocket and produced a coin.

'Here, boy. Take this for your trouble.'

'No, thank you, sir.' Jamie gave his head a vigorous shake. 'Mama says it's not mannerly to accept money from strangers.'

'Does she, be jove! Not exactly strangers, are we? Haven't I seen you at my place fetching messages? Here, lad, accept my thanks for looking after my Ebony.'

He tucked the money into Jamie's pocket, and was about to board the trap when Florence appeared from the house.

'Mama, come and meet Farmer Stanton Hayles of Twelve Trees. Farmer Hayles, this is my mother, Florence Drummond.'

'A pleasure to know you, ma'am,' Hayles said.

'And you, sir.'

Farmer Hayles, charmed by Florence's gracious demeanour, gazed at her for a moment.

'I hope we shall see yourself and your daughter at Twelve Trees before long.'

'We shall be delighted, sir,' Florence accepted with a smile.

Stanton Hayles turned to Nathan.

'I'll bid you farewell, Drummond,' he said. And shaking his hand in a crushing grip, the farmer clambered up into the trap and took up his reins.

'Hup-hup, Ebony!'

As his mother returned to the house, Nathan watched with relief as the horse and trap clattered out of the yard.

'Gone, has he?' Jim Merridew appeared at Nathan's side. 'How did you fare?'

'Oh, I think Farmer Hayles and I came to an understanding.'

'Aye, well, Hayles unna a bad fellow as men go. A hard taskmaster, mind. And not generous with pay. I reckon that's how he's got where he has.'

'Is Twelve Trees a family farm?' Nathan asked.

'No. Hayles came by it as a young man and built it up. His missus were a nice little woman. Folks thought a lot of her. The daughter's had the best of everything and it's turned her head a bit. Thinks the world revolves around her. Not her fault, of course'

Nathan's heart squeezed. It could have been Isobel Macnair the man spoke about.

'You'll know Hayles is a chapel man? He's in the Fellowship of Rechabites, an' all. He's highly respected in these parts you'd be wise to have him on your side.'

'I think I'd already worked that out,' Nathan agreed.

'Shall we go up to the hill pasture now and check those boundary walls that Hayles came about?'

'Could do. We might take a look at the winter hut while we're there. I noticed a few slates missing off the roof. Silas Turner always saw to that side of things, along with keeping the dry-stone walls and the penning folds in good order.'

'Turner had the other tied cottage, I take it. Was he a good shepherd?'

'The best. He's not the easiest of fellows to get on with, but he's conscientious. Silas is a union man. I'll not need to say more.'

'No.' Nathan was silent a moment. He had heard talk at the forge of union activity in the neighbourhood. There had been some unrest and it seemed to be growing. 'Hayles did hint at something.'

'Aye, he warned Silas when he took him on if there was any trouble he'd be out. Silas's wife is dead, but there's his son to consider. For the lad's sake I wouldn't have thought he'd take risks, but these things can take hold of a man.'

'True.' Nathan was thoughtful for a moment.

'Jim, about those Clun Forest sheep you mentioned. I spoke to Hayles about it. He seemed to approve.'

'Hayles knows what he's talking about, I'll give him that.' Jim Merridew collected the jacket he had left on a nail by the barn door.

'Right then, gaffer. Shall we go?'

The two men set off, climbing over the stile and taking a stony farm track that wound gradually upwards. They trudged on in silence. Once, Nathan threw a backward glance at his farm nestling in the valley below.

His farm. His blood stirred at the thought, surprising him. If Hayles as a young man had managed to make good out of bad, he mused, then couldn't he?

He turned to the man walking steadily at his side.

'When is the next beast market at Shrewsbury, Jim?'

'Second Wednesday in December. Why d'you ask?'

'Shall we get along there and see what's on offer in the sheep pens?'

'Could do.' The farmhand couldn't disguise the grin on his face. 'If there's anything suitable, shall you go for it?'

'That's the idea,' Nathan said.

'Strikes me you'll be needing a shepherd to see after them, in that case. Silas Turner might be at the Dog tonight. Want me to have a word?'

Nathan hesitated. The man was currently in Hayles's employ.

'If you're concerned about treading on any toes, then I wunna worry,' Jim said shrewdly.

'All the casual workers will get laid off in the next few weeks, and Silas has another reason to get sorted. Him and Edward are living in a cottage by Hadnall pond. Damp, 'tis, from the marshy ground. Unhealthy. Strikes me they'd be glad to have their old home back.'

'On the same terms as yours?'

'Happen. Glebe wages always dropped over the winter months anyway. If you could manage a bit for him and his lad, I reckon Shepherd Turner would be back here before you could whistle. Young Edward's a decent fellow and good with the stock. You won't be sorry you took them on.'

'Go ahead, then,' Nathan said, hoping that he was doing the right thing.

*   *   *

'Please say yes, Mama!' Aileen begged. 'Think of all those pears and apples we gathered from the orchard — how many fruit tarts they would make. Think of the *profit!*'

'In my young days, those apples and pears would have been stored away for the winter,' Florence said.

'That was then, Mama! Listen . . . ' Aileen plumped down on the settle beside her mother, taking her hands. 'I've thought how to raise some regular income. Chrissie gave me the idea with her veal and ham pies that Cook used to make.'

'But, Aileen, a market stall! Could you bear to stand there selling cakes and pies to all and sundry?'

'Yes, I could.' Aileen's chin jutted in a way that reminded Florence of Dorcas. 'I'd enjoy it. Chrissie wants to help, and I'm getting better at the baking, aren't I, Chrissie?'

The maid, who had been hovering in the background, came forward.

'Yes'm. Miss Aileen can turn out a pie as good as mine.' She dipped a curtsey, bringing a groan from Aileen.

'Oh, do stop all that bobbing, Chrissie! It's in the past. Let us forget it and concentrate on the future.

'See here, Mama.' She produced a sheet of paper from her apron pocket. 'I've made a list of everything we shall need and totalled it. We get the baking done on Thursday, the day before Hadnall market, and Nathan says he'll drive us there first thing in the morning. They'll be ploughing the Ten-Acre then so we can't take Captain from the farm for the whole day.'

'And how do you propose to get home again?'

'We walk, Mama,' Aileen cried.

'Darling, it is almost December. Think of the weather.'

'What's a little snow? Chrissie and I don't mind, do we, Chrissie?'

'No, Miss Aileen. And, madam, those wee pullets are laying a treat. We're getting more eggs than we can use. We could sell the surplus, and when we get some kine we can make butter and cheese and sell that, too!'

The memory of Glebe Farm butter, rich and smooth, with the farm's emblem of a clover leaf pressed into each golden mound, was too much for Florence.

'Very well; proceed. Though I don't know what your father will think.'

'Papa knows, Mama,' Aileen said gleefully. 'He thinks it a wonderful idea. He said I was a daughter after his own heart'

'Mmm.' Florence was studying Aileen's list of requirements. 'Fourteen shillings for sugar? Five shillings for a barrel of salt? Aileen, have you considered how we can meet this sort of cost?'

'Oh, yes. I intend funding it myself. You remember when Nathan went to Shrewsbury to see the solicitor on your behalf and I went along for the ride? Well, while Nathan was closeted with the solicitor, I went into the jeweller's and sold my jewellery.'

'Aileen!' Florence flung up her hands in horror.

'Oh, Mama! What do I want with pendants and bangles? A stout pair of boots would be more fitting. And who knows? If we make a fortune with our stall, I could buy jewels aplenty!'

'Heaven bless you, child,' Florence said faintly. 'You deserve to succeed.'

★ ★ ★

The next day Aileen drove to the village and returned excitedly with her purchases. Whilst sitting with Balfour — now up and settled in a winged chair by the fireside in the small parlour — Florence picked over and peeled basket after basket of fruit, which Aileen and Chrissie quickly turned into lattice tarts. They also cooked a dozen meat pies, rich with herbs and gravy, some crusty loaves of bread and a tray of little round pastries Chrissie called queen cakes.

First light the following morning saw them bound for Hadnall, their faces hopeful, their goods carefully placed in baskets on the cart and covered with cloths of cheerful red check to keep off the dust from the road. Aileen's only regret was that she would miss the expected visit from Dorcas Webb.

'Confound the woman!' Balfour was not in the best of humours. 'Never could stand her,' he grumbled. 'Mind you keep her out of my sight, Florence!'

'I shall, never fear,' Florence replied. She placed the tartan rug over her husband's knees. 'There. You shall be cosy in here and I shall entertain my sister in my kitchen.'

'To think what it's come to,' Balfour mumbled, his once-strong speech pitifully weakened and slurred from the crippling effects of the seizure.

Compassion for this man she had always been proud to call husband stirred in Florence's heart. Her father might have wanted better for her, but the marriage had turned out a true love match. And hadn't Father made his own money in trade?

She thought how Grandfather Webb's tableware company had been the making of them. Dorcas now held the reins of the firm. No wonder Balfour resented her presence in his current enfeebled world.

Florence planted a loving kiss on her man's cheek.

'There, now. Do not deny me my small pleasures, my love. I'm very fond of my sister. And she has been so good to us.'

Balfour's scowl expressed his thoughts on the matter, but he held his counsel and

Florence, sending him a smile, left to busy herself with broom and duster.

* * *

'Sister, you have worked marvels here!' Dorcas exclaimed some time later, taking in the gleaming surfaces and the dull sheen of pewter and copper on the dresser.

'Thank you, Dorcas. Come and sit by the fire and we shall take some tea.' Florence glanced through the window at the Wollerton trap, piled high with baskets and boxes that Nathan, back from ferrying his sister to market, was unloading. 'My goodness! What's all this?'

'Some china, amongst other items. It's such a waste having it languishing in a cupboard when it could be put to good use here. There is bed-linen, too. In Balfour's condition one cannot have too much. How does he?'

'Balfour gets stronger every day, thanks to our good Doctor Merrick and his pills and potions. They cost a small fortune, but the treatment does Balfour so much good one must not grumble.'

'I need to speak to you on the matter of finance,' Dorcas said. 'After we've had our tea will be soon enough. What delightful little cakes. May I take two?'

Florence placed the platter within her sister's reach and wondered, not for the first time, how anyone with such an appetite could remain as slim as a reed.

'How does Davina and her man?' Dorcas enquired. 'Are they settled in that outlandish place they went to? Barotse, was it not?'

'Yes, indeed. It is not the sort of life I would wish for myself, though Davina appears content. She writes regularly, though the post is spasmodic. But at least we are able to keep in touch. The children seem well. Two little granddaughters and I have never seen them. Ah, me!'

'So long as they thrive, that is all you need to worry about. Who knows, one day they may surprise you and turn up on your doorstep.'

'I cannot see Davina doing that. They seem very settled in Africa. Finbar is totally dedicated to his cause.'

'There, then, why are you fretting? I must say young Aileen's got plenty about her. What are these plans of hers for a market stall?'

Florence allowed herself a small smile. Nothing here remained private for long.

'That is where she is gone today. I only hope she doesn't overtax herself.'

'Don't be ridiculous! The girl's as strong as

an ox! Though I'm surprised at you allowing it.' Dorcas took a bite of cake with evident enjoyment.

'Aileen got Nathan and her father on her side before ever approaching me. What else could I do but agree?'

'She's a girl to be proud of and you know it.

'I had a word with young Jamie as I came in. Country air suits him. He looks the picture of health.'

'He's bursting out of all his clothes. They were bought with plenty of growing room and Chrissie has had to let them all out.'

Florence could have bitten her tongue. She hadn't meant to imply that they couldn't afford new.

'Would Chrissie be responsible for these delicious confections'?' Dorcas enquired, helping herself to another queen cake. 'I'm rather taken with that maid of yours. She's got a wise head on her shoulders.'

'She's been marvellous,' Florence said. 'Though she's finding the different voices here taxing. She was telling me the other day that Jim Merridew's broad vowels were beyond her. 'It's all unna and wunna with him, mistress,' she said. 'I can't be making top nor tail of it!''

'I expect Jim feels the same about her.'

'That's just the point. He does!'

They laughed kindly, and Florence reached for the teapot. 'More tea?'

Once the pot was emptied and only crumbs remained on the plates, Dorcas turned to her sister.

'Florence, please don't take offence, but clearly you will need funds if you are to get the farm on a proper footing. Let me help you. The firm has done exceptionally well this year. You are my only sibling. Do let me help.'

Florence looked away.

'I have my allowance,' she said. 'We shall manage.'

'You will manage a good deal better this way! Stop being such a prude, Florence. See, I have a purse of coin here. I have more than enough for my own needs. Take it; it will do more good here.'

Florence's mind raced. She thought of the sheep Nathan wanted to purchase. A small flock of in-lamb ewes they could afford. A larger one would bring in more profit.

'Then do it this way,' Dorcas said as the silence continued. 'Regard it as a loan. Here, take the money and pay me back when the time is right. And it will all come right, my pet,' she assured Florence, her tone softening. 'Believe me, it will. You have a loyal family and they're not too proud to get stuck in and work'

Looking into her sister's mobile face with its bright eyes and firm chin, Florence felt herself weakening. Dorcas meant well.

'Then, sister, I accept your offer with thanks,' she said. She would have to tell Nathan about it, but not Balfour. Never Balfour. If he were to learn that they were beholden to Dorcas Webb, it could be the end of him.

★ ★ ★

Chrissie spelled the letters out painstakingly. '*We went to Had . . . n . . . all Hadnall market and we so . . . sold all our wares.*' She looked up from the slate on which Nathan had chalked the words. 'We did, too, Master Nathan! By midday every last wee cake was gone!'

'Good for you, Chrissie. Did you enjoy the market stall?'

'Aye, I did. We'll need to bake twice as much for next week. Miss Aileen took some orders and wrote them down in a wee book. She said once I've got going with the reading and penning I can take over the accounts because I'm that quick at adding up.'

'Then we'd better get on. Here, you take

76

the chalk and copy underneath my writing. Let me help. Like this, see?'

Nathan guided her wayward strokes. The touch of his hand on hers made Chrissie's heart sing.

'Now try again by yourself,' Nathan said, bringing her back down to earth.

She began, her brows tight-drawn in concentration.

'Excellent, Chrissie. Next time we'll do away with the slate and use paper and ink, yes?'

'Aye, if you say so, Master Nathan'

Nathan pulled a face.

'I wish you would stop calling me that. All those airs and graces were left behind us in Glasgow. So why not Nathan?'

'I suppose . . . because I am still a servant and I'll no' forget it.' Chrissie's voice wobbled. She might wish things were different, but it could not be. She took a calming breath and went for safer ground.

'Will I soon be able to read the Bible the master gave me?'

Nathan smiled. Regardless of whether they could read it, and most could not, all the staff had been supplied with a Bible bound in soft black leather when they were employed.

'You will indeed, Chrissie. You'll be reading

Mr Dickens, too. You'll enjoy that.'

'Once I start getting some wages I shall save up and buy Mr Dickens's novels.'

'That day may be nearer than you think. Can you keep a secret?' Nathan's eyes danced. 'Jim and I intend being at the next beast sale at Shrewsbury. Jamie had best get that pup of his trained. We shall be coming back with some sheep.'

'Shall you get some kine as well?'

'Cows, Chrissie,' Nathan said, grinning. 'Jim won't know what you mean otherwise.'

'Cows, then. You didnae answer my question.'

'Let's wait and see,' Nathan said. He straightened in his chair. 'We'd best finish now. I need to write in my journal before the light fades.'

'Yes, Master Nathan,' she said, getting up.

As she crossed the farmyard, it occurred to Chrissie how alone she felt even though she was surrounded all day by people. She missed her friends at the Drummonds' old house in Glasgow: Cook, Agnes, young Jackie the boot boy . . . The villagers at the market were different. She'd found it hard to understand her customers, and they her, and a longing for home and the soft voices of her childhood had almost overwhelmed her.

But Glebe Farm was a good place and would be even better with the yowes and kine in the pasture.

Her spirits lifted. Of course she was not alone. Wasn't Miss Aileen always saying she couldn't do without her? Particularly now. And Master Jamie needed her, too, she thought, as she went into the orchard to make sure that he had shut in the fowl against marauding foxes. Pleased to find them safely at roost, she headed back over the damp grass.

And there was Nathan. Nobody must know how she felt about the young master. At least she was here, near him. The Drummonds had given her a home and a ready-made family, and that was worth a lot.

★　★　★

Shrewsbury beast market was crowded. Elbowing his way to the animal pens with Jim Merridew at his side, Nathan was aware of many a curious glance.

Word had spread that Glebe Farm was in the hands of new people. Conscious of being an outsider in this close-knit company, he acknowledged as many people as possible, meeting a gaze with a nod of his head or a brief greeting.

Jim, however, knew everyone and the banter was rife.

'Morning, Jim. Come to outbid us, have you?'

'You could be right there, Thomas.'

'Ho, there, Jim. I've heard the Glebe was going in for arable, with so much land going under the plough. Any truth in it?'

'Could be, Ben. If the price of corn goes up any more it mightn't be a bad move. What have you on offer today?'

'Half a dozen of my Red Polls. They're two-year-olds, in milk and in calf to my Hereford bull.'

'If you're serious about a couple of milch-cows for the house, you couldn't do better than Ben Harris's,' Jim said in a sideways whisper to Nathan. 'They'll be in the very best of fettle, and the breed thrives on poor pasture.

'The bidding will start shortly. Let's take a look.'

Nathan was immediately taken with the neat red cattle with no horns and mild, innocent eyes.

'Let's have those,' he said at once.

'Right.' Jim was in his element. 'Want me to do the bidding? It might keep the price from being pushed up.'

'Go ahead,' Nathan said thankfully.

The auctioneer, a rotund man with impressive side-whiskers and a loud voice, called for attention. The bidding was fierce and quick. Time and again Nathan saw his farmhand's forefinger go to his brow, and very soon Nathan became the owner of three healthy young cows.

They were heading back to the sheep pens when Nathan's way was barred by his neighbour, Stanton Hayles. 'Drummond! Thought I might see you here.'

Nathan raised his cap.

'Good morning, sir. Are you buying or selling today?'

'Bit of both, as ever. I've a fine young tup if you're interested. He's what you wanted — a pure-bred Clun Forest.'

'It's ewes I'm after today,' Nathan said.

Folk gathered round to find out what Hayles was up to. The farmer had made no secret of the fact that he had been keen to buy the neglected Glebe Farm at a knockdown price after old Reeve Webb died.

The arrival of the family from Glasgow had not featured in his plans at all, and it was common knowledge that he was not best pleased. Was he spoiling for a fight? They pressed closer.

'Ewes, is it?' Stanton Hayles boomed. 'Well, now, boy, that can be arranged. Come with me and I'll show you what I've brought in. Leave your nursemaid behind. Likely he'll take a jar with his mates while we're gone.'

Jim's face was impassive, though Nathan could imagine how he was feeling.

'Thank you, but we've already made our choice,' he said. 'Maybe next time.'

Sending his neighbour a nod, Nathan passed on his way. He was stinging at the slight to himself and to his man. There was disappointment, too. He had thought better of Hayles.

They saw the ewes as they walked the pens. Jim was not impressed.

'Hayles unna likely to sell anything worth keeping and you dunna need a tup just yet, gaffer.'

Typically, he made no further mention of the incident, and merely carried on with the business in hand.

* * *

By the end of the afternoon, two dozen in-lamb Clun Forest ewes were registered alongside the cattle in the books under the Glebe Farm name, and Nathan's purse felt considerably lighter.

The horse and cart had been left at the tavern yard. Nathan was just harnessing up for home when two characters appeared under the arched entrance.

'Mester Drummond?' A lean, sallow-faced man wearing a shepherd's smock over his fustian breeches and gaiters addressed him. 'Might we have a word?'

Jim quickly made the introductions.

'These are the two mates I were telling you about, gaffer. Silas Turner and Wilkie Hutch.'

Nathan nodded a greeting.

'How can I help you'?'

'I'll come straight to the point,' the shepherd said. 'I've got turned off. It wasn't unexpected. I'm a union man and the gaffer didn't hold with my beliefs.'

'It was only a matter of time anyway,' the other man added. He was older than Turner, a strong-looking fellow with ruddy cheeks and kind hazel eyes under bushy brows. 'Last taken on is always first to be laid off. I'm expecting the same myself any day.'

Nathan turned to the shepherd.

'I take it you want your old job back?'

'That's it, and I know the terms. I've a bit put by, enough to see us over the winter. Me and my lad will do fine in our old cottage. I'll be glad to get out of our present quarters. It's that damp the water rims down the inside walls and your clothes are never dry.'

'I wouldn't be too hopeful that the Glebe

cottage is any better,' Nathan said ruefully. 'I'm told your son is good with the animals.'

'That's right. Edward'll manage them cows you bought, no problem.'

'On such a small wage? Might he not wish to look elsewhere for work?'

'Not Edward. He met with an accident when he was a nipper and damaged his foot, see. He can still put in a day's hard graft, though. I'm telling you straight, mester. You take me and my lad together or we don't come. As to the pay . . . well, wages always were sparse at the Glebe during the winter, but anything's better than nothing, inna it?'

Nathan thought fast. He didn't particularly like the man and he thought the son sounded more a liability than an asset. But he trusted Jim's judgement. And if Hayles had turned the shepherd off, there surely wouldn't be any hard feeling if Glebe Farm accepted him back.

'What about you?' he asked the other man.

'I'm a Glebe worker through and through,' the ploughman replied. 'Me and Jim here were the last to go afore the stock were sold off. I've two handy young 'osses of my own. If you can find 'em a stable and some keep for the winter, plus a few shillings so I can pay our dues on the cottage, that'll suffice. The missus earns a bit taking in washing and we've no childer, so our needs are few.'

Nathan did some swift calculations in his head: their funds would stretch — just.

'We'll call it a deal,' Nathan said. 'But let's not be too hasty. There's no reason why Shepherd Turner and his boy can't move into the cottage immediately. Hutch, I'd rather you waited till you get officially turned off from Twelve Trees.'

'I understand, gaffer. I were thinking along those lines myself.'

It was done. The two men melted into the gathering gloom and Nathan and Jim Merridew set off for home.

* * *

Back at the farm, Florence was waiting with some news.

'I bumped into Farmer Hayles's daughter in the village. Verity. Such a pretty girl and so vivacious. I've invited them for supper this Friday week.'

Nathan's spirits plummeted. The thought of Stanton Hayles opposite him at the supper table was no longer a pleasing one.

'I see,' he said. 'We can't entertain in the kitchen. We'd best get the dining-room sorted.'

'If you please. I know you want to get the

outside to rights before doing any more to the house, but whitening the walls shouldn't take long, should it?' Florence paused. 'How did you get on at the auction?'

'Not bad at all.' Nathan told her about his purchases. 'The sheep will arrive next week, but the cows are due tomorrow. It looks as if some of the old staff are returning, too.'

'Wonderful!' Florence clapped her hands together in delight. 'Wait till I tell Chrissie about the cows. I caught her scrubbing out the dairy in anticipation! Oh, I almost forgot. There was a letter for you in the post.'

One look at the elegantly written address, and Nathan's heart began to thump. He'd know Isobel's hand anywhere. But what could she want?

He took the letter up to his room to find out.

My dear Nathan, Isobel began. *I fear as time passes that I have been remiss. I would like to apologise for how I behaved towards you at our last meeting . . .*

Nathan raked his hand through his hair. Glasgow and his life there was all in the past. He had a farm to run now . . . responsibilities . . .

He read on. Isobel would be in the area in the new year — she wanted to see him. Anger boiled up inside Nathan, bursting from his lips in a gasp. Well, she could want!

He made to slam the letter down on the shabby old pine dressing table. The sudden movement released a waft of perfume from the embossed writing paper, a piercing reminder of what he had lost. And then he saw the tiny lock of golden hair drift from the envelope to fall like a portent on to the faded wooden surface.

Isobel's hair. Trembling, he picked it up. How soft it was. Perhaps, for the sake of what had been between them, he should agree to meet . . .

4

'Och, will you look at them, Master Nathan!' Chrissie cried in delight. 'Have you ever seen such a fine sight as those wee kine?'

The three Red Polls in the stalls turned their heads as if in agreement, neck-chains jingling.

'You couldn't have sweeter wee creatures for starting off a herd, nor so willing. Why, they scarcely know me, yet the milk they let down for me this morning was so yellow and creamy I could hardly believe it. And Jim says they're in calf . . . '

Nathan looked into Chrissie's eager face and felt his heart tug strangely. His brow creased in bemusement and Chrissie caught her lip.

'Did I say something wrong, Master Nathan?'

'No, no, Chrissie. Just thinking. It's good news about the milk. Have you done anything with it yet? Apart from using it for the house, that is.'

'I should say we have!' Chrissie was off again. 'I've been showing Miss Aileen how to make butter. Och, the moans and lamenting!

She said her arm was dropping off with all the churning. 'You'll get used to it,' I told her. But dearie me!' Chrissie gurgled with laughter. 'She was like a dog with two tails when the butter came.'

Nathan chuckled.

'Actually, Chrissie, I came to ask if you happened to see our shepherd and his lad arrive. I was wondering how they're settling in.'

'Aye, I did. The poor young laddie walks with a terrible limp, and him so well-made and handsome, too. He had a friendly smile. Not like his father — a face on him like a wet weekend, that one!'

'Maybe he'll cheer up now he's back on home ground, eh?' Nathan said with a smile.

He was still smiling as he headed for the cottage behind the barns and outbuildings. There was something about Chrissie's good humour that made it seem as if the sun was shining even on the dullest day. His thoughts turned to Isobel and he sobered. He had replied to her letter, posting it himself in the village, away from prying eyes.

Filled with a terrible yearning for what might have been, he had agreed to meet her at the tavern in Shrewsbury where she and her father would be lodging. Almost as soon as he'd posted the letter, his misgivings had begun. Glasgow and everything he had known there was in the past. Though Isobel would have had his response by now, he still wondered whether he had done the right thing.

He squared his shoulders decisively. It would not happen for some weeks yet. He could put her out of his mind for the time being.

Nathan crossed the stackyard and arrived at the shepherd's cottage. As with Jim Merridew, the Turners were losing no time in going about the repairs. A ladder was propped against the gable end, and on the roof a young man with a mop of yellow hair was replacing a section of rotting thatch.

'Good morning!' Nathan called. 'I can see you're busy, so please don't come down. Thatching is a job that needs to be done while this weather holds.'

'You couldn't have said a truer word, gaffer. Pa's inside. Do go along in.'

Nathan knocked on the latched and studded door of the cottage. Two rangy sheepdogs, tied up in an open-fronted shed tacked on to the house, began to bark shrilly.

'The door inna bolted,' a voice shouted.

He entered the house to the now familiar and all-pervasive reek of tar. Silas was perched on a rung of a ladder, giving the rafters a good coating of preservative against the worm.

'Morning, gaffer.' The shepherd placed his brush in the pot of tar hooked over the end of the ladder and came down from his perch. 'What can I do for you?'

'I shan't hold you up. I simply wanted to know what you thought of the flock of sheep we bought from Shrewsbury.'

'The Clun Forest? They're a tidy bunch, in fine fettle. I reckon it wunna a bad move getting them.'

'Shepherd Turner,' Nathan said, 'I should make it clear that I am new to farming. I'm feeling my way and expect to be doing so for some time yet, so whatever you can tell me about the flock and their care will be welcome.'

'I understand, gaffer.'

'And if there is anything you need for repairs to the cottage, you must ask and we'll see what can be done. Help yourselves to produce, too: eggs, milk and such.' Nathan paused, not wanting to appear patronising. 'It can't be easy, with no woman to keep house for you.'

'Oh, we manage, Edward and me.'

'Yes, I'm sure. I'll leave you to it, man.'

Sending his shepherd a nod of farewell, Nathan went to seek out Jim Merridew.

He found him in the tithe barn, repairing a stack of hurdles.

'Morning, Jim. I've just come from the other cottage. It needed some sorting out. Those two seem to be knuckling down to it.'

'Aye, they will,' Jim said, without stopping what he was doing. 'Silas isn't the easiest of customers to get along with, but you can't fault his work. Did you meet his lad?'

'In a way. He was patching up the roof. He seems an agreeable sort.'

'Oh, aye, you'll not find better than Edward. Takes after his ma, he does. Beth was the prettiest creature that ever walked the earth. She had hair the colour of wild honey and the brightest smile you ever saw.'

'What happened to her?'

'She took scarlet fever and died. Edward must have been four or five at the time. I remember Edna Hutch having him at her place so he wouldn't take the infection. A good woman, is Edna.'

'What about Edward's leg? Will he be capable of working?'

'Surely.' Jim stopped weaving the twine through the slats of willow. He looked at Nathan steadily. 'I didn't mislead you, gaffer. Edward limps badly and his foot must pain him something terrible, but he works hard and you never hear a word of complaint.

'You'll find him gifted with the animals. He'll stop up all night with a cow that's calving and still be ready for work in the morning. I should say Edward Turner is the least of your worries.'

'I see. Well, that's reassuring. Can I help with those hurdles?'

'Gladly. I'll show you how it's done.' Jim reached for one from the pile. 'You remove the damaged slat like this, see. Slide in a new one so it fits nice and snug . . . '

* * *

The two men were working companionably, not saying much but concentrating on the task in hand, when the clamour of heavy iron-shod hoofs sounded on the road and Bess, Jamie's collie pup, set up a loud barking. Both men glanced up.

A broad grin crossed Jim Merridew's face.

'If I'm not mistaken, that's Wilkie and his team. I saw him the other night in the Dog. He said others had been laid off and he was expecting the same. Seems he was right.'

'I see,' Nathan said, putting aside his work and pulling to his feet. 'We'd better go and greet him.'

Out on the cobbled yard, Jamie was holding on to the squirming collie while

Wilkie Hutch bent to stroke her. Beside them stood two sturdy Shire horses, their harnesses gleaming in the wintry sunshine.

'Her name's Bess,' Jamie was saying. 'She's grown a lot. She was the runt of the litter and nobody wanted her.'

'Aye, I remember, young master. A right little tiddler she was. None of us thought she'd make it, and she wouldn't have, either, if it wunna for Jim and Edward Turner between them. By, but she's a bonnie thing. Will you get Silas to train her to the sheep?'

'I don't know. Is that the man that came earlier? He had two dogs with him.'

'They'd be his shepherding dogs.'

Ploughman Hutch straightened and re-moved his cloth cap as his boss and Jim Merridew appeared in front of him.

'Morning, gaffer. Jim.'

'I wasn't expecting you so soon, man,' Nathan said. 'Welcome back to Glebe Farm.'

'Thank you, gaffer. It's glad I am to be here.' The ploughman threw an interested glance around. 'Someone's been at work here all right. Proper run-down, the old place had got. It's looking more as it used to do a few years back.'

'Nice of you to say so. There's still a good deal to be done, I'm afraid. What's brought you here so early?'

'This morning Farmer Hayles said I wasn't needed any more so I came straight round. Well, I thought there might be some ploughing as needs doing before the ground gets too hard.' He pointed to a hilly field known as Mean Acre. 'That old patch needs attending to double sharp. She unna called Mean Acre for nothing. The ground's shallow, see, and the weeds love it. Will I start there?'

'Yes, go ahead, man. I'd be grateful. We'd put dealing with that field aside for now. Isn't that right, Jim?'

'It is. It needs a more expert hand than mine, and the man from Wollerton Manor wunna tackle it, either. He said it'd be too hard on old Captain.'

'He were right. My Rosie and Jack will have that ground turned over in no time. You'll be growing potatoes on it next year, gaffer.'

'I hope you're right,' Nathan said.

The door of the farmhouse opened and Florence came to greet the new arrival.

'I tell you straight, mistress. I'm happy to be back,' Wilkie Hutch declared. 'There unna nowhere like the Glebe.'

'Oh, let us hope we can return it to the way it was,' Florence said.

'It'll come in time, mistress. You may see

something of my Edna before long. She always lent a hand in the house where she could. Very fond of the old gaffer, she was. Looked after him during his last illness. Mortal sad we both were when he went.'

'I was, too,' Florence said. 'My uncle Reeve was a great favourite. I shall look forward to seeing your wife. I don't think I knew her before.'

'No, you wunna have, mistress. Me and Edna were wed after you'd gone off up north. Well, then, I'd better get on.' Wilkie looked at Jamie.

'Are you coming to see how to hold a plough, young master? You'd best leave that pup behind. We don't want her getting under the horses' feet. Want to get up on Jack and ride there?'

'Yes, please.'

Nathan felt the first lifting of the tension that had gripped him these past weeks. With men like these behind him, his chances of success looked distinctly brighter.

★ ★ ★

Florence was sweeping out the long-neglected dining-room when there was a light knock on the door. She shook the dust from her pinafore and went to answer it.

On the step stood a trim little woman with bright brown eyes and a clear complexion. Her gown and shawl, though much mended, were spotlessly clean.

'Good day, mistress,' she said. 'I'm Edna Hutch. I used to work here. I'd be glad to make myself useful at the Glebe again. Wilkie has explained about the wages. Those terms are acceptable to me as well.'

Florence looked into Edna Hutch's plain, good face and knew another gem had appeared in their midst.

'Please come in,' she said. 'You must excuse my appearance. I was cleaning the dining-room.'

At that moment there was a shout from the sick-room.

'Florence? Where in the world have you got to, woman? I want my cup of tea.'

Mortified colour touched Florence's cheek-bones.

'My husband,' she said, with an apologetic little gesture of her hand. 'He is not himself. His illness, you know.'

'I had heard,' Edna said calmly, divesting herself of her shawl and bonnet and hanging them neatly on the peg by the door with the ease born of familiarity. 'The poor master. You run along and see to him, mistress. I'll see what's what in the dining-room. It was never used much after the old master took bad. It'll be a treat to get it up shining bright again.'

'Florence?' Balfour's cry came again, frail and querulous. 'Where's my tea?'

Florence heaved a sigh. There was no denying it; despite all their efforts and the diligent ministrations of Dr Merrick, Balfour was growing more difficult with every day that passed.

'Give me strength!' she murmured, and went to attend to her husband.

⋆   ⋆   ⋆

Thanks to Nathan and Edna Hutch — who polished up the shabby old farmhouse furniture till they could see their faces in it — the room was ready to receive the Drummonds' first guests.

A fire of apple logs blazed in the massive grate, filling the room with fragrance. The curtains of crimson plush, made over from an old pair from better days, toned perfectly with the Turkey carpet Edna had hung over the line and beaten until not a speck of dust remained. Small occasional tables were strategically placed over the carpet's worn patches. Oil lamps gave a mellow glow over gleaming cutlery and crystal — the small amount Florence had saved after the Glasgow Bank crisis. The Hayleses, thankfully, would not know about that.

Jamie was in bed, his disappointment at missing out on the event mollified by the presence of Bess, who had been banished upstairs for the evening. Chrissie was serving at table and Edna Hutch had volunteered to sit with Balfour, with whom she got on astonishingly well.

Florence wore her dove-grey and Aileen her favourite blue. The pleasure of rustling silk after weeks in everyday woollen brought smiles to both their faces. Aileen, exhausted after a demanding day at Hadnall market, felt a cheering surge of energy.

'Such a pity you sold your jewellery,' Florence said at the sight of her daughter's bare neck. 'I shall fetch you my silver locket and chain. It will look well with the sky-blue.'

Aileen did not demur, for she had felt the loss of her trinkets more deeply than she cared to admit.

Nathan, out of his working togs and now in a dinner suit, his hair smoothly combed, was undeniably handsome. He had a new maturity about him that Florence liked.

Under her approving eye, they assembled to greet their guests.

Stanton Hayles and his daughter arrived on the dot of seven in a covered gig drawn by the farmer's strong black cob.

'Oh, what a pretty house!' Verity cried, looking up at the timbered and brick dwelling that glistened with frost under the stars.

'Indeed, m'dear,' her father said. 'This building will have stood a good two centuries. Ours is a newcomer by comparison, though I like our stone and slate, myself. Ah, here's our host. Evening, Drummond.'

'Good evening, sir. Ma'am. Do come in out of the cold.'

They went into the low-ceilinged, candle-lit hallway. Proudly, the farmer presented his daughter.

'Drummond, my girl, Verity. Verity, this is Mr Nathan Drummond.'

Verity Hayles, her cheeks glowing from the cold, sent Nathan a coquettish blue glance under long lashes and offered her hand. Her flaxen hair fell in ringlets about her heart-shaped face, and her mouth made the sort of pout that no man with an eye for a pretty girl could possibly resist.

'Miss Hayles. Charmed to meet you. Let me take your cloak and muff. And your topcoat, sir. Ah, here's Chrissie,' Nathan said as the maid arrived, a touch breathless and bringing with her a waft of good cooking smells, to take the guests' outdoor clothes.

Nathan ushered the pair directly into the dining-room where Florence and Aileen waited.

'Mama, come and greet our guests. Aileen, I don't think you have met Farmer Hayles and his daughter. This is my younger sister, Aileen.'

'What a charming room,' Stanton Hayles said, glancing round. 'There's nothing like a woman's touch. Makes a house into a home.'

Aileen went to chat with Verity. The two girls were much the same age, but while Verity spent her time more or less as she wished, Aileen's days were driven and constructive, and it showed.

'Do you ride, Miss Drummond? But of course you do. We shall go riding together one day very soon,' Verity trilled, clearly taken with the prospect of a friend with whom to exchange gossip and confidences.

Aileen was saved the embarrassment of replying by Chrissie announcing that the meal was about to be served, and would the company please care to be seated.

Chrissie had done them proud. The ox-tail soup and fried fillets of cod, followed by croquettes of fowl and pork cutlets and the crown of lamb, would have brought a nod of approval from Cook at Langsdale Avenue, where Chrissie had learned her skills.

Nathan was more discomfited by providing beverages suitable for their neighbours. Members of the Order of Rechabites were renowned supporters of the Temperance movement. In the end, he had settled for cordials produced by Chrissie and Aileen from the Glebe orchards.

'I see you went for those Clun Forest I recommended, Drummond,' Farmer Hayles said, accepting more cordial. 'A wise decision.'

'It seemed so to me,' Nathan replied, apparently unmoved by the implication that the choice of breed of sheep had come from the farmer, which it had not. 'My mistake was not going for more. We have a great deal of rough ground to be grazed off.'

'Indeed? That's no drawback, sir. I'd put the lot down to corn come spring. You've got the acreage. It's good soil. You're not without an experienced ploughman, either.'

Florence saw Nathan swallow hard, and prayed that their guest would not spend the entire evening riling her son.

'Indeed,' Nathan acknowledged neutrally. 'I shall certainly give the matter some thought.'

Finally, they settled round the fire with

coffee from the supplies that Dorcas had sent and, mellowed by the excellent meal, the conversation became easier. Aileen, suddenly sleepy in the warmth, stifled a yawn.

As the clock struck ten, their neighbour said he must not keep the horse out any longer and rose to leave. Verity thanked their hosts prettily for a delightful evening and repeated her request for Aileen to go riding with her.

Chrissie appeared with the guests' outdoor clothes. The Drummonds gathered on the front porch to see them off.

'I've enjoyed myself hugely. Please give my compliments to your cook. That was a feast fit for a king,' Farmer Hayles said as he handed his daughter up into the gig. 'We must return the honour, aye, Verity?'

'Do you know, I rather like Stanton Hayles,' Florence announced after the carriage had gone rolling away. 'Oh, I know he likes to throw his weight about a little, but he's not without a certain charm. And Verity is a picture. Do you not agree, Nathan?'

'Indeed, Mama.'

Florence hid a smile. Verity Hayles was young and pretty. She would make a very suitable match for Nathan. What a joy if the two farms could be joined at some point. She let the idea rest for now and headed off to the small parlour to see how Balfour had fared.

Florence found her husband snoring soundly in his bed and Edna, having stowed her knitting away in her basket, putting on her bonnet and shawl.

'There you are, mistress. The master has had a bite of supper. He's been quite cheerful. I think he enjoyed the change of company. I've built up the fire for you — you'll not want it getting cold in here. Did the evening go well?'

'Very well, thank you, Edna. I am so grateful for your help,' Florence said. 'It is late. Nathan must see you home.'

'No need, mistress. My man was going to the Dog on the Upper Astley road for a game of darts. He'll be waiting for me at the lane end. I'll say goodnight, mistress.'

Florence watched Edna walk briskly away across the frosted cobblestones, and thought that somewhere a guardian angel had to be watching over them to have sent such worthy staff to Glebe Farm.

* * *

'I met the post-boy in the lane, mistress,' Chrissie said. 'He gave me this letter for you. It's from Africa.'

She handed it over, proud to have

deciphered the envelope.

'Oh, joy! Word from Davina at last!' Florence put aside her mending and ripped open the envelope, her eyes sparkling. 'I've been so worried. There's been nothing since December. Let us hope all is well.'

Christmas had come and gone. January snow lay thickly over the countryside.

'Oh . . . ' Florence murmured, frowning over her letter.

'Is something wrong, mistress?' Chrissie enquired.

'Well, not exactly, but . . . ' Florence looked up, her eyes anxious. 'Davina speaks of unrest in the district. Some of the other missionary families are talking of removing to another station. Dear me, I hope Finbar will do the same. When I think of those two babes . . . '

'Mr Finbar will take good care of them all,' Chrissie assured her mistress. 'Try not to worry yourself too much, mistress. When was the letter dated?'

'The third of November. It's been weeks getting here. Anything could have happened in that time.'

'Now, now, mistress. You mustn't fret. You have enough on your plate here without worrying about things that might not even be happening.'

'You are right. And, I suppose, if he were

really troubled, Finbar would be the first to remove his family to safety.'

Florence looked Chrissie over closely and the girl waited, aware that her achievements at the reading and penning had made her more self-assured. She was even losing her soft Highland brogue; her speech was taking on the clarity of Miss Aileen's, brought about by the need to make herself understood quickly at their increasingly successful market stall.

'Are you happy here, Chrissie?' her mistress asked now.

'Yes, mistress,' Chrissie replied truthfully.

She had developed a certain status at the Glebe, she realised. The men looked up to her and there were times — heart-stopping times — when Master Nathan treated her almost as an equal, including her in the conversation when he and Jim Merridew were making plans for the year ahead.

'I wouldn't change places with anyone.'

'I am very glad to hear it . . . Listen!' Florence broke off. 'Do I hear hoofbeats?'

'I think so. Will I go and look?'

Chrissie hurried to the door, letting in a blast of bitter air and a few drifting flakes of snow.

'It's Miss Dorcas, mistress. She's on her horse and she's leading another one.'

Florence smiled and shook her head.

'Trust my sister not to be beaten by the weather. Where is my cape? Ah, I have it. Is the kettle boiling? She'll be ready for a hot drink.'

Out in the farmyard, Dorcas was dismounting from her lively grey mare. With her, wearing a bridle and side-saddle, was a chestnut, sturdy in bone and boasting the pretty dished face and noble carriage of the Arabian.

'Good morning. What a lovely day. Would my niece be about?' Dorcas called, her breath smoking in the sharp air.

Aileen came speeding from the dairy where she had been skimming cream for the butter.

'Ah, Aileen. I had my stableman look around for something suitable for you, and he's found this young mare. Her name is Firefly. Suits her, does it not?'

For a moment Aileen was speechless.

'Oh, Aunt,' she gasped. 'She's beautiful! Oh, Mama, Chrissie . . . isn't she gorgeous?'

They gathered round the little mare, fussing her. It crossed Chrissie's mind to wonder what Master Nathan would make of the new arrival. Horses at the Glebe had to earn their keep and this was a riding horse, and a lady's mount at that.

No sooner had the thought struck than

Nathan emerged from the tithe barn where he had been mending a broken ploughshare. His hands were black with grease and there was a smudge across one cheek. One look at the group gathered around the horse, and his expression tightened.

'Morning, Aunt. What's this?'

'It's a horse, Nathan,' Dorcas responded archly. 'Your sister cannot continue to tramp round the lanes on foot, and that vehicle of yours is likely to fall to bits before long. Aileen has a birthday coming up soon. Regard this little mare as my gift to her.'

'But, Aunt Dorcas . . . ' Nathan struggled to find the right words. 'This is a very generous gesture, but a saddle horse is a luxury. I'm sorry, but you must take the animal back.'

'Nathan!' Aileen rounded furiously on her brother. 'This is unfair. I've worked my fingers to the bone and this is all the thanks I get. When Verity Hayles mentioned going out riding I felt mortified. Thank goodness the snow came and she couldn't pursue the subject. And now I have a chance to hold up my head in society you want to ruin it all. Well, I won't have it!'

'Aileen — '

'Don't Aileen me!' Her voice throbbed on the verge of tears.

She cast a desperate glance at the dismayed faces around her. 'Mama, say something!'

Florence put her hand on her son's arm.

'Nathan, perhaps we should go inside and discuss this in private.'

'There's nothing to discuss, Mama. Believe me, I would have looked for a mount for Aileen if it were possible to keep one here. But it isn't.'

'Stuff and nonsense!' Dorcas said, brisk but kindly. 'Nathan, I have to confess there is method in my madness. I'm a selfish woman and I have a liking for company when I ride out on Gemini.

'I know my niece's presence is required here. But she's young, and believe me, Nathan, all work and no play can make Jill a very dull girl. Would you deny your sister a little light recreation?'

'It's not that, Aunt.' Nathan ran his hand hopelessly over his hair, where flecks of snow were settling. 'To be blunt, we have enough oats and hay to last Captain and Wilkie Hutch's two horses the rest of the winter, and that's it. I cannot afford to buy more fodder for an animal that cannot pull its weight on the farm.'

'Nobody expects you to, Nathan, my love. Did I not mention it?' Dorcas assumed a look of utter candidness. 'Firefly comes with her own supplies. Being gently bred, she cannot be fed the same rations as those great lumbering farm-horses. As soon as I get back to Wollerton I shall send my man along with her feed. Best meadow hay, of course. And crushed oats and barley. There's sufficient to last well into the spring.'

There was a small silence. 'Shall we go in for tea, sister?' Florence said. 'Nathan, will you join us?'

'I think not, Mama. I had better prepare a stall for the new horse.'

'And I shall take a turn at riding her.' Aileen, all smiles, delivered her brother a grateful peck on his cheek. 'Thank you, Nathan. Oh, and darling, darling Aunt Dorcas, how can I ever thank you enough?'

'Your face says all, my dear,' Dorcas replied.

The sisters went indoors.

'I know those two, once they get cosy over a pot of tea,' Nathan said, with a nod at the house, 'they'll be there for the best part of an hour. Chrissie, could you put my aunt's mare in the stall, please, while I fetch some straw?'

'Gladly,' Chrissie said. 'Master Nathan?'
'Yes?'

'For what it's worth, you've done the best thing. Miss Dorcas was right in what she said.

Too much work does make for dullness; no-one knows that better than I. Miss Aileen is a gentlewoman. She should mix with her own sort, and she needs some time to herself to enjoy what she likes doing. The mare will give her that.'

'I'm sure you're right, Chrissie.' Nathan shot her one of his increasingly rare smiles. 'And, Chrissie?'

'Yes?'

'Even if you worked until you dropped, you could never be described as dull!'

* * *

Nathan whistled cheerfully as he screwed the final bolt on the ploughshare into place. There, it was done. He always had enjoyed tinkering with defunct machinery, and there was plenty of it on the farm.

As soon as the snow melted he would have the blades sharpened at the forge, and that would give them a spare ploughshare for the coming spring.

Jim had not been keen on Farmer Hayles's suggestion of putting the land down to corn.

'What if the weather turns against us? You've got all your eggs in one basket. A drought or too much rain, and you stand to lose the lot.'

'That's always the risk with crops,' Nathan argued.

'Yes, but you don't have to use all the ground. Leave some of it fallow. With luck we'll more than double the flock, once the ewes lamb. Fifty head of sheep will soon nibble off the rough grass, and what doesn't get eaten can be ploughed in as green mulch.

' 'Course, 'tis up to you, gaffer.'

But the thought of acres of waving golden corn was too much for Nathan to resist.

He imagined the stackyard filling with neat round corn ricks, and a fine, full feed loft once the miller had done his work. He should have enough left over to sell at the corn market, too . . .

'Nathan?' Jamie hollered. The boy appeared in the doorway, his face flushed and eyes bright. Bess was at his side.

'Nathan, there's someone coming up the lane. I was up in the barn, getting some hay for Firefly, and I saw them. It looked like a mother with a baby. There was a little girl, as well. The lady was loaded up with stuff. She looked awful lumbered, Nathan.'

'A woman? Coming here? We'd best go and see what she wants'

They crossed the snowy yard and reached the gate that now hung on new hinges.

Nathan stared, squinting his eyes against the cold red sun.

The figure trudging wearily up the road towards him seemed vaguely familiar. Her bonnet had fallen back, and the sun glinted on her bright auburn hair.

She carried a baby wrapped in a shawl on one arm, and had a bundle strapped across her back. She held the hand of a very small infant.

The child's voice carried plaintively over the air.

'Mama, are we nearly there? I'm very tired, Mama.'

Then the woman's voice, gently pleading.

'There, child. Look, there's a house ahead. I do believe this is it. Just a little further. You've been so very brave.'

Recognition dawned, and Nathan caught his breath.

'Davina! Good heavens, what now?' He turned to Jamie. 'Jamie, take the dog indoors and fetch Mama. Tell her we have a visitor. Look sharp.'

The boy raced off, Bess at his heels. Nathan opened the gate and hurried to greet his sister.

At closer quarters he could see how utterly exhausted she was. Gratefully she placed the sleeping baby in his arms.

'Brother, at last,' she said, dropping the bundle of belongings into the snow on the verge with a small sigh of relief. 'How glad I am to see you. These are your nieces, Annabel and Catherine. Nathan, we have come home!'

5

'Now then, my love,' Florence said to her elder daughter. 'Let us be cosy here by the fire, and you shall tell me all your news.'

She drew up two chairs invitingly to the kitchen hearth and they both sat down, Davina a little apprehensively.

After a rapturous reunion, the weary travellers had been swept into the house and treated to a good hot meal. Nathan had tactfully withdrawn to see to the animals, taking Jamie with him. Aileen went to the stables to bed Firefly down for the night.

Throughout all the bustle and excitement, Balfour Drummond slept soundly. He slept a lot these days. Dr Merrick had told Florence it was to be expected.

The little girls — Annabel, three and a half, and eighteen month-old Catherine — had hardly been able to keep their eyes open and were now tucked up in the bed Chrissie had hastily made up in the largest of the spare bedrooms.

It had been nearly five years since the Lennoxes had left for Africa and Florence saw changes in her daughter. Always sturdy, with the Drummond bright-auburn hair and sharp blue eyes, the bearing of children had rendered Davina's figure plump. The pallor and sheer exhaustion on the young woman's face had been a shock. But now, fortified by food and hot sweet tea, a little colour had returned to her cheeks, and her eyes, though guarded, were less heavy.

'Mama, I scarcely know where to begin,' Davina said.

'Well, what of Finbar? He's not — '

'No, no. Finbar is well and whole . . . or was when we left.'

Some sixth sense cautioned Florence to brace herself. Granted, it was feasible for the wives of missionaries to travel alone, but it seemed unlikely that Finbar Lennox would be happy for his own wife to do so, given her condition and the fact that she had the two children with her. She took a deep, sustaining breath.

'I've left Finbar, Mama. I had no choice.'

'You . . . you've left your husband'?' Florence's hand went to her throat in shock. 'Mercy on us, Davina! Not a word of this to your father!'

'So what do you suggest, Mama?' Davina retorted with more than a touch of her old spirit. 'That I lie to him?'

Florence struggled to gather her scattered wits.

'No, of course not. We shall have to think what to tell him. But on no account is he to be upset. The shock could . . . ' Florence could not say the words. 'You do understand?'

'Yes, Mama, I understand perfectly. But Papa will have to know some time. I have come back to this country to live and Finbar wishes to remain in Africa.'

'Davina, please forgive me if I pry, but could you be more specific?'

Davina darted her mother a hard glance.

'I think I explained some of what happened when I wrote to you. Barotse seemed ideal at first. We had our bungalow, our servants and a reasonable social life. The other wives were admirable, on the whole. I became very friendly with one in particular, Annie Platt. She and her husband were the first to leave after the trouble began.'

'Trouble?'

'I didn't like to go into too much detail in my letter for fear of worrying you. Oh, Mama, words cannot express how frightening it was. There was an uprising. The natives . . . nothing could get through to them. The word of God was meaningless. They regarded us a threat and wanted us gone.'

In a few graphic words Davina described what had happened. The authorities had moved in and tried to bring the situation under control, but the servants, afraid of reprisal from their own people, would no longer work for the missionaries. Gradually, the settlement became depleted as, one by one, families left for safer ground.

'In the end it was just us, a few single men and the couple who ran the Stores. I begged Finbar to come away. I begged him. He would not entertain it. He was there on the Lord's work and there he would stay. I could not make him see how nonsensical it was. Mama, you have no idea what he was like.'

'Oh, yes,' Florence said sorrowfully. 'I think I have.'

'There were such stories going round. My children and the new babe had to come first. I told Finbar I was coming home and he could do as he wished. He has made his choice.'

'Perhaps in the fullness of time he will have a change of heart,' Florence said soothingly.

Davina gave her head a fretful little shake, as if she doubted it.

Florence sighed.

'I'm sorry, my darling. You know you have our love and support.'

'Thank you. I was afraid . . . oh, I hardly

knew how you would respond. If I hadn't been expecting again . . . You know how it is, Mama. One has a yearning to be safe and secure.'

'I understand, my dear. Well, then, we must try to look on the bright side. A new little babe! When is it to be?'

'The beginning of April. Mama, I was thinking of returning to Glasgow eventually. I still have friends there, and there will never be anywhere else for me. But for the time being . . . if we could stay here it would be a great weight off my mind.'

'Davina, of course you must stay with us. You know you don't even have to ask.'

'I have a little money, but I don't know how long it will last. The girls and I had to travel steerage — it was all so different from last time. We stayed overnight at the cheapest lodgings I could find in Portsmouth, and took the first train north this morning.

'The walk here from the station was the worst. Catherine was so heavy to carry. I had to keep stopping for a rest, and then Annabel cried because she was cold, poor sweet. Neither of them had seen snow before. I think the novelty soon wore off.'

'Never mind, you're here now and safe, the children, too. What darlings they are. I can't tell you how thrilled I am to see them at last.

And how nice for Jamie to have his nieces here. He'll be able to take them under his wing.'

Davina just smiled and covered a yawn. Florence was at once contrite.

'My dear, here I am keeping you talking when you must be quite worn out. Why don't you go on upstairs? A good night's sleep and you'll feel much better tomorrow.'

'But there's Papa. Should I not see him tonight?'

'Leave it till the morning. Let me explain first that you are here. It will be less of a shock for him.'

'Very well.' Davina stood up, swaying visibly. 'Dear me, Mama, you are right. I am so tired I can scarcely stand . . . '

*   *   *

Much later, after the household had retired for the night, Florence and Nathan sat discussing what was to be done.

'I've told your father that Davina had to leave Africa because of the dangerous situation, which is nothing but the truth,' Florence said.

'How did he take it?'

'Oh, very well, considering. He was surprised, of course. He can't wait to see

Davina again, and the little girls, naturally. I didn't need to go into details. He seemed to accept that Finbar would have to stay where he was until his term of office expired.

'Nathan, I know this will sound shamefully unworthy and penny-pinching, but three more mouths to feed? How shall we manage?' Florence's voice faltered.

'You mustn't reproach yourself, Mama,' Nathan replied. 'My thoughts have been running along the same lines. It seems to me that Davina turning up like this might be put to our advantage.

'Chrissie will have her work cut out now that I've agreed to take on those extra cows Jim wanted. Edward doesn't mind lending a hand in the dairy and the milking-shed, but he's needed elsewhere, and we put on Chrissie too heavily before, if you remember.'

'Yes, but what has all this to do with Davina?' Florence asked.

'I was thinking of employing a girl to help out. Davina could do the work instead.'

There was a shocked silence. The fire crackled and Nathan bent to stroke Bess, who had settled down before it, her nose on her front paws.

'Davina?' Florence's voice split the quiet. 'Nathan, Davina's in a delicate condition. She may not be fit enough.'

'Oh, fie, Mama! Davina's as strong as an ox. She could surely churn a pound or two of butter and help Aileen with the market bakes? We were none of us cut out for this sort of life, but we've adapted and so will she.'

Florence shrugged, seeing the sense in the argument.

'Very well. Let us put it to her in the morning, but not until after she has seen her father. What a joy that will be for him. He'll want to know all about missionary life in Africa, right down to the last detail. It will keep him amused for hours.'

'There is that. I must say I'm still in shock myself. Who'd have thought Davina would turn up out of the blue like that? It'll be interesting to know what she makes of what we've decided. Let us hope she agrees, eh?'

Davina, it turned out, was far from impressed.

'Work on the farm? Mama, you cannot be serious? It's hardly respectable. Anyway, you know I never did like the country. It smells, and there are too many flies.'

'But you will have seen worse in Africa,' Nathan said. 'It must have been more primitive, as well.'

'Indeed it was not. We lived to a civilised standard, let me tell you. I had my own servants. There were plenty of staff to see to the manual work. Nathan, Mama — you cannot expect me to do this.'

'I'm sorry, Davina, but the matter is settled,' Florence replied in a voice that brooked no argument. 'We have all had to adapt. There's no reason why you should be different. If we are to survive here it is crucial that we all pull our weight.'

'Pull our weight? Is that what you call it? Milking cows and sweeping floors? My own brother, cleaning out cowsheds? Jamie running wild like a village urchin. As for Aileen — '

'Davina, please!' Florence said with an anxious glance towards the sick room. 'Your father: he must not be upset.'

'I'm sorry.' Davina collected herself and went on more quietly, 'But truly, I am shocked at how you live here. When I think of how it used to be. And now, this . . . '

She flicked a disparaging hand at the bright, homely kitchen.

'You should have seen it before,' Nathan put in dryly.

Florence sent her daughter a look of appeal.

'Davina, dear. Do try to see this from our point of view.'

'Or at the very least, look at it practically,' Nathan added, twinkling. 'If the house doesn't suit, I'll mix you up a pail of whitewash. You can give the walls a fresh coating.'

Davina went pale.

'Don't listen to him, Davina,' Florence said, laughter in her voice. 'He's only jesting. As to the rest, I'm afraid it still stands. Chrissie will show you what to do in the dairy. The work is not heavy, and anyway, a little exercise will be good for you. I'm sure Aileen will appreciate your company at the baking, as well.'

Davina opened her mouth to protest, took one look at her mother's face and closed it again. Florence, knowing she had won her case, gave her daughter a conciliatory kiss on her cheek and went through to the small parlour to check if Balfour needed anything.

*　*　*

'Where's the gaffer off to, then?' Silas Turner said. 'All dressed up like a dog's dinner! I scarcely recognised him!'

''Tes business in Shrewsbury,' Jim Merridew answered. 'The family deal with the accountant there.'

'That were fancy dressing to see a dry stick of a man like Weston Roseberry. Unless of course he's taken on a dandy new lady

124

assistant,' Ploughman Wilkie Hutch put in.

Edward Turner, as always, remained quiet.

The four Glebe workers were seated in the open door of the barn, taking their midday snap of bread fresh from the oven, a wedge of hard red cheese and an onion.

Silas bit into his with a crunch that made the eyes water.

'I dunna hold with females taking on a man's job. They're too flipperty by far. They unna got the brain for it.'

'Oh, come on now, Da,' Edward piped up, causing the other three to stare in surprise. 'There must be plenty of ladies who can tackle an office job, and make a good fist of it, too. Look at Chrissie. She can reckon up in her head as quick as a wink, and she reads and pens as good as anyone. Miss Dorcas is another. Runs the manor and that business as well as any fellow, she does. What's flipperty about that?'

'I daresay the lad has a point,' Ploughman Hutch said.

'Mebbe, but show me the female that can do all them things and still have a bonnie look about her,' Silas remarked.

'There's Chrissie,' his son said indignantly.

Jim Merridew threw the lad a grin.

'What's this, then, Edward. Are you sweet on Chrissie Ross?'

'Nah. No point. A maid like her wouldn't look twice at a cripple.'

Edward shifted his position to ease the damaged ankle that pained him so, and retreated once more into his shell.

There was a sympathetic silence, broken by Jim Merridew.

'Good thing the snow's gone at last. Mind you, March can be bad. When are those Clun Forest due, Silas?'

'The gaffer said towards the middle of the month, but I reckon it could be earlier. Two dozen ewes when there used to be a few hundred cropping the Glebe heights. Who'd believe the like?'

'It'll be a short lambing, look at it that way,' Hutch said. 'If you manage to triple the numbers, we'll be on the road to building up a decent flock again.'

'Amen to that,' Jim Merridew said.

'Twin lambs all round?' The shepherd looked wry. 'It's possible, though there's bound to be losses, especially with first-timers. So long as it doesn't turn wet, that's all. Newborn lambs can do without it.'

He chewed thoughtfully on a mouthful of bread.

'I can't say I'm in any great hurry for big numbers just yet, not with those tumbledown walls to tackle and the roof on the shepherd's hut needing repairs.'

'I'll give you a hand with the walls,' Jim offered. 'There's still snow up on the heights, but once it's gone we can make a start.'

'Right-oh,' Silas said.

'What about your cottage? Have you got it to rights yet?' Ploughman Hutch enquired.

'Aye, it'll do. Why d'you ask?'

'There's a darts match tonight at the Dog. I thought you might be interested in going.'

'Well, I unna. I got other things on.'

'Oh, aye?' Jim Merridew's eyes narrowed. 'Would that be union business?'

'That's my affair,' Silas growled.

Jim took a swig of cold tea.

'The gaffer was saying a barn had gone up in flames at Shifnal. That's a mite too close for comfort, if you ask me. You wouldn't know anything about it, I suppose?'

'I might and I might not,' Silas said.

Edward kept his gaze firmly lowered and the men finished their midday meal in silence.

★   ★   ★

The train rattled towards Shrewsbury. Nathan moved in his seat and eased his finger round the stiff neck of his collar. The hard physical work of the past months had honed his figure to a muscled toughness and his suit of fine grey worsted — made by a Glasgow tailor and once a perfect fit — felt unfamiliar and uncomfortable. His shirt, pristine and crackling from Edna Hutch's ministrations, felt fresh against his skin, even if the collar did threaten to choke him.

Isobel, Isobel, Isobel.

The carriage wheels drummed her name as the train sped ever closer to its destination. The meeting they had arranged for January had been postponed because of bad weather. It was almost spring. The signs were everywhere. Catkins hung delicately on boughs that were bursting into tender leaf, and only that morning Chrissie had come across a pale drift of primroses under the hedge — her favourite spring flower, she said.

Recalling the eager glow on her face, Nathan's lips twisted into a smile. Chrissie had flowered herself over recent months. But he felt a fleeting regret for the old Chrissie, with her quick looks and quaint turn of phrase . . .

Not for the first time, he regretted having responded to Isobel's letter. She belonged to the past, as surely as did the clothes on his back and the boyhood dreams of university and life as an engineer. Nathan sighed, and the man opposite looked up from his newspaper with a frown.

The train rolled into Shrewsbury station and fifteen minutes later Nathan was entering the foyer of the Lion and Pheasant, the comfortable sixteenth-century coaching inn where Isobel and her father were staying.

Alistair Macnair greeted Nathan distantly and at once excused himself, saying he had urgent business to attend to and he trusted Nathan would not keep his daughter too long. Inwardly bristling at the slight, Nathan turned to face Isobel.

She was more beautiful than ever, and he caught his breath. She wore an afternoon gown of delicate pink silk, and the violet-blue eyes that gazed up at him from beneath a golden fringe of curls shone in silent appeal.

'Nathan, how wonderful to see you again. You look different. More . . . mature?'

Behind her, a maid hovered in attendance, a mouse-haired girl Nathan remembered of old, whose keen eyes and ears never missed a thing.

'And you are as lovely as ever,' he said gallantly, and taking Isobel's hand he pressed it to his lips.

'Have you had luncheon? No? Then perhaps you will join me?'

They were shown to a table close to the fire in the cosy beamed and flagged dining-room.

Isobel's maid remained in attendance, though at a discreet distance.

'Isobel, delighted as I am to see you again, I must know what has brought all this about,' Nathan said as the waiter left them. 'During our last encounter, it seemed to me that you made it perfectly clear where your wishes lay.'

Isobel fluttered her lashes in a well-remembered way.

'I felt I should apologise for what I said then. Not in a letter, but in person. I'm sorry, Nathan. I behaved abominably. What happened was none of your doing.'

'None of my father's, either. He did the noble thing and paid all he could to the creditors, and at the expense of the family's happiness and wellbeing. You know of his illness?'

'Only what you told me in your letter. I was sorry to hear of it. How does he now?'

She might have been talking about a neighbourhood acquaintance.

'Father does well enough,' Nathan replied coolly. 'He'll never be robust again, and of course, there is always the fear of another seizure.'

'How trying for you. Are you intending to return north in the near future?'

'No, of course not,' he said a trifle shortly. 'I have a farm to run, responsibilities

. . . Now that Father is incapacitated it is up to me to head the household. How could I possibly dally away the time in a holiday?'

Isobel's mouth turned down pettishly.

'I didn't mean that. What I meant was, when will you return for good? Nathan, you are not a farmer. You are far too genteel for that. You cannot actually *like* what you are doing?'

'On the contrary, I don't mind it in the least.'

It was true. His lips twitched as he realised how much he had changed.

Isobel, believing the smile for her, reached out to touch his arm lightly.

'Oh, Nathan. Perhaps I should not say this, but there will never be anyone else but you in my heart. Please, do you think we might start again?'

He shook his head.

'It's out of the question, Isobel. Your papa would never allow it. Can you see yourself as a farmer's wife? Working in the dairy, seeing to the poultry, getting your hands dirty'?'

The look in Isobel's eyes was answer enough.

'My papa might help us. He could find you a position in the business.'

'I'm sorry to have to be so blunt, Isobel, but your papa was not generous with his help when it was most needed. It would have taken but a word to prevent what happened to my family. If he had given us fair warning of the troubles with the bank — and it was clear he knew, or he'd have been floundering with the rest of us — then we'd still be in Glasgow and flourishing. A few quiet words were all that was required. That's what my father would have done in his place.'

At that point the waiter arrived. Anything else Nathan might have said — and perhaps regretted later — was lost. He mustered a smile, feeling suddenly strong and in command.

'There now, Isobel. Let us enjoy our meal. I'm afraid this will be a short reunion. I have a train to catch at four . . . '

The look Isobel shot him would stay in his memory for quite some time.

★ ★ ★

Sunshine filtered through trees and the early April air felt soft on Chrissie's face as she set off for Wollerton Manor. In the nursery fields, the new lambs frisked and frolicked — the flock almost tripled, thanks to Shepherd Turner's skills.

Old Captain strode out with a spring in his step, the empty cart rumbling lightly along. It would be a different matter on the return journey, Chrissie thought, fetching the reins a flip. For Dorcas Webb had promised them several sacks of seed potatoes and some raspberry canes, and since now was the best time for planting, the items had suddenly become urgent.

She guided the horse and cart under the clock-arch, where a weathercock of a rearing horse spun in the breeze, and reined in on the stableyard. A stable lad appeared to take the horse, sending her a cheeky grin.

'Morning, Chrissie.'

'Good morning, Dan. And it's *Miss* Chrissie, if you don't mind.'

The lad grinned all the more and led the horse away, cart wheels rattling over the well-kept cobblestones.

'Chrissie! Good morning,' a voice hailed her, and Dorcas Webb appeared from the direction of the kitchen gardens.

She wore a battered straw hat on her springy curls and a shapeless smock over her gown. From the deep pockets protruded a trowel and a small fork. Her gardening boots of brown leather were thick with mud, which she removed by scraping her feet vigorously on the black-iron shoe-scraper by the back door.

'I was weeding the strawberry beds. You

wouldn't think any self-respecting weed would grow after all that snow we had, would you? But they do, the imps!'

'I'm sorry. Am I holding you up?' Chrissie said.

'Holding me up? I should think not indeed. I'm only too glad to have a visitor. Shall we go indoors and I'll ring for some tea? You must be ready for it after the drive here. Grand weather we're having. Mind you, we haven't seen the last of the winter yet. Frost in May we had last year, and all the blossom nipped . . . '

Talking nineteen to the dozen, Dorcas led the way into the house, along rambling corridors and through to the shadowed hall, where a bright fire crackled in the grate and two large hounds and a small spaniel dozed before it.

'Come, Chrissie, let us sit here by the fire. There, I must say I'm quite relieved to take the weight off my feet.'

The tea arrived, together with a plate of fresh-baked gingerbread, dark and moist.

Chrissie had long learned to let her hostess do the talking and simply to respond when necessary. She had come prepared for a grilling, since Dorcas was always keen to know how her family fared, and considered Chrissie the perfect one to ask.

Sure enough, over the refreshments the questions came thick and fast.

'How copes my younger niece with the little mare? Well, I hope?'

'Oh, yes. Miss Aileen loves to ride, and she looks after Firefly very well. My mistress says she's the most spoilt animal in the county, but Miss Aileen will have none of it. She says Firefly is the best thing that ever happened to her. Riding certainly gets her out and about. She goes out a lot with Miss Hayles. They've become quite friendly.'

'Stanton Hayles's daughter? There's a pampered miss if ever there was one. I don't envy the man she weds. A merry dance she'll lead the fellow, to be sure.'

Dorcas passed her the plate of gingerbread, nodding approvingly when Chrissie took a large slice.

'What of Davina? Is she settling any better into the fold?'

'Well, no, not really. Mrs Lennox has no love of country life. I suppose it takes all sorts but . . . dear me, there have been ructions!'

Over the weeks, Chrissie had learned that she could speak plainly to Dorcas Webb. At some point, servant and mistress of the manor had reached beyond the boundaries of status and become friends.

Dorcas looked up from pouring more tea,

curiosity all over her face.

'Ructions? How interesting. Do tell me more.'

'It was over the dairy work. I've shown and shown Mrs Lennox how to use a butter churn, but a few turns of the handle and she puts it aside. It makes her arm ache, her back hurts, her feet are cold standing on the stone floor . . . '

'She needs to wear two pairs of knitted stockings. That'll keep her warm enough.'

'I told her that. Mrs Lennox threw up her hands in horror and said she wears only silk.'

'Silk, is it? And here's me thinking that missionaries had to sing for their supper!'

'Not Mr Finbar. I heard he was granted a generous allowance on his marriage, so as the couple wouldn't want for much,' Chrissie said confidingly. 'I . . . I'm not sure what will happen now.'

Chrissie looked down at her feet. The mistress had drawn her to one side and whispered what had happened between the young couple, warning Chrissie that — where the master was concerned, in particular — Davina Lennox had come home to await the birth of her child and Finbar was to follow at a later date. Chrissie, already accustomed to keeping her counsel in the face of the villagers' curiosity about the

136

family's move from Glasgow, found it hard to escape the feeling that Glebe Farm was fast turning into a house of secrets.

'Ah!' Dorcas said with a nod of understanding. 'A sorry business all round. My niece did a brave thing to travel all that way with two tiny tots, and her carrying, as well. Could she not be given some light work in the house for now?'

'It was suggested, but Mrs Lennox was displeased with the notion. Master Nathan said he'd look for a girl to help out in the dairy but the mistress insists. She says everyone must do their bit.'

'Yes, I can see my sister's point. The trouble is Davina's like her father — stubborn as they come! If all fails you might try for a village girl. Edna Hutch might know of someone reliable.'

An impish gleam appeared in Dorcas Webb's sharp storm-grey eyes.

'What's this about my nephew taking luncheon with a pretty young miss? My manager was in Shrewsbury a few weeks ago and saw them. Have you any idea who she was?'

The jealousy that flamed within Chrissie shocked her. She had seen Isobel's letter awaiting Nathan's attention all those months ago and had guessed, from the feminine hand

and perfumed envelope, who the sender might be. When Nathan had asked her if she would mind running a sponge over his suit of best woollen worsted, before his meeting in Shrewsbury, it had not taken much to work out what was going on.

'Yes, ma'am,' Chrissie said, astonished at the calmness in her voice. 'It would be Miss Isobel. She and Master Nathan were betrothed, if you remember.'

She swallowed and turned her attention to the gingerbread, which tasted all at once like straw.

The dogs had come to sit beside them and were throwing pleading looks at their mistress, when the clatter of hoofbeats outside had them woofing and bounding to the door.

The hasty approach of footsteps on the passageway beyond was followed by the door bursting open and Aileen appeared. She was out of breath and looked distressed.

'Aunt Dorcas, I'm so sorry to intrude,' she cried, 'but Chrissie must come at once. It's Father. He's been taken badly. Nathan has gone for the doctor but . . . oh, Chrissie, I fear it may be too late!'

6

The ploughshare cut cleanly through the hard earth and steam from the horse's flanks rose into the sweet upland air. Nathan stumbled inexpertly behind, lead rein in his right hand, foot in the furrow, the plough-breast moving with a rustling scrape over compacted soil and stone.

On the lower levels, Wilkie Hutch's team thudded their deliberate course, the plough-man in firm control, the cold, unyielding earth churned to a sea of furrows in their wake.

Sorrow had come to Glebe Farm with the early spring. Balfour Drummond had suffered a second seizure from which he had died. With the family thrown into mourning and Nathan now officially head of the household, he had quietly taken stock. Part of him still yearned for the engineering career he had once set his heart on, but now he felt driven to make a success of the farm, not only for his family's sake, but also to prove that he could do it. He sat up far into the night, reading the farming manuals on the shelf in the office, making plans.

Glebe Farm boasted a great deal of open pasture and as yet did not carry enough stock to graze it down. It seemed feasible to Nathan to turn the unproductive acres into something that would bring rewards. Why not put the unused acreage under the plough and plant crops?

Jim Merridew had been sceptical.

'Plough up the high ground?' Jim had removed his threadbare cap and scratched his grizzled head in bemusement. 'I dunno 'bout that, gaffer. That's always been sheep pasture as far as I can recall.'

The other men had sided with Merridew. The Glebe had always been a mixed farm. Making pasture over to arable was taking a risk, and — as Ploughman Hutch warned — it was getting late in the season for ploughing.

Nathan had gone ahead anyway. They had stripped the surface from meadow and upland, burned the turves and scattered the residue on the land. Ploughman Hutch, his weathered face set and disapproving, had harnessed up his team and set to work. The coulter had swiped cleanly through the tangled roots of dandelion, speedwell, bindweed and ancient billets of rotted gorse. And while he was thus engaged on the lower levels, Nathan had made a start on the upland.

140

He was approaching the end of the field. Bringing the horse in on a tight rein, he negotiated the turn and began on the next furrow. He was halfway there when he spotted Chrissie making a way up the steep, stony cart-track.

'Whoa, Captain!'

Nathan drew the horse to a stop, fetched the nosebag of oats from where he had left it by the drystone wall, and fixed it on the animal's bridle. Captain gratefully lowered his head and began to eat. Nathan, fetching the old horse's neck an affectionate couple of claps, went to greet Chrissie.

'Chrissie! Is that the time? I had no idea.'

'I'm a wee bit early, Master Nathan,' Chrissie admitted, out of breath from the climb. 'I want to get on with the ironing while I'm not hindered with the children. Miss Aileen is taking them down to the brook to pick cowslips. There's such a lot of laundry these days, with the new little one.'

Davina's baby, John Balfour Finbar Lennox, a strong, healthy boy, now resided, loved and spoiled by all, in a crib secretly carved by Jim Merridew and presented to the mother with a shy smile once the birth was safely over. Inevitably, the bulk of the extra work brought about by having a new infant in the house fell to Chrissie.

'Not that I'm complaining,' she said. 'I think the world of the little mite and he's such a good baby.' She smiled, pert and pretty, and Nathan's heart twisted strangely. 'Shall I leave your snap here by the wall till you're ready? It's ham and vegetable pasty and new bread.'

Nathan's stomach growled. Breakfast had been a long time ago and Chrissie's baking tempted.

'Thank you, Chrissie.'

She sent him another smile and left, her basket swinging from her hand.

Nathan watched her go, troubled. Chrissie had been a rock during the difficult days of the second seizure that had ended his father's life. It was she who had supported Mama through the distressing tasks that followed. She was the last to retire at night, the first up in the morning. There were times when Nathan wondered if she ever slept at all.

Taking out his kerchief to remove the worst of the grime from his hands, he went to sit on the wall and eat his meal, appraising his work as he did so. He had a long way to go before his ploughing matched that of his men, but for a novice the work was passable and Nathan was not displeased.

★　★　★

142

Much later, the job completed, Nathan was in the stable seeing to the horse when there was a sudden clatter of hoofs on the lane and Dorcas Webb rode into the farmyard.

'Nathan! The very one I've come to see,' she cried as he hastened to help her dismount. 'I wonder if I might have a word? I'll just put Gemini in the box, shall I? Come along, girl.'

She clicked her tongue to the mettlesome grey mare and led her into the stables. Mystified, Nathan waited while she tied the animal to the manger and came out again, shutting the door of barred iron with a clang.

Dorcas, typically, came straight to the point.

'I am concerned about young Chrissie. It's none of my business, I know, but I have a fondness for the girl. Chrissie Ross is worthy of more than being a slave to the whims and fancies of the Drummonds.

'Must Davina have Chrissie at her beck and call the day long? Someone, I allow, had to attend her following her lying-in, but Davina is no simpering miss, fit for nothing but languishing on a couch from morn till night. She's like the rest of you Drummonds, tough and hardy.'

Dorcas paused for breath and Nathan managed to get in a word himself.

'I understand, Aunt. You think Chrissie is being put upon?'

'Indubitably so. Housework, cooking, laundry, not to mention the dairy-work and the hours involved in the market stall venture. One day, Nathan, Chrissie is going to crack and the Drummonds will be to blame.'

'You are quite right,' Nathan admitted. 'I've been thinking along those lines myself. I shall have to speak to Mama. She hasn't been herself these past weeks . . . It didn't seem right to burden her . . . '

'Pshaw! A little straight talking could be what Florence needs. Sitting about moping isn't going to bring Balfour back, is it? I know it sounds brutal, but it's the truth.'

'I think Mama feels responsible in some way for what happened.'

'Stuff and nonsense. The man ailed. His days were numbered and that's all there is to it. You all gave him every care under difficult circumstances. I've told your mama as much myself, so let's have no more of that. It seems to me that it's Davina who needs the chivvying.'

'Aunt, my sister is recently out of childbed — '

'Oh, fiddle! The whelp must be getting on for six weeks old. A little light work would do Davina no harm at all and keep her mind from fretting over her man.' Dorcas looked at her nephew and smiled. 'Well, then, I've had my say. Shall we go inside? How fares my sister?'

'I'm sure Mama will be all the better for seeing you, Aunt.'

'Charmer! Save your silver-tongued words for others, nephew. They won't cut any ice with me.'

Delivering Nathan an affectionate tap on the shoulder, Dorcas swept out of the stable block.

It was a sad fact, Nathan reflected, that as Davina's pregnancy had advanced, so had her resentments and demands, and Chrissie seemed to have borne the brunt of it. John's birth had done nothing to soften his sister's attitude. Something had to be done.

With little more than a year between them, he and Davina had always been close. Nathan sensed a deep unhappiness behind her behaviour. But how to get a moment together to talk things over? With so much work for him to do outside, their paths rarely crossed.

The opportunity arose sooner than he expected.

It was the evening after Dorcas's visit and the day was just beginning to thicken to dusk. Nathan was crossing the farmyard, intending to put in a couple of hours' work in the office before bed, when he caught sight of Davina by the orchard gate. She stood motionless, a silent, rather solitary figure, a warm black shawl clutched about her against the evening chill.

'Davina?' He went to join her. 'It isn't often we see you out here.'

She smiled, a little wanly.

'Oh, it's you, Nathan. I was afraid when I heard footsteps that it might be one of the farm hands. Merridew with his everlasting talk of animals and crops is not the sort of company I relish.'

'Isn't that a little unfair? If it wasn't for Jim I dread to think where we would be now.'

'Jim! The man is a hired hand, Nathan. Call him Merridew.'

'In company I might, but in private it is different. I value Jim's friendship and I admire the man and . . . oh, what does it matter? Times are changing, sister. Many of these snobberies are dying, and better so.'

Faint colour touched Davina's pale cheekbones. Nathan saw how drawn her face was and his heart stirred with pity.

'Davvy, you are not yourself,' he said. 'Can't you tell me what is wrong?'

'Oh, 'tis nothing. I came out here for some fresh air and started to reminisce, that is all.'

'You were thinking about when we were young?'

Davina nodded.

'We had a wonderful childhood, didn't we?'

There was a poignant silence.

'Ah, me.' Davina sighed. 'How it has all changed.'

'But not necessarily for the worse,' Nathan said, surprising himself. 'We have a roof over our heads, albeit a leaky one. We have an understanding workforce prepared to work for almost no wages for now, and we have kindly neighbours. Look how they all rallied round when Father passed on. People couldn't have been more helpful. Even Stanton Hayles!'

'That girl of his was probably whispering in his ear. She's sweet on you, if you but knew it.'

Nathan groaned.

'Please, Davvy, don't you start. I get enough from Mama. She's constantly singing the praises of Verity Hayles. I think she wants me married off, and a son and heir for Glebe Farm.'

'Well, there's nothing wrong in that.'

'Maybe, but I should prefer a bride of my own choosing when the time is right, thank you.' His mind went briefly to Isobel. 'Davvy, I've neither the time nor the desire for this sort of debate. Let us speak of other things. What of those two scamps of yours? Are they happy here?'

'Oh, well enough, I dare say. They miss their father . . . as I do.'

Davina's voice trembled, and Nathan reached out and gave her hand a comforting squeeze.

'Then why not write to Finbar and tell him? He knows about the new babe, I take it?'

'I wrote and told him when John was born. There has been no reply.'

'These things take time. I remember how anxious Mama used to be when she heard nothing from you for weeks on end, and then several letters would come at once.'

A steely look entered his sister's eye.

'There is no point in our keeping up a communication,' she said. 'Spreading the word of the Lord is more important to Finbar than his family.'

Her lips snapped together in a thin line.

'You believe he has survived the unrest in Barotse, then?'

'I've no doubt the good Lord will look after his own.'

She slid her gaze away, focusing on the darkening orchard whence drifted the delicious scent of blossom.

'This isn't what you've come here to talk about, is it? You wanted to say 'Come on, Davvy. Snap out of it. We've a farm to run here. You've got your babe safe and sound and he's thriving, so why not lend some help when it's due?''

'I wouldn't have put it so bluntly.'

'Of course you would. And you'd be right. I'm a crosspatch and I can't seem to stop myself. I'm sorry, but there it is.'

She gave a hopeless little shrug and left, chin up, shoulders straight, her pride burning fiercely. Nathan, recognising a strong streak of their late father in Davina, shook his head wordlessly and carried on to the office and the paperwork that awaited him.

★   ★   ★

The days continued to draw out and all at once spring was really upon them. There was a rush to till the newly ploughed ground and sow the seed; barley and oats, and on the higher slopes, leas of the good red clover that would make prime feed for the cattle in the winter. Nathan walked his land with a smile, whilst behind his back the disgruntled faces of the men said plainly that no good would come of it.

Chrissie, emerging one evening from the

milking-shed, a large pail of creamy milk in each hand, a vastly oversized smock over her gown and hair tucked haphazardly into a milkmaid's cap, came across Nathan in the yard.

'There you are, Master Nathan. Edward was looking for you. He wanted to tell you what a difference the better weather has made to the milk yield. We're getting an extra four pails a day!'

'That is good news. Here, let me carry those for you.'

He took the pails from her and as he did so his hands lightly brushed hers. At his touch Chrissie's heart began to thunder.

Just then, Jamie's collie ran across the yard and began darting round them in crazy circles, her ears flattened and tail low.

'Look at Bess,' Jamie cried gleefully, rushing into the yard after his dog. 'She's rounding us up. She thinks we're sheep.'

'She's deluding herself, the daft animal,' Nathan said, mindful of the brimming pails. 'Call her off, Jamie, before I spill the milk and get into Chrissie's bad books.'

The boy laughed and called the dog to heel.

'Are you frightened of Chrissie, Nathan?'

'Terrified, especially when she's wearing her dairymaid things.'

Chrissie, conscious of looking a sight, blushed to the roots of her hair.

'But why?' Jamie persisted. 'Chrissie always puts that old smock on for milking so she dunna get her dress mucky.'

'Does not, Master Jamie. And it's soiled, not mucky, if you don't mind,' Chrissie said.

'But why? Jim says it all the time. Chrissie, why have you gone all pink?'

'Because I'm vexed,' Chrissie said breathlessly.

Nathan's eyes danced merrily.

'There, what did I tell you?'

'But you don't have to be scared of Chrissie, Nathan. I'm not. I'm not afraid of anybody.' Jamie looked suddenly pensive. ''Cept Father when he used to frown at me. He looked terrible fierce. I miss him, though.'

'We all do, Master Jamie,' Chrissie said. 'Now, stop your chatter and let's get on, or the milk will be soured in the sun and there'll be no butter for market.'

As they continued to the dairy, Nathan nodded towards the bare brown back of the field he had insisted on ploughing.

'It doesn't look bad at all, does it, Chrissie?'

'No, Master Nathan. You did fine.'

'That's not what Jim said,' Jamie cut in. 'He said Nathan's furrows were straight as a dog's hind leg. They were, too. Wilkie Hutch's were good and straight. I 'spect it'll take till Nathan's about thirty before he can plough as good.'

'Why thirty?' Chrissie asked, frowning.

'He'll be old then, like Jim and Silas and Wilkie. I 'spect he'll need a stick to get about with.'

'I'd best put this milk down on the step, before my poor old arms drop off.' Nathan fetched Chrissie a wink. 'Remind me not to overdo things in future, being as I'm heading towards my dotage.'

Chrissie choked on a giggle. Nathan grinned, and the next moment they were both laughing properly.

It was a release after the weeks of strain and sobriety and, once started, Chrissie could not stop. She laughed and spluttered, her hand to her side, while Nathan mopped streaming eyes with his fist. Bess began to bark excitedly and Jamie stood staring up at them in puzzlement.

The back door of the farmhouse opened and Davina appeared, shepherding her two small daughters before her. Chrissie sobered instantly, a closed look crossing her face.

'Jamie,' Davina said. 'Take the girls into the orchard and play with them, please.'

Jamie pulled a face.

'Do I have to? Annabel got stuck in a tree last time and Catherine wouldn't stop bawling.'

'I'm not surprised,' Davina said. 'Little girls shouldn't be climbing trees. Mind you look after them and don't let them get their clothes dirty. I've just run the smoothing iron over today's washing and I don't want to have to do any more.'

Chrissie gawped.

'Oh, but — ' Jamie began.

'Master Jamie, that's enough,' Chrissie said calmly, collecting her scattered wits. Mrs Lennox with a smoothing iron in her hand she would have loved to see. 'Please do as your sister says. Why don't you and the girls look for a four-leafed clover in the grass? It's lucky if you find one.'

Jamie indicated to the girls that they follow and strode off, his nieces stumbling after him.

'Well, then. I'll carry the milk inside for you ladies before I start on the books, shall I?' Nathan offered.

In the cool of the stone-floored dairy, Davina turned to Chrissie.

'The mistress and Edna Hutch are taking down the bed in the room that poor, dear Papa occupied,' she said in her well-modulated tones. 'Edna is going to give everywhere a scrubbing down. Mama says it

153

will make an excellent parlour for use in the evenings. I thought it a good sign.'

'Yes, Mrs Lennox,' Chrissie agreed.

'My husband always said that acceptance was halfway to coming to terms with grief.'

'I'm sure that is so. And the mistress would not have wanted the master to suffer — we none of us would,' Chrissie said gently.

Davina looked as if she wanted to say more. Instead, she shrugged and ran an eye over the dairy shelves.

'Shall I try the churn? I might as well occupy myself usefully while the baby sleeps.'

Thinking her ears had deceived her, Chrissie sprang into action, fetching bowl and skimmer.

'This old churn is a heavy thing and you mustn't maul yourself around just yet. If you could skim off the cream, Mrs Lennox, I'll see to the churning for now.'

They set to work, the only sound the slap-slap of the churn until the butter came. Together they patted it into golden rounds and stamped each one with the Glebe Farm emblem of a clover leaf. Chrissie, her mind on the carefree incident in the yard, was aware of a small bubble of pure happiness within her.

'What are you smiling at?' Davina asked suddenly.

'I . . . I can't say, Mrs Lennox. It's maybe the sunshine cheering me up.'

'I became tired of the sun in Africa. It was endless.' Davina paused. 'Was there any post this morning, do you know?'

'I don't think so, Mrs Lennox.' Chrissie regarded the other woman curiously. 'Were you expecting a letter?'

'Not particularly,' Davina said.

She placed the final round of butter on the tray and then went to see if John had woken yet.

Chrissie, folding a crisp white cloth over the tray of golden rounds, went to the door to get some air. What she saw in the main farmyard made her freeze. Verity Hayles had called for Aileen to go riding. A colourful figure in peacock-blue velvet, she was talking to Nathan and smiling down at him from the saddle, her eyes coquettish beneath the broad brim of her feathered hat. Nathan laughed up at her and their voices mingled, for all the world as if they were meant for each other.

Chrissie's bubble of happiness burst instantly. Slowly she turned and went back into the dairy, shutting the door behind her.

* * *

Time rolled on and the pall of sadness that had hung about the old farmhouse began to lift a little.

One warm afternoon in June, Chrissie and Aileen took the little girls shopping to Hadnall. They had called at the haberdashers for some thread and were about to cross the street to the general store, whose window sported a tempting array of barley sugar twists, when Stanton Hayles came around the corner on his black cob.

'Miss Aileen. Chrissie,' he greeted them. 'It's a grand day.'

'Indeed, sir.' Aileen inclined her head. 'I'm surprised you are not at the market.'

'Oh, my man has taken some ewes in for me. I can leave it to him to get a fair price.

'I see you've put some of your upland down to crops. Bit late in the season for sowing. It's to be hoped we get some rain to start it off.'

'The ground is greening up fine,' Chrissie said, not liking the implication.

'Really? Well, well. Beginner's luck, aye? 'Course, it's stony ground for crops. High up, and all. Gets the brunt of the wind and the weather.'

The farmer's expression said plainly what he thought of the move. His attention returned to Aileen, who looked neat in her

156

dark gown, her tawny hair drawn back from a face that was arresting rather than pretty.

'Miss Aileen, we haven't seen you at Twelve Trees in a while. Not tired of riding out, I hope?'

'Not at all. There has been much to do at home, that is all.'

'Ah. The weekly produce stall must keep you busy. My housekeeper bought some of your excellent pies last week. Never tasted better.'

'Thank you, sir,' Aileen said. He raised his cap once again and continued on his way.

'Miss Aileen,' Chrissie said, picking up little Catherine who was starting to grizzle. 'I wouldn't be at all surprised if Farmer Hayles doesn't pay his addresses to you in due course.'

Aileen stared.

'Don't be ridiculous, Chrissie. He's too old for me. Too . . . devout. Besides, it's too soon after poor Papa.'

'The time will pass. Farmer Hayles will come calling, you wait and see.'

Chrissie hoped she was wrong. It was true that Miss Aileen would want for nothing as mistress of Twelve Trees, but that independent spirit trapped in wedlock? Chrissie could not see it. She joggled the child in her arms.

'All right, Miss Catherine. Let's go and buy

those sweeties. Miss Annabel, hold your auntie's hand. That's right. Quickly now, let's cross while the road is clear.'

★   ★   ★

Shopping done, they arrived home to find the kitchen swept and Davina placing the suppertime broth on the hob.

Chrissie blurted out her thanks.

'It's a good help, Mrs Lennox. I can get straight out to the milking now.'

Davina's response was lost as Jamie came bounding in.

'Guess what? I've come top in arithmetic and composition. Miss Cartwright says I'll get two prizes on prize-giving day!'

'That's wonderful, Master Jamie. You're doing well at the school,' Chrissie said.

'I like it better than my other one. The boys here don't call me names. Andy and me are going fishing when it's holidays.'

Annabel tugged hopefully at his sleeve.

'Jamie, shall we look for lucky daisies again?'

'Clover, you mean. Can't. I'm busy.'

'Shan't give you what we've brought from the shop, then.'

'Annabel!' Davina said warningly. 'Hand Jamie whatever it is at once, please.'

158

The little girl brought out a bright-red lollipop from behind her back.

'Here y'are, then. I only licked it once.'

'Yuk!' Jamie backed off. 'No, thanks. I'm going to find Silas. He's showing me how to train Bess to the sheep.'

'Mind you change your school clothes first,' Chrissie said.

Jamie thundered off upstairs. Davina confiscated the lollipop. Annabel began to bawl and her sister joined her in sympathy.

The door to the passageway opened to admit Florence.

'My, my, children. What a noise,' Florence cried.

'Chrissie, what's to be done with them?'

Before Chrissie could answer, Davina stepped forward.

'Girls, that will do. If you are good maybe Chrissie will spare you a nice drink of fresh milk in a little while.'

'Gladly,' Chrissie said and made her escape.

As she crossed to the milking-shed she saw Jamie hurtling off in the direction of the sheep pasture with Bess loping along beside him. She was not altogether in favour of this sudden friendship of Master Jamie's. There was something about Silas Turner that alarmed her. The shepherd was

159

so silent, so dour . . . so deep, if talk was to be believed, into the union activity that was causing such unrest across the countryside.

Edward, fortunately, did not appear to involve himself in his father's activities. She smiled at the thought of Edward, his tall frame, his good, eager face, the thatch of blond hair and mild blue eyes.

Reaching the milking-shed, she found the cows already milked and Edward about to let them out into the meadow.

'I picked these for you,' he said, and shyly handed her a posy of wayside flowers. The sweet scents of columbine and bee balm winnowed up, poignant, evocative.

'Thank you, Edward. My favourites. How could you know?'

'I just did,' he said quietly. 'Can you manage the pails? I'd do it myself if it were possible. I've used the smaller ones. They shouldn't be too heavy.'

'I'll manage just fine.' Chrissie knew what it must have cost him to acknowledge the limp that so blighted his life and was conscious of a piercing sorrow that he should be so afflicted.

Tucking the posy into her bodice, she began the task of transporting the milk across the yard.

'I'm telling you,' Silas Turner said. 'This is the only way. The union needs more members. What about it, men?'

The four Glebe workers sat on the stone seat outside the door of the Dog In The Lane tavern, brimming tankards in hand. Before them, the narrow road wound away towards Upper Astley, the hedgerows brimming with fragrant ranks of yellow bedstraw.

'I dunna like trouble,' Merridew said stoutly.

'Me neither,' Hutch concurred.

Edward nodded in agreement.

'There are better ways of making folks sit up and take notice than firing barns and frightening the animals out of their wits. It's no good, Da. You'll never convince me that the union is going about this the right way. Negotiation, that's the way forward.'

'Negotiation!' Turner took a long swig of ale. 'You talk like a politician, boy. No, us working men know how to get a rise in wages.'

Hutch brightened.

'Talking of an increase — that was a bit of good news today.'

The proceeds from selling some of that spring's lambs and calves at the auctions,

161

added to the growing income from the market produce, had allowed Nathan to increase the men's pay to the going rate.

'Aye. Better than wasting it on more grains for crops, I reckon,' Turner growled. 'Daft idea, that was. 'Course, it still unna a decent wage, the union says.'

'Oh, give it a rest, man. I bet young Chrissie unna for ever werritin' over money. A real sassy little lass, she is. And human with it,' the ploughman said.

Edward sipped studiously at his ale.

'Asked her out yet, have you, boy?' Merridew enquired.

'None of your business,' Edward said.

'Oh, getting narky now, are we? That's a sure sign of being moonstruck. I reckon we'll be hearing wedding bells come next spring, Silas. Spick as a new pin your place'll be, with Chrissie Ross in command.'

'Spare me,' Turner said. 'I'm happy with things as they are. An' talking of womenfolk, what's this about the Glebe getting a new milkmaid?'

Everyone sat up.

'Go on?' Merridew said.

'Well, a union member whose brother's son's wife does a stint at the stores at Hadnall overheard Edna Hutch enquiring 'bout a milkmaid, being as we've got more cows come in milk after the calving.'

'My Edna did?' Hutch said.

'That's what I said.'

'Edward, lad,' Merridew put in, 'seems like you'll have a bit of pick and choose.'

'Who's ready for another round?' Edward asked abruptly.

Tankards were duly drained and offered up.

'Since you're asking, boy, we all are,' Merridew said.

* * *

Florence lay wakeful, watching the moon-shadows make slow progress around the bedroom walls. As on every night since Balfour's demise, fear and guilt surfaced. If she hadn't brought him to Glebe Farm, if she had followed his wishes and stayed in Glasgow, would he be alive still?

Dr Merrick had said that Balfour's health had already been seriously undermined by the problems that had befallen them. The memory of her husband's drawn face and haunted eyes during those last weeks at Langsdale Avenue gave credence to his words. Balfour's days had been numbered from the moment the City of Glasgow Bank met its crisis.

Turning over in the bed, plumping up the feather bolster, Florence tried to count her blessings. Though it was still early days since they had come to Glebe Farm, she was grateful for the progress they had made. The stock they had bought in had multiplied gratifyingly that spring. The men were now being paid at the accepted rate. Nathan had exceeded all her expectations. The children were well and happy, Davina seemingly more relaxed. The new milkmaid would give Chrissie the help she needed . . . Indeed, they had much to be thankful for.

Gradually Florence began to notice a pleasant languor was stealing over her. She let herself drift, eyes closed . . .

A sudden series of shrill barks from the shed where the collie slept brought her instantly to wakefulness. Bess's alert was joined by the shepherd's two dogs from the cottage behind the farm buildings.

Florence rose and went to the window. Moonlight flooded the farmyard and fields, making the landscape almost as bright as day. As she watched, a shadow detached itself from the deeper shadows of the barn. A figure was stealing along the length of the outbuildings.

The barking increased to a frantic pitch. Florence thought of the recent outburst of union activity in the area and her heart clenched with fear. A fire in the feed-store and barn was the last thing they needed.

She reached for her wrap. She must alert Nathan — and quickly.

7

'Finbar!'

Davina's voice resounded with shock and disbelief. 'Good heavens, so it is!' Nathan gasped.

Finbar Lennox, gazing, rapt, at his wife, opened his arms. With a glad little cry, Davina rushed to him. Nathan lowered to his side the kitchen poker he had seized for the anticipated fray.

Bess continued to bark hysterically. By now the entire household was assembled — apart from Davina's children, who still slumbered.

A shiver touched Florence, though the night was far from cold. She pulled her woollen wrap closer over her thin cambric nightgown and turned to Chrissie.

'Chrissie, you had better stoke up the range and put the kettle to boil. I'm sure we could all do with a hot drink. And Mr Lennox will need something to eat.'

'Yes, Mistress. Miss Aileen, I'd appreciate a hand, if you please.'

Aileen was regarding her sister in amazement. After all Davina's proclamations of never wanting to see Finbar again, the way she had greeted him was beyond belief.

'Coming, Chrissie,' Aileen replied.

'And Master Jamie, what are you doing out here with nothing on your feet? Inside with you this minute!'

Bess, seeing her young master, increased her barks to top pitch and strained eagerly against the chain that held her, tail thrashing.

'Look lively, laddie,' Nathan chivvied his small brother. 'And make that dog stop her din before she wakes half the county.'

'It seems she already has,' Florence said wryly.

Jim Merridew approached, his breeches over his grey flannel nightshirt, his boots unlaced, still wearing his nightcap.

Silas Turner followed, a stumbling Edward in his wake, old sacks thrown over their night clothes. The sheepdogs were with them, snarling and grumbling. All three men had reached for the first weapon to hand. Merridew had his shotgun and Turner and Edward bore stout sticks.

'It's all right, men,' Nathan shouted to them. 'You can drop your weapons.'

Jim Merridew uncocked his gun.

'I dunno, gaffer. I thought we were under siege,' he said with spare humour.

'We all did, man,' Nathan replied.

The other two hands stood silent, weapons

thrown aside, the dogs now quiet and subdued. Turner seemed suddenly conscious of their state of undress.

'If you're all right then, gaffer, we'll be getting back to our beds,' he said.

'Thank you for coming to our aid. You, too, Jim.'

'That's all right, gaffer,' Merridew said.

Sliding a whimsical glance at the still-embracing couple, the men headed back to their cottages.

Thinly into the silence that followed, came the hungry wail of an infant. Davina disengaged herself from Finbar's arms.

'That's John. I must see to him before he wakes the girls. This way, my love.'

She led Finbar into the house and the others followed.

Chrissie rustled up tea and a platter of cold meat and pickles, while Aileen sliced and buttered bread. Finbar and Davina entered, with the baby cradled in his father's arms.

'My son,' Finbar said, gazing down at the child's furious red face in wonderment. 'Aye, but he's a bonnie lad.'

'He's a hungry one,' Davina said robustly. 'Here, let me have him. You look fit to drop. Sit down, husband, and eat. Then perhaps we can hear what you're about, waking us all up in the middle of the night!'

The look she bestowed on him belied the sharpness of her words and Finbar, swaying wearily on his feet, sat down gratefully to his first meal for many hours.

'You must be wondering what I'm doing here without first sending word,' he said after he had eaten. 'I'm sorry to be the cause of such disturbance. It was late when I got here so it seemed best to bed down in the barn till morning. I was heading there when the dog set up barking.'

'I thought it was the union men when I heard Bess,' Florence declared. 'You cannot imagine what trouble we've had in the district, Finbar. Barns set alight, machinery smashed, all kinds of uproar.'

An odd look crossed Finbar's face and he frowned.

'They must be desperate men,' he said with compassion.

Davina reappeared, without the baby.

'He's fast asleep, the lamb. Have I missed anything'?'

'Nothing, my heart.' Finbar made room for her beside him on the settle and she sat down, placing her hand in his.

'You must also all be wondering why I left the mission when I had been so intent on remaining. It was the strangest thing. A young chaplain joined us during another violent uprising. Well, this fellow and I got talking. When he heard about my wife and children back here, he looked at me askance, and it brought home to me what I'd done.' He looked at Davina. 'I was a fool, Davvy. I should never have let you leave like that — the long sea voyage with the girls, and you in a delicate condition.'

'It's over,' she said softly. 'I was hasty, too. Let that be an end to it.'

Nathan cleared his throat.

'I take it this young minister has taken your place at the Barotse Mission?'

'Something like that, yes. He's a single man. No responsibilities.' Finbar pressed Davina's hand lovingly. 'My ship docked yesterday morning . . . or was it the day before?' He stared blankly ahead through bloodshot, sleep-starved eyes. 'I arranged for my trunk to be delivered and caught a train here. I've a valise somewhere — must be still in the barn.'

'I think,' Florence said, rising, 'that we have heard enough for the present. Let us all retire and get some sleep.'

The sky was now washed with pre-dawn greyness and from the pear tree on the orchard wall, a blackbird tried out a few first fluting notes.

'It's hardly worth my while going back to

bed,' Nathan said. 'I'll get dressed and see to the animals. Finbar, man, it's grand to have you with us. Get yourself a good rest and I'll see you later on.'

He pulled to his feet, and Florence's eyes followed him as he crossed the kitchen. She knew he must be as concerned as she. It was wonderful for Davina and Finbar to be reunited, but with yet another mouth to feed, she wondered what would become of them all.

*   *   *

A few days later, Finbar sought Nathan out. 'Nathan? Could I have a quiet word?'

'Of course.' Nathan put down the harrow he was mending and straightened, glancing around. 'We're private enough here.'

Finbar, he noted, was looking more himself. His crisply curling sandy hair had been given a trim and he was cleanshaven, and now that the trunk containing his clothes had arrived, his professional mien had returned.

'I'll come straight to the point,' Finbar said. 'You've given my wife and family a home when you could ill afford it and I'm grateful. I know only a part of what happened in Glasgow — just what your mother wrote in her letters to Davina — but I could read between the lines. It must have been very distressing for you all.

'Nathan, I'm not without means. I shall reimburse you for the expense of these past months. I shall have to apply to the diocese for another position. A parish in the suburbs would suit me well.'

'Will you go back to Glasgow?'

'Davina would like to. We shall have to wait and see what turns up. Of course, my parents are there . . . I daresay we could stay with them if we're an encumbrance here.'

'Don't be a fool. You're welcome to stay here as long as you wish.'

'In that case, you must let me earn my keep about the place. I learned how to make myself useful around a farm during my term in Africa.' He grinned.

'Anything that needs doing about the farm or house, I'm your man!'

'It's a deal,' Nathan said, offering his hand, and they shook on it.

★   ★   ★

The weeks rolled by and summer came in hot and dry. The wheat, barley and leas of good red clover on the lower levels that had always been put over to crops were looking well, despite the lack of rain. But up on the heights growth was slow and worryingly sparse.

'I can't understand it,' Nathan said to Jim Merridew, shaking his head. 'I did everything according to the book, and look at it. What has gone wrong?'

Merridew was silent for several seconds.

'Well, gaffer, we tried to tell you. You only get out of the ground what you put into it, and this high land has been starved since Adam was a lad. Sheep do all right on it and that's about all it's fit for.'

Nathan felt a terrible sense of having made a blunder, a not unfamiliar sensation since coming to Glebe Farm, but in this case one they could ill afford.

Day after day he walked his land searching for signs of progress, but while the lower leas continued to flourish, the upper levels did not. Nathan was beginning to despair, and quite welcomed the distraction one morning when Verity rode into the farmyard on her pretty bay mare.

'Whoa, Melody,' she cried, reining in beside Nathan. 'Why, Nathan, have you no smile for me on this glorious morning?'

Nathan obliged, and placed his hands on Verity's waist to help her down. She jumped with practised ease.

Eyes like speedwells twinkled at him

coquettishly from under the broad brim of her feather-trimmed hat, and Nathan's heart lifted. What was it, he thought, about young women and their eyes? Verity's were candid and childlike — sometimes stormy if things did not go her way. Chrissie's, more green than blue, were thoughtful, deep and wise. While Isobel's . . .

But he wouldn't think of Isobel.

'What is it?' Verity said. 'You've gone all gloomy again.'

'Nothing. I was wondering when this heatwave would end. The land needs rain.'

'Oh, phooey — the land! That's all you farmers think of. Papa is the same.'

'Well, how else do you suppose he could buy you all your lovely dresses?'

'There are other ways of earning a living: investments . . . things like that.' Verity waved her hand airily as if such weighty matters were not for her and Nathan let it pass.

'May I get you a cup of Chrissie's lemonade? And your mare might like a turn at the water trough.'

'Oh, I'll see to Melody in a moment. She's rather warm after the gallop along the tops. But I'd love a drink.'

Nathan went off and returned with a brimming jug and two tall cups, setting them down on the farmyard wall.

'Oh, lovely. Shall I pour?' Verity, reins looped over her arm, deftly poured the drinks and passed one to Nathan. 'Isn't this jolly? Quite domesticated, don't you agree?'

Nathan almost choked on his drink. He was saved from having to reply by the unmistakable clatter of a spirited horse. Dorcas Webb rode through the gateway, two huge hounds and Pirate the spaniel swarming alongside.

'Morning, Nathan. Dashed hot, isn't it? Confounded weather. My gardener says if we don't get some rain soon we may as well forget about the summer greens this year.'

She reined in beside them, acknowledging Verity with a curt bow from the saddle.

'Miss Hayles. Haven't seen that mare before. New, is she?'

'Yes. Papa bought her for me. She's by Dark Minstrel.'

'Really? She doesn't take after him. Were you just off? I need to consult my nephew on a matter of some urgency and it won't do to keep the animals hanging about in this heat.'

The dogs had gone to quench their thirst at the water trough and now returned, dribbling messily. Nathan laughed and fussed them, but Verity, thwarted of what had promised to be a pleasing interlude, pushed them away. Placing her empty cup on the wall, she draped the long train of her skirt over her arm and turned to Nathan.

'Help me up, do. I shall call again when you are less occupied.'

Nathan laced his fingers together and Verity, placing her foot in them, sprang nimbly up. Nodding farewell, she touched her whip to the mare's flanks, sending her whirling out of the farmyard.

Dorcas watched the retreat through narrowed eyes. 'Too straight in the stifle,' she said with a sniff.

'Aunt?'

'The mare. Jogs you about something dreadful when they're straight in the stifle. Dashed uncomfortable. Mind, of the two, I think I prefer the horse, and that's not saying much!'

Nathan spluttered with hastily suppressed laughter.

'What's she doing here, anyway?' Dorcas went on.

'Mama encourages it. I fear she has aspirations of Miss Hayles becoming the new Mrs Drummond.'

'You and that little puss?' Dorcas gave a snort. 'Stuff! It's about as likely as a swallow in winter. Look for a girl with a bit of mettle about her, Nathan. Farmers' wives have to be strong.'

'What was it you wanted to see me about, Aunt?' Nathan said, steering the conversation away from the uncomfortable turn it was taking.

'What?' Dorcas was watching the dogs. One of the hounds snapped irritably at a fly and Pirate settled down for a good scratch. 'Oh, I happened to notice you'd ploughed up the sheep grazing. Have you decided not to extend the flock?'

'No, it's not that.' Nathan sighed. 'I thought since we're short on grazing stock as yet, it might bring in extra revenue if we put the fallow ground down to crops in the meantime.'

'But you'll never grow anything up there, boy! It's as bleak as a beggar's pocket. Twopenny Rise is sheep ground.'

'Don't you start, Aunt. Merridew and the others did warn me. I'm afraid I took no notice and it appears I'm paying the price.'

'Oh, well.' Dorcas looked at her nephew kindly. 'Never mind, Nathan. We all make mistakes. Got to have something to learn by, haven't we?'

'I dare say, but it's a bitter lesson.

'One good thing,' he went on. 'The sow farrowed yesterday.'

'She did? How many d'you get?'

'Twenty-one! They seem a healthy bunch. I

hope she rears them all. D'you know, Aunt, I rather like pigs.'

'Me, too. They've got more sense than sheep or cattle and you don't get a scrap of waste off the beast. If it wasn't for Gemini I'd take a peep at the babies, but you know horses where pigs are concerned.'

'Some in particular!' Nathan gave Gemini's neck a couple of slaps. 'Rogue! When are you going to calm down?'

'She's no youngster, so I'm not holding out any hope. Doesn't bother me one jot. I like fire in a horse.' Her memory jogged, Dorcas became suddenly serious.

'There was something else, Nathan. Wollerton Old Hall had a brush with the union folk last night.'

'Oh? What happened?'

'They lost a whole hayfield. Went up in a wink, hedges and all. It took an age to put the fire out. It's this heatwave. The grass was dry as tinder. Wouldn't have taken much to set it alight.'

'No.' Nathan frowned. 'You've not had any problems at the manor?'

'Not yet. They seem to be leaving us alone, for some reason.'

'Maybe they're looking after you. You've always cared for your workers and the poorer families of the parish. Folk know a generous hand when they see it.'

'Perhaps, but it doesn't take much to start a riot. Your shepherd is one of them, isn't he? Does he ever give you any trouble?'

'Not a whisper. Turner isn't the easiest of men, but he's a first-rate shepherd and he's good with Jamie. Edward Turner is different again from his father. That's him up on the roof. He and Finbar are mending the damage from last winter's storms.'

Dorcas followed his direction, squinting her eyes against the glare.

'Bless us and save us, look at that! I never thought to see a man of the cloth so close to heaven!'

Nathan spluttered again, wiping watery eyes.

'Aunt Dorcas, you beat all — you've given me an idea, though. A man of Finbar's persuasion invites confidences and he talks quite often with the hands. I could ask him to keep an ear out for trouble.'

'That would be helpful,' Dorcas agreed.

Gemini started to sidle restlessly.

'Time I was away,' Dorcas said. 'Do give my regards to everyone, and don't take any chances with those union hotheads!'

'I could say the same for you. Farewell, Aunt.'

Dorcas called to the dogs and sent Gemini

clattering away, and Nathan, seeing Finbar descend from the ladder, went to speak to him while the idea was fresh in his mind.

★ ★ ★

'Finbar — you're doing a good job there!'

'Save your praise for Edward. It's he who's shown me the ropes. There's a knack to laying tiles.'

'I'll believe it. Finbar, there's something I wanted to ask you. It's about the union followers.'

'That's odd,' Finbar said. 'I was only thinking about it earlier. Remember the night I got here, and you all mistook me for one of the rioters?'

'I do indeed. You were lucky not to get your head blown off.'

'That did occur to me afterwards.' Finbar made a rueful face. 'But that night, on my way here from the station, I spotted a band of men crossing the fields. The moon was bright and they kept to the shadow of the hedges so they couldn't be seen. They looked furtive, so I hid in the bushes until they'd gone past.'

'How many were there?'

'Ten or twelve. Turner was with them.'

'You're sure?'

'Absolutely. I recognised him as soon as I

180

saw him here. You can't mistake that nimble way he has of moving.'

Nathan sighed heavily.

'I wish it were otherwise. Do you think you could keep a discreet watch for trouble? Aunt Dorcas says the Old Hall had a field set ablaze in the night.'

'Yes, I can do that. I shouldn't think Edward or the other men here would be party to what goes on. I imagine there are some arguments in the Turners' cottage behind closed doors.'

'I'd agree. The trouble is it only takes one to cause problems. We'll have to trust nothing happens here.'

'Aye.' Finbar passed a hand over his sweating brow.

'It's hot. I could drink the river dry. Is there any of that lemon juice left in the jug?'

'Not much. I'll fetch you some. Edward, too. Won't be long.'

Breathtaking heat met Nathan from the red glow of the fire in the range. He went to the dresser and took down two of the pewter tankards that hung there, checking at the same time for any morning mail.

'Would this be what you're looking for, brother, dear?'

Nathan turned to see Aileen standing at the passage door with several letters in her hand.

'It would. Thank you.'

He noticed the broad-brimmed poke bonnet newly trimmed with white ribbon and the lacy shawl his sister wore over her white muslin dress.

'You're all dressed up. Going somewhere special?'

Aileen made a pained face.

'Only for a drive with Mr Hayles. Mama thinks he wishes to pay his addresses to me. I'm really not interested, Nathan. He's far too old.'

'He'd be a good catch,' Nathan mumbled, riffling through the letters. Most were bills but the one he wanted from the lawyer in Shrewsbury was there . . . and another: perfumed, elegantly addressed — Isobel.

He stuffed it into his top pocket to read later and turned his attention back to his sister.

'A very good catch indeed.'

'Oh, don't speak of it like that,' she cried. 'As if he were a fish on the end of a line. I don't even like Mr Hayles all that much. He's so pompous.'

'Goodness.' Nathan stared, flummoxed. 'All the same, Aileen, you'd not want for much with a man like Hayles. Nice house, servants — you'd never need to bake another pie again!'

'But I like baking my pies! I fancy I shall not wed at all. I shall work hard at my market bakes and open up a shop, like poor, dear Papa.'

'All right,' Nathan said. Aileen in an argumentative mood was a force to be reckoned with and he gave in with good grace.

She sent him a hard look, then glanced round as the rattle and clop of a trap was heard on the road.

'That'll be Farmer Hayles now.'

Nathan watched her go, his mind racing. A wary truce existed between himself and their neighbour. He still had no real liking for the man. He recalled how supportive Hayles had been to their mother at her bereavement, quietly providing the vehicles for transporting the mourners to and from the church, and other, smaller favours that meant much at such times. Even so, he no more wanted the man for Aileen than he relished taking the daughter to wife.

The clatter of Hayles's carriage leaving broke his train of thought, and remembering the thirsty roof-repairers, Nathan went hastily to see to their refreshment.

★　★　★

Nathan ascended the stone steps to the office over the barn to investigate in private the news from Dennison and Poleworthy, his mother's lawyers in Shrewsbury. The missive confirmed that his mother's trustees had now given him full power over the farm's business dealings and commitments and while, for the present, the Glebe and its lands were still held for Florence's benefit under the terms of her uncle's will, the day-to-day management was now under his control.

While it came as a relief to have the question settled, the weight of responsibility that rested on his young shoulders felt awesome.

The Lord will provide.

How often had those words resounded through the lofty rooms of their old home, and how empty they had seemed. Balfour Drummond had stuck rigidly to his principles and sold everything to pay off his creditors. Yet the steady ship that had been their business and their succour had sunk, taking them with it.

Nevertheless, he had loved his father. Now he was gone and there was nothing for it but to press on, like old Captain in harness ploughing the furrows. And he'd do it, he vowed. By all that was good, he'd do it!

Isobel's letter was wearying. She missed

him, she swore. She must have been unhinged to have spoken to him the way she had on that fateful day when she had ended their betrothal.

Nathan was mildly irritated by her flowery speech and her refusal to accept what he had told her when they had met in Shrewsbury earlier in the year. He'd pen an answer when he had a spare moment, he decided. Ramming the scented pages back into the envelope, he tucked the letter behind the clock in the office and promptly forgot about it.

★ ★ ★

'That hayfield was set alight at Wollerton Hall, Silas, and we all know who was responsible,' Chrissie admonished the shepherd as she distributed the men's snap. 'The whole lot lost and the hedges, too. If that were to happen here, it could spell ruin for all of us.'

'It wunna happen here,' Turner growled. 'It hasn't yet, has it?'

'Well, no.' Chrissie pursed her lips in thought. 'But those men are like sheep. It only takes one to barge through a gate and all the rest follow.'

Edward sat apart, thoughtfully observing

while chewing on a hunk of bread.

Wilkie Hutch took a swig of cold, refreshing cider and looked up.

'You have a point there, Chrissie. Folks at these meetings get all fired up. If one of them decided to target this farm there'd be no stopping them.'

'That's my thought, too,' Jim Merridew said. 'I sleep with my gun at the ready. Have done ever since we had that scare when Parson Lennox showed up.'

'Master Nathan does, too, so the mistress says.' Chrissie looked over to where the fields lay green and golden under the sun. 'The hay is so close to the house and buildings,' she said. 'If it should go up the house could catch as well and we'd all be burned in our beds!'

'Enough!' Turner pulled furiously to his feet, scattering crumbs and the remains of his cold meat pasty, which the dogs duly pounced on. 'Stop your rattle, girl. I've said it won't happen at the Glebe and that's that!'

His eyes blazed angrily in his swarthy face and Chrissie drew back in alarm.

'Steady on, man,' Merridew said. 'That's no way to talk to a lady.'

'What lady? All I see is a servant same as us. A bit of a lass that does the work of three and dunna get what's due for one.'

There was an uneasy truth in the

shepherd's words and the men stared in discomfort.

'That's my business.' Chrissie's voice choked with humiliation and distress. 'The Drummonds have been like a family to me and I'll not forget it.'

'Maybe, but d'you think they'd care if you left? Oh, they'd miss you all right. They'd have no-one to skivvy for them any more, would they? It wunna be Chrissie Ross they'd miss. It'd be the servant who works her fingers to the bone for 'em!'

'Da, that'll do!'

Edward's voice rang out.

'The lad's right, Silas,' Merridew muttered, once he'd got over his astonishment. 'We dunna want any of that union talk here. Sit down, man, and finish your meal. Here, have some of mine. The dogs got yours.'

'You shouldn't have spoke to the lass like that,' Ploughman Hutch said quietly.

'Happen you should apologise.'

'He needn't bother.' Chrissie glared. 'I'm going. But I'll say this, Silas Turner. Another word against the Drummonds and you can get your own snap, for I'll not wait on you any more!'

She seized her basket and whirled out, tears coursing down her cheeks. Edward glowered at his father then blundered after her. He caught up with her in the cowshed, where she was trying to control her raging emotions.

'Chrissie, I'm sorry,' Edward began. He reached out his hands as if he longed to touch her, but could not bring himself to take the liberty. 'Da doesn't mean it. He goes to the meetings and comes back full of their talk. It's a kind of fervour. He was at one last night. He'll calm down in a day or two.'

'It wasn't right what he said. The Drummonds do think a lot of me.'

Even she heard the doubt in her voice.

'Chrissie, you're so sad.' Edward came closer. 'You mustn't worry. Whatever happens, I'll look after you.'

She looked up sharply.

'What do you mean?'

'I wasn't ever going to say this. But, Chrissie, I love you. I know I'm not much of a prospect, what with my bad foot and all, but do you think — '

He got no further. Rose Hutch, the new dairymaid and niece of Wilkie and Edna, came hurrying towards them.

'Oh, there you are, Chrissie,' she cried. 'I've been looking everywhere for you. It's those childer. They're in the orchard scrapping like cats. You'll have to come, for they'll take no notice of me.'

Chrissie ran to the orchard, where a furious Annabel, her face as red as her hair, was laying into her young uncle with a stick. Jamie was fencing the attack and laughing, which only made matters worse. Little Catherine sat indifferently in the grass, calmly dissecting a daisy with fat, meticulous fingers. Beside her, Bess the collie sat panting in the sunshine.

'Children, children!' Chrissie cried. 'What a to-do! Master Jamie, how many times have I told you not to entice the girls into rough games?'

'I wasn't. Silas said we'd have another go with Bess and the sheep. She wanted to come as well.'

'Who's she? The cat's mother?'

'Annabel, then. Anyway, I told her only boys could be shepherds and she said she could shout and wave her arms about as good as any boy. So I said if she could get over the orchard wall she could come and watch.'

'I felled off and ripped my dress,' Annabel fumed.

'Never mind, my pet. Chrissie will mend it. Calm yourself, Miss Annabel. It isn't seemly to be shouting like a fishwife. And Miss Catherine, will you please get up off that grass? That's a clean pinafore — or was!'

Catherine held up a chubby fistful of wilting flowers.

'Daisy chain?' she lisped hopefully.

'Not now, sweetheart. Chrissie's busy. Maybe later.'

Chrissie picked the child up, smiling. Pink-cheeked and solemn, no-one could be cross for long with Catherine.

Jamie heaved a sigh.

'I wish school would hurry up and start again,' he said, scowling. The village school was temporarily closed for the haymaking. 'When we go back, Andy Fox is going to show me how to climb the school wall with a rope. Andy's good at climbing. He went up the bell tower once and fixed the bell so it couldn't ring at all for afternoon lessons.'

'The bell tower?' Chrissie felt suddenly faint.

'Yes,' Jamie continued blithely. 'I was going to show Annabel how to — '

'Master Jamie, that's enough! Don't you even think about it.'

Jamie darted his small niece a look of sheer disdain.

'Why wasn't John born first? He'd be more fun. Why does he have to be the baby? I don't like babies. Puppies and calves are much nicer. And lambs,' he said as an afterthought.

'Isn't that Silas now, with the dogs?' Chrissie parried neatly. 'He'll be on his way to the sheep. You'd better get after him,

Master Jamie, or you and Bess will miss your lesson.'

Jamie shouted to the dog and the pair went bounding off to join the shepherd.

Seeing Annabel's bottom lip quiver suspiciously, Chrissie held out her hand.

'Dear me, how hot you are. Shall we go and have a nice cool drink? And Chrissie shall mend the rip in your frock.'

She headed towards the house, the rosy toddler on one arm, the small, defiant girl in tow. And Nathan, rounding the corner from the stables, couldn't help thinking what a charming picture they made against the quiet background of burgeoning fruit trees and flower-strewn grass.

* * *

Hearing the sound of hoofs on the road, Nathan went to the gate to see if his delivery of wood from the village had arrived. A gleaming black brougham drawn by a pair of matching bays met his astonished gaze.

'You had better wait here, coachman,' a female voice called — a voice that was impossibly, puzzlingly, familiar.

The coachman swung down from the high driving seat and went to open the door of the carriage.

191

'Nathan, thank goodness!' the fashionable creature who emerged called out. 'I feared we had come to the wrong place. How quaintly rustic you are here. Are you not going to greet me?'

Nathan, shocked to the bone, found his voice at last.

'Isobel! What the blazes are you doing here?'

8

'Dear me, Nathan. A fine way to greet an old acquaintance, I must say.' Isobel swept a pouting glance under long lashes. 'Not pleased to see me? After me venturing all the way from Shrewsbury in this dreadful heat!'

'You've travelled from Shrewsbury?' Nathan managed a small smile. 'A fair distance indeed.'

'Papa is here again on business. He's out today, so I took the opportunity to come and see you.' She gestured to her maid to follow.

At the entrance to the house, Isobel paused and ran her gaze over the half brick, half-timbered frontage. Mellowed by centuries, the house had a timeless quality. Nathan felt his heart respond with a curious tug of affection for the place he now called home.

'How quaint,' Isobel said, with a twirl of her parasol. 'Who would have thought you would end up in such a rustic setting? Indeed, you look quite the part, Nathan.'

Nathan had been out on the fields since daybreak. His sturdy breeches and sweat-soaked shirt, he was acutely aware, were hardly suitable for entertaining a visitor.

'Yes, well. If you'll excuse me, Isobel, I shall hand you over to Mama and go and tidy myself up.'

'But of course. How does your dear mama? She is well, I trust?'

'Exceeding so, thank you,' Nathan replied dryly. Less than twelve months ago Isobel had not wanted to know his mother, nor indeed any member of his family.

Florence, who had observed the arrival from the house, appeared at the door. Her face was commendably calm as she welcomed the visitor.

'Isobel, my dear. What a lovely surprise and how charming you look. Do come inside out of this dreadful sun. I vow your complexion objects as much as mine to being scorched.'

She ushered Isobel into the cool confines of the small parlour and Nathan, pointing her maid towards the kitchen, made his retreat.

Nathan was vigorously towelling dry his hair in his bedroom, when more hoofbeats sounded on the road. Glancing out the window, he saw, to his dismay, that Verity had returned. She must have espied Isobel's carriage on her way home and turned back to investigate, he thought.

'What timing!' Nathan muttered. 'What confounded awful timing!'

He ran a hairbrush over his still-damp hair,

reached for his coat and hurried from the room, arriving in the hallway as Verity came breezing along the passage.

'Back again?'

'As you see.' Flushed and breathless, she sent him her most charming smile. 'Nathan, I seem to have mislaid my whip and Melody does need a touch now and again. Could it be here, do you think?'

'I doubt it. You didn't enter the house when you were here before, did you?'

'But someone could have come across it and brought it inside for safe keeping. Do help me look, Nathan — oh!'

She broke off as Chrissie came through with a tray of tea things.

'Miss Verity, I thought it was your mare I saw tied up outside. Shall I fetch another placing for tea?'

'Please do,' Verity said. 'I find I'm quite parched again. A cup of tea would be perfect.'

Nathan gave in.

'You might ask one of the men to stable Miss Hayles's mare, Chrissie. Can't leave the poor beast standing about in this heat.'

'I'll see to it right away, Master Nathan. Rose has taken the coachman some ale. He looked ready to drop with thirst, poor man.'

She returned to the kitchen and Nathan ushered Verity into the parlour.

195

It wasn't the easiest of company and all welcomed the diversion when Chrissie reappeared with the tea. She also brought a dish of scones, warm from the oven, with butter, jam and cream. The maid's cheeks were flushed; her chin sported a tell-tale smudge of flour.

'Thank you, Chrissie. This looks delicious,' Nathan said.

He held the door for her, giving a smile as she left. He hadn't missed the disapproving line of Isobel's mouth as she took in the crumpled dairy-smock the maid wore under her pinafore and the frilled cap, hastily donned and slightly askew.

'Do you always address servants so familiarly, Nathan?' Isobel enquired, accepting a cup of tea from Florence and declining the offer of further refreshment.

'Always,' Nathan replied solemnly. 'Especially Chrissie. She's more one of the family than a servant.'

'I think Nathan has a perfectly lovely manner with people,' Verity said, helping herself to a scone and spreading it liberally with jam and cream. 'It's what makes him so popular.'

'Is that so?' Isobel remarked archly.

That was all she said, but it brought a rush of embarrassed colour to Verity's cheeks and

196

was, so far as Nathan observed, the only time Isobel addressed the girl as long as she remained.

Eventually, the talk wearing thin, Verity took her leave.

'Such precocity,' Isobel declared, the moment she was gone. 'I do believe the chit is sweet on you, Nathan. Are you not flattered?'

'No more than any other fellow would be.'

She gave a light laugh and glanced around. 'What a charming room. I'm longing to see more of this farmhouse of yours. Aren't you going to show me?'

'It would be my pleasure, though I fear there's little to see as yet. Glebe Farm stood untended for quite some while and the house had fallen sadly out of repair. The land, too, was in poor heart and that, naturally, is where our priorities lie.'

'Do you have stables? I noticed a rather well-bred horse when I arrived.'

'That would be Aileen's mare,' Florence said.

'Oh, really? How is Aileen?'

'She is out at the moment. She'll be sorry to have missed you,' Florence said, rising from her seat. 'And now, if you don't mind, my dear, there are matters that require my attention. I shall leave you to Nathan. Do call again if you are in the district.'

Bestowing a light kiss of farewell on Isobel's cheek, Florence left the room.

'The farmyard, then?' Nathan offered Isobel his arm. 'You must see the dairy. We've recently taken on a new girl.'

Isobel couldn't have looked less interested.

'Well, perhaps a quick glance. I mustn't keep the coachman waiting.'

'Oh, I think your man's been taken care of. This way. Don't forget your parasol.'

He escorted her along the maze of passageways and out into the scorching afternoon heat. Nathan, to his shame, was beginning to enjoy himself. If Isobel wanted a taste of rural life he was happy to oblige. Dairy, stables, pigsties; nothing was left out.

'Did I mention the barn we've restored? My man, Jim Merridew, did the best part of the work. Don't know what we'd have done without Jim. He and Finbar have gone today to look at some pigs. You remember Finbar Lennox, Davina's husband? Davina must be out with the children. A pity, you'd have enjoyed meeting them.'

His words provoked a token gesture of acknowledgment. Drawing Isobel into the shade of an elm, Nathan looked directly at her.

'Admit it, Isobel,' he said. 'This is not for you.'

There was a lost look in the violet eyes. It brought a pang of remorse. He had loved her once.

'Isobel, be honest with yourself,' he said reasonably. 'Search your heart and ask what you truly value above all else. There must be something.'

For a moment she just stood looking at him.

'Actually,' she said in a voice quite unlike her own, 'I like to paint. I always have. Oh, I don't mean the wishy-washy daubs that ladies are supposed to produce. I mean real painting ... There are some artists working in Glasgow now — Nathan, you should see their work. They're just beginning to become known — '

'The new group? Aren't they rather controversial?'

Her lips twitched.

'That's right. They advocate open-air painting; 'en plein air', as they call it — Papa would have a fit if he knew, but I took a folio along and showed it to one of the artists. He said I had talent.'

'He did? You've had this dream all along and I never knew?'

'Perhaps you were too wrapped up in your thoughts of engineering and university to be aware of where my interests lay.'

'Perhaps I was — much good it did me. But go on, what else did this artist fellow say? Did he want to paint your portrait?'

She dimpled.

'Actually, he did.'

'Oh, Isobel.' He smiled at her. 'I'm sure your papa could be persuaded to see things your way. If it's the right path for you, it will work out.'

'Do you really think so? It's all right for men. They can follow their dreams. It isn't the same for women.'

'Times are changing, Izzie. Maybe it won't be so long before women take their place alongside men — and you could be in the vanguard . . .'

Fifteen minutes later Nathan stood watching Isobel's carriage drive away. It hadn't been the easiest of visits but Nathan felt they'd reached a new understanding. He wished her well with her painting . . . and with her artist acquaintance.

Listening to the hoofbeats growing fainter, Nathan smiled at the recollection of Chrissie's hastily donned parlourmaid guise, and that smudge of flour from her thoughtful baking for their unexpected visitors.

How long was it since he and Chrissie had had a proper conversation, the way they used to, he wondered. While he was waiting for the woodman to turn up with the posts for the new fence he'd go and seek her out. Removing the stock at his throat, Nathan thrust it into his pocket and strode off in search of her.

★ ★ ★

'Look at it!' Rose Hutch sighed. 'My butter never comes all creamy like yours, Chrissie. I wish I knew your secret.'

'Wheesht, it's no' so bad,' Chrissie said, pausing to examine the offending substance. 'It might be a tad greasy but what else can folks expect this weather? Next time, try cooling the churn with well-water — hot water in winter. And gentle is best for churning.'

She put aside the whey for the pigs and made a mental note to go up to the cheese room to turn the cheeses. She was just leaving for the pigsties, her mind on the myriad tasks of the day, when she heard a voice.

'Penny for them, Chrissie?'

'What?'

Nathan stood leaning against the door frame smiling at her, his teeth very white in his sun-browned face.

'Och, I'm sorry, Master Nathan. I was miles away. Was there something you wanted?'

'It crossed my mind to wonder how someone manages to produce refreshments out of thin air. Or did you raid tomorrow's market bakes for the occasion?'

'The scones, you mean? Och, that was nothing. Plum cake might be fine for country appetites but 'tis hardly ladylike fare. The oven was good and hot. It disnae take a minute to rub a bit o' flour and fat together and bake a round of scones.'

'It was much appreciated.'

'Aye, well . . . If you'll let me pass, Master Nathan, I'll be away to the swine.'

'Here, let me.' He took the pails of whey from her. 'After you, Chrissie.'

They left the dairy and set off through the yard towards the pigsties. Heat lay in a haze over the fields. Cows lay chewing the cud, tails swishing against pestering swarms of flies. In the afternoon silence even the fowl were quiet.

The pigs had heard them coming and squeals of delight greeted them as they rounded the corner of the tithe barn. Nathan poured some of the whey into each of the troughs. Placing the empty pails on the ground, he leaned his back against the wall of the pen of a favourite Old Spot sow.

'D'you know, Chrissie, I never imagined when I was dreaming about engineering that

202

I'd end up farming for a living. The two don't seem compatible.'

'They are, though. You tinker about with the machinery and get it working again.'

He looked at her in amusement.

'My grandfather Drummond had a flair for putting defunct objects to rights — maybe that's where I've got it from. Clocks were his speciality, I remember. He and Grandmother were a fine pair. You'd have liked them . . . ' He paused and looked at her. 'Do you miss the old days, Chrissie?'

'I couldn't say, Master Nathan. But sometimes . . . ' She stopped, looking down at the sow guzzling her food.

'Go on,' Nathan prompted.

'Sometimes before I'm properly awake I think I'm back on the croft where I grew up. I hear the cries of seabirds and the tide lashing the shore. I can almost smell the heather.'

'It's your birthplace. It'll be with you till the day you die.'

'Aye, I ken you're right.' Chrissie sighed. 'Ah, well, this isn't getting the work done.'

'Let the work go hang for a minute. Tell me, are you keeping up with your reading?'

'I am. Mr Finbar loaned me an anthology of the Misses Brontë.'

'Are you enjoying it?'

'Aye. There's one poem I really like:

'Love *is like the wild rose-briar,*
Friendship like the holly tree —
The holly is dark when the rose-briar
  blooms,
But which will bloom most constantly?'

Nathan took over.

'*"The wild rose-briar is sweet in spring,*
Its summer blossoms scent the air;
Yet wait till winter comes again,
And who will call the wild-briar fair?'

'I'm familiar with that one. It's called 'Love And Friendship', if I remember rightly. I wonder what your choice would be, Chrissie? Wild rose or stalwart holly?'
'Love can grow out of friendship, can't it? That must be the best and most enduring love, I think.'
'Oh, Chrissie.'
There was a long silence. Distantly the voices of the men and the calls of cattle and sheep carried through the heat. But for Chrissie it seemed as though nothing existed but herself and the tall young man who stood gazing at her with an unfathomable expression in his grey eyes.

The moment was shattered by the rattle of an approaching vehicle.

'Hello? Anybody there?'

Nathan straightened.

'That's Joe Ferris with the timber, at last. I'd better go and help him unload.'

He strode off, and did not see Chrissie visibly collect herself before picking up the empty pails and heading back to her work.

*   *   *

They were unloading the last of the posts when Stanton Hayles's black cob and trap pulled up to let Aileen out by the gates.

'Hello,' she said as she approached Nathan. 'Busy?'

'You could say that. You're looking very fetching. Been anywhere special?'

Aileen shrugged.

'There was a Rechabite meeting in the chapel hall. Farmer Hayles offered to take me.'

'What did you make of it?'

'It was what I expected. Men giving speeches.'

'You don't sound as if you enjoyed it.'

'Well, I grant the Fellowship is an excellent cause. They made me very welcome. They do commendable good works and I can see what an advantage it might be to a person to join.'

'But?'

'There was rather a sense of the iron hand within the velvet glove. A little too much emphasis on control for my liking. Telling people what they must and must not do. Members have to sign the pledge. I couldn't help recalling Aunt Dorcas and her passion for a good Rhenish. There's no better person than Aunt Dorcas, or more good-living.'

'You're right there.'

'So what harm can a sup of wine do? And another thing,' Aileen said, into her stride now. 'It was all about what men can do. We women have brains, too, you know.'

'It hadn't escaped my notice. I saw an example today. We had a visitor, Ails — Isobel.'

'Isobel Macnair?' Aileen's blue-grey eyes widened. 'What on earth was she doing here?'

'Looking into the prospect of becoming a farmer's wife, I think. It didn't seem to appeal. She said she was sorry to have missed you.'

'Well, I can't say it's returned,' Aileen said with a toss of her head. 'Isobel Macnair never was my favourite person, especially after the way she treated you. Give me someone like Chrissie Ross any day.'

Unsettled without knowing why, Nathan

was suddenly aware that the man had finished stacking the timber and was waiting for his payment. Taking his leave, he went to attend to him.

★   ★   ★

It was no good, Chrissie thought. Tired though she was, sleep eluded her. No sooner did she close her eyes than a vision of Master Nathan's face swam before her. It hadn't been laughter she'd seen in his gaze today, it had been something entirely different.

Punching her bolster, she lay back with her fingers laced behind her head and gave herself up to speculation. She couldn't go on like this. Her love for him was pure torment. How long before she gave herself away? It had nearly happened today. She had wanted — oh, how she'd wanted — to step into his arms and surrender herself to his kisses.

What should she do? Go right away from here and start afresh? Did Glebe Farm need her any longer? Rose Hutch was becoming a dab hand in the dairy, and with Edna Hutch's bustling presence in the house her own load was considerably lightened.

And maybe it would be no bad thing to remove herself from Edward's lovelorn gaze. She thought of him; his good, honest face, the untidy sun-bleached hair and big, square hands, strong and capable. He'd make a fine husband for some lass — though not this one.

Where could she go? Back to Glasgow? Her savings were meagre. She might manage to scrape together the fare, and what then? She'd need lodgings and food until she found work. Her funds would not stretch to that. No, it would have to be closer to Hadnall. But not too close.

She almost shocked herself with her thoughts. She'd be leaving behind so much: the family who had been good to her; the farm she had come to look upon as home; the people she'd grown fond of hereabouts. She dared not think of her true reason for leaving . . .

Her eyelids were growing heavy. She slept.

★ ★ ★

'More gingerbread, Stanton? I know 'tis your favourite.' Smiling, Florence offered the plate to her guest. This was the farmer's second impromptu call this week. He seemed to be showing more than a passing interest in Aileen. Would a little delicate probing be in order, she wondered.

'Thank you kindly, m'dear.'

The farmer helped himself to the last slice

and sat back in the chair.

'Aileen tells me you took her to a Fellowship meeting the other day,' Florence said.

'That's right. Don't know what she made of it. She's a bit of a dark horse, your girl. Doesn't give much away. Bright as a button, mind.'

'Indeed. Aileen has inherited her father's head for business.'

'Oh? You were in business before you came here?'

Too late, Florence realised her slip and hastened to rectify it.

'There were . . . considerations. My husband's health, you know. We thought the country air might help. Sadly it was not to be.'

'No. I'm sorry. I found great solace in the Rechabite cause, myself. They were particularly good to me after my dear wife passed on. The Chapel was good, an' all. In its own way, of course.'

'Quite,' Florence said. 'Balfour found enormous strength in the Kirk.' A shadow passed over her face. 'But one must not grow morbid, not when there are the young people to consider.'

'Indeed. I'd not be without my girl for the world. She's everything to me, my Verity. My dearest wish is to see her settled with a decent young fellow who'll treat her well.'

Florence was about to respond when an outer door slammed. A moment later, Nathan entered the room. He was formally dressed in a dark grey suit of broadcloth from earlier times and the whitest of linen. His unruly hair was trimmed and tamed with a dab of pomatum, also a relic of earlier days.

'Mama, Hayles. No, please don't get up, sir,' he bade the farmer. 'I'm needed outside shortly. Just thought to join you for a sip of tea before changing my clothes.'

He went to sit beside his mother on the sofa. That morning he had taken the train to Shrewsbury to see Dennison and Poleworthy, the family solicitors, in order to clarify the remaining legal questions regarding the terms of the family trust that governed their occupancy of Glebe Farm.

Florence hoped the situation had now been resolved. She threw her son a searching glance. To judge by his demeanour there did not appear anything untoward. The fact that she had been considering asking the trustees to turn over the property legally to him was a point of discussion for the future.

'Started hay-making, Drummond?' Hayles enquired. Nathan shook his head.

'Not yet, though I see you have at Twelve Trees.'

'Aye, well, a wet May brings the hay, so the saying goes. We didn't get it this time and the grass is nothing like it should be. Still, we should have sufficient at Twelve Trees to see us through the winter. If you find yourself short, Drummond, there could be a bit going spare at my place.'

'Thank you, that's good to know. Though we should be all right for hay. It's wheat and barley we might be short of.'

''Tis a concern, I agree. Still, the weather's sure to break eventually. We'll get a cracking good thunderstorm and that'll be it. Not yet, though — not till the hay's in, eh?'

Listening to them, Florence couldn't help thinking back to when they had first arrived and how hostile their neighbour had been initially. She knew Nathan still harboured doubts as to the man's integrity. Hayles had wanted the Glebe acres for himself and Nathan thought he still might. Like her, he was worried that somehow Hayles might learn of their past and use it against them.

She rued her earlier blunder again. The undeserved shame they had suffered in Glasgow seemed far away, but the fear that discovery of those events might shatter the

211

peaceful haven they had found here lingered yet.

Feeling a sudden weariness at the effort required to keep hidden their past sufferings, Florence put her tea aside.

Through the open window she could hear the voices of the little girls as they played in the shade of the trees. What comfort the children brought. She must remain strong for their sake.

★　★　★

A few days later hay-cutting began at the Glebe. Nathan, working alongside the men, felt the ache in his muscles as he wielded the scythe. Next to him in the line, Finbar toiled doggedly. On his other side Edward, despite his lame foot, kept up a steady rhythm.

Swish, swish, swish. The flow of movement was becoming soporific.

At midday, Chrissie and Rose appeared with the food hamper and ale cooled in the well, and the men left off work and sought the shade of the elms to eat.

Nathan took his repast with Jim Merridew. 'We had big harvests here in the old days,' Jim said, pausing to slake his thirst with a swig of ale. 'The hay leas went as far as the eye could see and folks came from the village to help. I remember how hot the sun was and how the hay pricked inside your shirt. We'd stagger home bone-weary yet content after a day's work well done.' He paused again.

'You love these lands, don't you, Jim.'

'Aye, gaffer, I do. Before I die I want to see it back as it was when the old gaffer were a young man, and a fellow felt proud to be part of it all. And then I'll know that same feeling I had as a lad, of a job well done.'

Nathan's throat tightened.

'I let you down,' he said, sending a nod towards the hillside and its disastrous crop. 'You told me it wouldn't work and I wouldn't listen. I honestly believed I was doing the right thing. I warrant Reeve Webb never made such a mistake.'

'I'd lay a pound to a penny he did. We've all made 'em. Thing is to learn by them. We can always rake over that grumbly ground an' throw down some grass seed. A drop of rain will soon see it back as it was.'

'That's what we'll do, then,' Nathan said.

They exchanged a smile. Nathan was aware that a pact had been made. The advice had been graciously given. This time he would follow it.

★　★　★

They were just finishing their meal when Jamie came racing across the shorn ground, the dog streaking ahead. Bess made it first and flung herself down beside them, flanks heaving, tongue dripping, hopeful eyes on the food hamper. Nathan tossed her a piece of fat bacon and turned his attention to his small brother.

'No school, Jamie?'

'We were sent home. None of the others turned up 'cause they were needed on the fields. Can I help with the hay? Can I?'

'When you're big enough to use a scythe, you can join us with pleasure.'

'But I want to now. I'm strong — I'll show you.'

He made a lunge towards the row of scythes propped against the drystone wall. Merridew shot out a sinewy arm and yanked him back.

'Careful, boy. One false move and you could lose a limb. Them tools are for men.'

Jamie looked suitably chastened.

'Sorry.'

'How's the book-learning going?' Jim asked. 'Still liking it up at the school?'

'It's not bad. I've got a new teacher.' He pulled a face. 'I don't much like it in Mr Moseley's class. He's terrible strict. Miss Cartwright used to shout at us nicely, but Mr Moseley doesn't.'

'Oh, that's hard luck.' Jim's eyes were bright with amusement. 'Had the cane yet?'

'No. Andy Fox has. He said it's not so bad if you think of summat else.'

'Something else,' Nathan corrected him, then stopped. A rider was approaching. He could guess who it was from the dancing gait of the horse.

'Here's Aunt Dorcas coming to see if we're slacking. Better look lively, eh, Jim? Jamie, run back and tell Chrissie we're done here and she can come and collect the hamper. And tell Mama your aunt's on her way.'

'Right-oh,' Jamie said. 'Come on, Bess.'

They sprinted away. Soon afterwards, Dorcas arrived, the grey mare pirouetting energetically in defiance of her rider's request to halt.

'Afternoon, Nathan. Jim,' Dorcas bid them.

'How do, Miss Webb,' Jim said, pulling a forelock. 'Mare's looking well.'

'Thank you.' She fetched the dripping grey neck a slap and Gemini responded by dancing on the spot.

'Whoa, girl. That's quite enough. How's your mama, Nathan? More herself, I hope?'

'I think so, thank you, aunt.'

'I see you've made fair progress with the

hay,' Dorcas said, glancing round. 'We've made a start at Wollerton. The grass isn't up to its usual standard but at least we've got some to cut, unlike others who've lost theirs to the flames. No bother with union folk here, I take it?'

'None at all,' Nathan replied.

'That's good to hear. Let's hope it stays that way, eh? Anxious time, this, without added worry. But still, there's nothing quite like hay harvest.'

Bestowing on them a beaming smile, she nodded her acknowledgement to Finbar and the others a little way off and gathered up her reins.

'Ah well, I shall carry on to the house. Farewell for now, Nathan. Keep up the good work.'

She sent Gemini thudding away along the avenues of cut grass. As she neared the farmhouse, she came across Chrissie heading slowly in the direction of the harvesters. Her head was down and she looked dejected.

'Ho there, Chrissie,' Dorcas hailed her, pulling to a skittering stop.

'Good-day, ma'am.'

'You don't seem quite yourself,' Dorcas said bluntly.

'No. Yes. I mean . . . ' Chrissie bit her lip.

Dorcas, easing her right leg over the high

pommel of the side saddle, slid nimbly to the ground.

'Come on, Chrissie. This isn't like you. Want to talk about it?'

'Talk about it?' She seemed to make up her mind. 'Truth is, ma'am, I feel I'm not needed here any more.'

'What?' Dorcas's snort of incredulity sent Gemini's ears flattening to her head. 'You're deluding yourself. Without you this household would fall apart.'

'No, it would not — begging your pardon, ma'am. I allow it was that way to begin with. 'Twas how I came to be here in the first place. I played on the fact and got them to bring me along wi' them, instead of leaving me behind to find another place like the rest of the staff.'

'So? You did the right thing for everyone.'

'It's different now. People have learned how to do so much themselves, and I'm not as vital to them as I was. Master Jamie's growing up. He won't need a nursemaid for much longer. And I don't suppose the minister and Mrs Lennox and the children will be here for ever. They'll want a home of their own.'

Dorcas's eyes narrowed.

'Were you contemplating leaving the fold, by any chance?'

'Maybe. You'll not say anything, will you?'

'Of course I won't. But think very hard about it, Chrissie. It's not just my sister and the girls who would regret your going. Nathan would feel the loss enormously, if he but knew it.'

The maid's face went so white that Dorcas put out a hand towards her in alarm.

'I must go,' she whispered. 'I have to collect the hamper.'

'Indispensable, eh?' Dorcas said dryly. 'Well, take care, Chrissie.'

She carried on to the house thoughtfully on foot, Gemini's reins looped over her arm. She hoped her sister had got the kettle on the boil. On second thoughts, perhaps Florence might be persuaded to produce something a little stronger; Chrissie's words had upset her exceedingly.

★ ★ ★

A few nights later, Chrissie waited until the household was asleep and crept down the back stairs. In the kitchen all was quiet. Taking an envelope from her pocket, she propped it against the clock and continued to the back door.

Outside, there was no moon but the night was starlit. The last leas of hay had been cut that day and the scent of drying grass hung

218

sweetly on the air. Chrissie knew she would never again catch the scent of new-mown hay without remembering this moment. She paused, her resolve almost broken. Then, straightening her back, she pulled the door closed with a decisive click.

She shouldered her bundle and set off across the farmyard, shushing Bess who had woken in her kennel. Chrissie headed for the stile and the route across country. Scrambling over, she set off briskly along the meadow path and was soon lost to view.

9

'Chrissie, gone?' Nathan stared at his mother. 'Gone where?' In silence Florence handed him the letter she had found on the kitchen mantel.

Frowning, Nathan ran his eye over the missive, written in the careful hand he had himself watched Chrissie master.

> *My Dear Mistress,*
> *I am writing to say that I am leaving your employment and hope to make a life for myself elsewhere.*
> *I shall always remember you all with warmth and affection, and hope I shall be forgiven for leaving in this way.*
> *Your devoted servant, Christina Ross.*

The page shook slightly in Nathan's hand.
'I never knew her name was Christina,' he muttered absently. 'She was always Chrissie to us. Christina. It's lovely, dammit!'

In sudden fury he thrust the letter back at his mother.

'How long has she been gone?'

'Nathan, I really cannot say.' Florence

recoiled at his response.

Nathan ran his hand through his unruly mop of hair.

'Have you looked in her room?'

'Of course. She's taken all her belongings. The bed is made. There is no trace of her at all.' Florence spread her hands in despair. 'Where can she be?'

She swung round as the door burst open to admit Aileen.

'Well?'

'I've looked everywhere,' Aileen said, her breath coming in short, sharp gasps. 'There's no sign of her. Silas Turner says the dogs were grumbling in the night. He couldn't be sure of the time. Edward is demented. He's gone tearing off to Hadnall Station to see if she's there. I told him to take the cart but he wouldn't listen. He blames us for what's happened.'

'But that is ridiculous,' Florence said.

There was a hesitant tap on the door. Jim Merridew stood twisting his cap agitatedly in his big red hands.

'Begging your pardon, but I think Chrissie dinna leave by the road. She wunna heading for the station like Edward thinks. She's gone off in the other direction — over the stile and across the fields. There's a trail in the grass.'

Nathan reached for his coat. 'She can't

have got far. I'm going after her!'

'Take Firefly,' Aileen said. 'She's quicker than Captain.'

'If you follow the trail to the brook, gaffer, you'll see how she's cut across Long Meadow. There's a chance she were making for the Shrewsbury road. Want me to saddle the mare for you?'

'No, it's all right, man. With Chrissie gone and Edward rushing off like that, the cows must be crying out to be milked. Could you see to it, Jim?'

'Aye, I'll do that.'

Nathan followed him out.

The inner door opened and Jamie trailed in. He was still in his nightshirt, his face flushed from sleep.

'Where's Chrissie? My school things aren't ready an' school starts again today. I'll get a skelping off of Moleface if I'm late.'

'Mr Mosely, if you please, Jamie!' Florence said in rebuke.

'All the others call him that,' Jamie replied, aggrieved. 'Where is Chrissie?'

'She's not here,' Aileen said. 'Good gracious me, Jamie, it's high time you got yourself ready for school, a big lad like you. Come on, let's get you sorted.'

She hustled him away. Florence, reaching for the kettle for a much-needed cup of tea, was then waylaid by the arrival of Edna and Rose Hutch. Both were red-cheeked and out of breath, as if they had run all the way.

'Oh, ma'am!' Edna gasped. 'We met Edward on the road. He told us what's happened. What was she thinking?'

'I have no idea, Edna,' Florence said wearily.

From the bedroom above, John let out a hungry wail. It was echoed by the two small girls, who had woken to find no-one present to wash and dress them. Davina's voice answered, gently chiding. Florence raised her eyes heavenwards.

'What a fine state of affairs! Edna, would you be so kind as to help Mrs Lennox for now? Rose, could you see to the breakfast? Someone must go to Wollerton and let my sister know what has happened. Perhaps Mr Lennox would oblige.' She threw a glance around. 'Where is Mr Lennox?'

'Fetching the water, ma'am. I saw him as we came in,' Rose answered.

★   ★   ★

The morning chores were completed somehow and the sun was high when Nathan arrived back on a lathered Firefly.

'No trace. It's as if she's vanished off the

face of the earth. I've been all the way to Shrewsbury. She must have taken the train after all.'

'It seems not,' Florence said, handing him a cup of tea. 'Edward enquired. The station master hadn't seen her.'

'I've been thinking . . . there's a chance she'll have headed back to familiar ground.'

'You mean Glasgow?'

'It's possible. She'd know we'd make enquiries at Hadnall Station. She could have walked on to the next stop and boarded a train there.'

'Then we don't have the remotest chance of tracing her.'

'No, we don't.'

The words were loaded with despair. Gulping down the strong, reviving tea, Nathan considered the prospect of life at Glebe Farm without Chrissie. Could this be his fault? Had he not protected her enough from the never-ending demands of the farm and his family? His chest ached unbearably and the cold meat and pickle his mother had put before him stuck in his throat. Pushing the food aside, he went out.

In the yard he came across Finbar, a set of harness on his arm.

'No luck?' Finbar greeted him.

'None whatsoever. Where are you headed'?'

'I'm away to the manor. Your mother says your aunt Dorcas will want to know what's happened. It seems she had a soft spot for Chrissie Ross.'

'I wouldn't mind a word with her myself. I'll go in your place. I was about to give a hand with the hay. Could you take over till I get back?'

'Aye, of course.'

Nathan had barely gone half a dozen paces before Jim Merridew accosted him with the news that one of the cows had gone down with what looked like lead poisoning. He'd given her a drench but the poor beast's joints were swelling badly.

Nathan was desperate to be off, but this latest news gave him pause.

'Lead poisoning, you say? How the devil could she have got that?'

Merridew hesitated, his face pensive.

'Contessa will lick the manger during milking. She never did it before we gave the byre a doing out. I reckon she's got a liking for the taste of that new-fangled paint we used.'

Nathan made no reply. It had been his idea to use the paint instead of the usual tar; he'd had a surfeit of the strong fumes. Was this yet another error on his part?

Leaving Jim with instructions to act as he

thought best, Nathan continued to Wollerton with a heavy heart.

★ ★ ★

In the manor, all was blessedly cool after the blistering heat outside.

A maid appeared with a laden tray which she set down on a low table next to Dorcas's chair.

'Sit down, Nathan, do,' Dorcas said. 'You make me dizzy pacing up and down like that. What ails you?'

Nathan flung himself into the chair opposite and one of the hounds padded up and placed a sympathetic paw in his lap. Absently Nathan rubbed the massive, rough-pelted head. His face was grim.

'It's Chrissie Ross, Aunt. She's left us. Went in the night, no-one heard a thing.'

Dorcas abandoned the coffee and went instead to raid the dresser for something more fortifying. Pouring a generous measure of good French brandy into two cut-glass goblets, she silently handed one to Nathan and took her own and the brandy back to her seat. She tipped a wedge of game pie on to a plate, topped it with a slice of cheese and pushed the dish at her nephew.

'Eat, boy. Then tell me from the beginning.'

Nathan did as he was bid.

'Chrissie confided in you, didn't she, Aunt? Has she said anything that might make you think she was contemplating something like this?'

'Not as such. She seemed a bit low last time I saw her.' Dorcas sipped brandy, frowning. 'This wasn't what I expected when you rode up. I thought it was union problems. There was more trouble here in the night.'

Nathan stiffened, his drink halfway to his lips. 'Here? At the manor?'

'No, no — at least, not yet. A well was poisoned at Snab Farm. It's a wretched business. The Snellgroves rely on the well for the house as well as the animals. Jack Snellgrove came here wanting fresh water. I could hardly refuse him, could I?'

'Of course not.' Nathan swirled the brandy in the glass, watching it catch the light from the window. 'I see your dilemma. The manor has been left alone so far because of your goodwill in the district. Being seen to help the targeted farms might go against you. How long then before they turn on the manor?'

'You've put it in a nutshell. I'm not normally one to worry, but this latest development has got me concerned.'

'What about your staff? Would they support you?'

'Oh, they'd put up a fight, though I'd rather it didn't come to that.' Dorcas paused, indicating the brandy. 'More?'

'Thank you, but I must keep a clear head. There's a great deal to think about.'

'The runaway? You're a fool, boy. Chrissie Ross was in love with you and you were too blind to see it.'

He stared.

'Chrissie? But she's — '

'A servant? Is that what you were about to say? Well, what of it? Tsk, we're not landed gentry ourselves. Your grandfather Webb was ordinary working stock blessed with a keen intellect and the wit to use it. Balfour Drummond was the same and so, in her own way, was Chrissie. And she was a beauty, and if you hadn't been so bedazzled by Miss Flibbertygibbet Hayles you'd have seen it!'

'Me, taken in by Verity? I certainly was — '

'Admit it, Nathan. You relish the attention the chit lavishes on you.'

'Verity is a dashed fetching young woman. What man wouldn't be flattered? But I have not encouraged her. I've a farm to run. A wife would be a hindrance.'

'Even a wife like Chrissie Ross?'

There was a short silence.

'Think about it, boy,' Dorcas continued remorselessly. 'Why have you come chasing over here in such a tizz? You love her, if you but knew it. I've tried to tell you before, but would you listen? It's as I said. You've been blinded and now you've lost her.'

Nathan opened his mouth to speak and then closed it again. He put aside the empty goblet and said he ought to go, the men would be expecting him.

Long after the hoofbeats had faded away, Dorcas sat on, her mind on this new turn of events at Glebe Farm. She'd miss Chrissie Ross sorely. Where in heaven's name could the wench have headed for? For the first time in her orderly life, Dorcas Webb was at a loss . . .

★　★　★

As the sky lightened towards dawn Chrissie had heard the clop of hoofs on the road behind her. The carrier was heading for Nantwich. It seemed as good a place as any. Gratefully she had tossed her bundle on to the cart and clambered aboard.

After what seemed like hours of comfortless, joggling miles Chrissie was dropped off at the square in the centre of the town. She must find lodgings. Shouldering her bundle, she crossed the square and asked a wrinkle-faced flower-seller who sat at the foot of the church steps.

'Try Mrs Huxley on Monks Lane, dearie,' the woman said. 'Cut through the church-yard, turn right and it's first on the left. You won't get better.'

Chrissie found the lodgings easily: a tall house with a green-painted front door and gleaming lion-head knocker. The landlady appeared to her rap.

'Mrs Huxley? My name is Christina Ross. I'm looking for lodgings and you were recommended. Please, have you a room? I can pay.'

Stiffly corseted and dressed in rusty black, the landlady looked her up and down.

'You're in luck, miss. A room was vacated yesterday. This way, please. Mind you wipe your feet.'

The room was small, square and clean. There was an iron-framed bed with a faded coverlet, a scuffed and wobbly table, a single chair and a small chest of drawers. On the far wall, oh joy, was a fireplace complete with oven.

'I'll take it,' she heard herself say as if from a long way off.

'Wood and coal are extra,' the landlady said. 'Rent is due every Friday night sharp. I want a week's payment in advance.'

Minutes later Chrissie had paid her deposit

street and men with clogged feet clattered to work. It might have been Glasgow . . . but this was Nantwich.

Her landlady had told her that Nantwich held two markets a week, Saturdays and Thursdays. Today being Friday she could get her fire going, her oven hot and her goods baked. Tomorrow she would discover if her wares would bring custom.

She settled for simple bannocks and the little mutton and vegetable pies so beloved by Hadnall villagers. Before seven the next morning she was at her stall, setting it all out as attractively as her trembling hands would allow.

'My, those look good enough to eat!' a voice exclaimed.

Looking up, Chrissie discovered a young man smiling at her from the next stall. Not much taller than she was and stockily built, he had thick brown hair and kind brown eyes in a homely face.

The smile broadened.

'My name's Daniel Jolley. What's yours?'

'It's . . . Christina.'

'Nice knowing you, miss — you're not from these parts, I'd say.'

'No, I'm not,' she replied. The less she said about herself, the better. Nantwich was miles from Hadnall but one never knew who might pass through market places.

'Have you been on the market long, Mr Jolley?'

'Practically all my life, miss. You must call me Daniel. If there's anything you need to know, you have only to ask.'

'Thank you,' Chrissie said. 'And it's Christina.'

Daniel Jolley sold household wares, every-thing from fire tongs to pots and pans and basting spoons. Over the next weeks Chrissie came to rely on him, not least for obtaining more requirements for her work at a good price. Plan as she might, she never seemed to have enough baking trays and skillets for the demand . . . and the demand was there. Word spread rapidly that a pretty new stallholder was trading in pies and other foodstuffs that melted on the tongue, and by midday her stall was always cleared.

'What did I tell you?' Daniel said, a month later.

'Let's hope it continues.' Chrissie caught his gaze and smiled.

★   ★   ★

Florence put the rolling pin aside and straightened to ease her aching back.

'There, that's the pie tins lined. What

fillings are you putting in them?'

Aileen, taking a large batch of cherry scones from the oven, dumped the tray down on the table with a clatter and turned to her mother. Her cheeks were crimson and the tendrils of reddish hair that hung about her face were dark with damp.

'It will have to be apple,' she said, mopping her brow with the back of her hand. 'There may be a last jar of apricots as well. And that's about it till the new season stuff comes in. We must see about increasing our stock of jams and bottled fruit next time. I'm always being asked for pies and there's never enough.'

'Well, we were late getting the crop in last year. I think we did an excellent job, in the circumstances,' Florence said.

'Just think, Mama,' Aileen said, 'we'll have our own raspberries and blackcurrants this time. I picked a few this morning. They're ripening nicely, though I did expect a better yield. Jim says that soft fruits can take a year or two to establish.'

'You could always ask Aunt Dorcas for some of theirs. They have far more than they can use at the manor. While I remember, Aileen — last night I had an idea.'

'Oh? Do tell me,' Aileen said.

'You know these remedies of Davina's?

Why don't we get her to make extra and sell them on the stall?'

To everyone's surprise, Davina had brought back from her time in Africa an astonishing knowledge of plants and cures. These days she scoured the hedgerows for herbs and roots — tansy, marjoram, feverfew — and bound them in bunches which she hung to dry in a small room off the larder, her stillroom. All manner of medicinal requirements had appeared on the shelves; a brown jar of liquorice sticks for the cough, pots of goose-grease and marigold for chapped hands, oil of cloves for the toothache. The cocktail of odours when the door was opened fairly took the breath away.

'Mama, what a perfectly splendid idea!' Aileen said. 'Would she mind?'

'I don't see why not. Davina's never happier than when concocting her tisanes and tinctures.'

'You could be right. I thought I might try making more wine this autumn, too. The elderflower we did in the spring sold well.'

'Excellent. What made you think of it?'

'I didn't. It was Chrissie. She maintained that a perfectly acceptable wine could be made out of virtually anything that grew at the roadside or in the garden.'

There was a long silence.

'Ah, me.' Florence sighed. 'I think about Chrissie all the time. I do hope she is all right.'

'Rest assured, Mama, she will be. Chrissie Ross would thrive anywhere.'

Aileen, still vexed at being left to manage the market stall alone, drew her lips together in a thin line. She looked up as hoofs and the rumble of trap wheels sounded on the yard.

'Oh, no! That will be Mr Hayles. Tell him I'm occupied, would you, Mama?'

'Indeed not. I shall offer him tea in the parlour, since he's taken the trouble to call.' Florence whipped off her pinafore, and put up a hand to tidy her hair. 'May I take one or two of these scones for the tray?'

'Yes, by all means.'

An alarming whiff of burning sent Aileen flying to the oven.

'Oh, fiddlesticks! I'd left a tin right at the back and now the scones are ruined!'

Opening her mouth to remonstrate, Florence thought the better of it and went to welcome their guest.

⋆   ⋆   ⋆

Sitting in the cool confines of the parlour, watching her caller consume new-baked scones spread lavishly with thick yellow

237

butter, Florence broached the subject of the missing maid.

'I was talking to Aileen about Chrissie just now. We feel the loss dreadfully and I don't mean as a servant. We miss her as one of us.'

'She was a remarkably attractive young woman. Beautiful eyes, I remember.'

'Attractive? Yes, I suppose she was. We never really look at the people around us, do we? I do recall her eyes. They always reminded me of the sea along the coast where she came from. She must have found Glasgow very different.'

'Glasgow?' He looked up. 'Is that where you moved from?'

Florence let her gaze fall. This was not the first time she had slipped up. She must be more careful . . .

'Not far from there,' she said lightly, picking up the teapot. 'More tea?'

'Thank you kindly.' Stanton Hayles was not easily distracted. 'Glasgow, eh? A fine city, by all accounts.'

A door had opened and the smell of overdone baking wafted in. He glanced round, inhaling.

'Begging your pardon, ma'am, is something burning?'

Silently applauding Aileen for her mishap, Florence reassured him.

'Oh, 'tis nothing. We overlooked a batch of scones.'

'Ah. Well, it happens. Nothing wrong with these!'

The last scone on the plate was contemplated with interest.

'Do help yourself.' Florence smiled. There was much to like in this uncomplicated man who appeared to enjoy her own company as much as he did her daughter's.

'I had ideas of a match between Chrissie Ross and Edward Turner, you know,' she said.

'What, the cripple?'

'Oh, please do not refer to him so! Edward is such a delightful young man. I vow Chrissie scarcely noticed his lameness.'

'And yet the fellow didn't tempt her enough to make her want to stay.'

'That is true.' Florence frowned.

'I confess I also had hopes of a liaison between our two children. Though I fear events are not progressing favourably.'

'Aye, well, they're young yet, ma'am. Give 'em time.'

Thoughts chased behind the farmer's shrewd hazel eyes. To his shame he had never really forgiven Balfour Drummond — God rest his soul — for snatching the Glebe from under his nose. Looking around the comfortable parlour, contemplating the acres that lay beyond the walls, he knew he wanted the farm still. By Jove, he did!

From somewhere within the depths of the house he heard childish voices raised in play.

'The little ones have woken from their afternoon nap,' Florence said fondly. 'I promised them a walk. It gives Davina time to devote to other things and I do so love having them to myself.'

''Course you do, m'dear, 'tis understandable.' Stanton Hayles finished his tea and returned the cup and saucer to the tray. 'I ought to be moving, mustn't keep Ebony waiting about too long in this heat.'

He stood up, showering crumbs.

'Well then, ma'am, I shall bid you good-day.'

Seeing him out, Florence went to find her grandchildren.

* * *

'Grandmama!' Annabel cried. 'Will you take us to the hens?'

'Will you take us, *please*,' their mother corrected, following with the baby in her arms.

'Please. You promised.'

'I know I did, my lamb. Yes, we shall go through the orchard and see how many birds we can count. What is this?'

'A picture I drawed of Grandpapa Drummond. Mama said he was with the angels so I drawed him with wings.'

'Drew,' Davina said. 'Drew him with wings, Annabel.'

Florence cast her eldest a beseeching look. She looked at the drawing.

'Oh, my, it's very good. How clever you are, Annabel.'

The little girl beamed and submitted to having her sunbonnet put on, while her sister looked on, waiting her turn.

In the dappled shade of the orchard trees the hens were busily pecking the ground in search of insects.

'Oh, look!' Florence exclaimed. 'This one's starting to moult.'

'What's moult?' Annabel asked, frowning.

'It's when they lose their tired old feathers. They stop laying then for a while. It gives them a rest, you see. Then they grow beautiful new plumage and we get eggs again.'

Annabel's frown deepened.

'What happens to angels when they moult? Will Grandpapa Drummond be able to fly with no feathers?' Laughter and tears sprang to Florence's eyes.

'Oh, I shouldn't think it happens to angels,

darling, would you?'

'No,' Annabel said, smiling.

* * *

Nathan stood at the crest of the hill and cast a look around. Far below, in the Glebe stackyard, six new hayricks huddled together in a satisfying cluster, and over at Twelve Trees the final leas of grass were being cut. He watched the teams move slowly and patiently over the ground. There was something deeply moving and peaceful in the sight.

His thoughts turned to the encounter he had overheard the previous day, when he had come across Finbar castigating Silas Turner.

'Man, you're risking everything: job, home, friends.' The usually measured tones had been harsh. 'It's come to my ears that the union might target a property close to here shortly.'

Nathan had frozen in the deep shadow of the hayricks. Could they mean Twelve Trees?

'So what?' Turner had responded. 'There are some that need showing what's what.'

'That isn't the point. I'm sorry, but if anything untoward should occur I shall have to tell what I know.'

'That's up to you, Parson. Right is right.

The common man has to be supported.'

'One doesn't support one's brother man by poisoning water systems and firing hayricks. Arbitration and negotiation would achieve better results.'

'Words! It's not words people want. It's action.'

'But this is wilful violence and destruction. Can you not grasp that?'

'No, I canna,' Turner had said.

Finbar had looked at him steadily for a long moment before striding wordlessly away.

Nathan recalled finding his brother-in-law making a frenzied attempt to clear a ditch of decades of growth a short while later.

'You'll do yourself no good going at it like that in this heat,' he'd told him.

Putting down the billhook, Finbar had wiped the sweat from his face with the heel of his hand.

'Maybe not, but it's got rid of a lot of frustration.'

'Turner, you mean? I overheard what you said.'

'Aye, well, maybe I was pushing it a bit. I'd noticed a furtive conversation by the cattle pens at Shrewsbury market. Three of the group were Twelve Trees men, I'd swear to it.'

'You think they were planning something?'

'It looked that way. We might be wise to

watch out for trouble. From what you've said Hayles hasn't been the best of neighbours, but you wouldn't want to see his property harmed.'

'No, I wouldn't. I almost wish I'd not taken Turner on. I was warned about his union sympathies, and yet he's a damned good shepherd and Edward couldn't be bettered.' Nathan looked at the other man. 'There's more, isn't there?'

'Aye. I'm concerned for my wife and bairns. A farmhouse caught ablaze the other week. Those inside were rescued in the nick of time. It could have been disastrous. If it should happen here . . . '

His voice trailed.

'You want to move on,' Nathan said flatly.

'If it were just me I'd stay put and see this confounded business out. But I have to think of my family. I've decided to apply for a ministry back in Glasgow. There must be a place for me somewhere.'

'Yes, well, I can't blame you. It's your calling, after all.'

'I'm sorry, Nathan. I feel bad about leaving you to this.'

'You mustn't think that way. Of course you must put your family first.' Nathan paused. 'Shall you break the news to Mama, or would you like me to do it?'

'No, I'll tell her.' Finbar sighed heavily. 'Poor woman, she'll not take kindly to being separated from the girls and wee John.'

High above a curlew called, piercing Nathan now with a melancholy that was almost unbearable. Whistling to the dog, he turned and set off down the hillside for home.

In the farmyard, he saw Stanton Hayles's black cob tied to the tethering post. He supposed the farmer had come to see Aileen again. As he passed the barn, Hayles emerged from the shadows. His chin was high, his expression set.

'Drummond! I want a word.' Hayles came closer, his eyes narrowed beneath the bushy brows. 'A short while ago I found my girl in tears. It seems you've led her on and disappointed her.'

'Sir, believe me,' Nathan said, taken aback. 'I've done nothing to encourage Verity.'

'That's not what she says. Sobbing her heart out, she was! I'll not tolerate it, I tell you!'

'Sir, I'm sure you will agree that there is a vast difference between a mild flirtation and serious courtship — '

'Mild flirtation, is it? I'll not have Verity's feelings played about with! You either court a girl or you do the right thing and keep your distance. I know your mother has hopes of a union. Up till now I've let things take their course. But enough is enough.'

The eyes grew cunning.

'I've been asking a few questions, Drummond. You had good reason for moving all the way down here from Glasgow.'

Nathan's heart quailed. This was it, the situation he had dreaded ever since setting foot on Glebe soil. Squaring his shoulders, he faced the other man calmly.

'We can't talk out here,' he said. 'You had better come up to the office. I'll hear what you have to say there.'

10

Grim-faced and silent, the two men ascended the steps to Nathan's office over the stables. Nathan flung open the door and gestured the other man in. He indicated a chair and, bracing himself for what was to come, went to sit at the desk.

'I'll not beat about the bush,' Hayles began, lowering his solid frame on to the carved wooden seat and fixing Nathan with steely gaze. 'I know all about your father's fall from grace.'

'Through no fault of his own, sir!'

'That's as maybe. Myself, I'd have thought a man of business would have been more astute. Drummond's Grocery Stores, I hear, was a thriving enterprise until he went and lost the lot through unwise speculation.'

'My father was a prudent man, Hayles. It was the collapse of the bank that was the cause. My father made the decision to pay back what was owed. He was an honourable, God-fearing man and I won't see his name blackened. He did the right thing according to his own conscience, and in doing so we lost our home and our livelihood.'

'And all that went with it, I warrant. Respect, goodwill. It must have been dashed hard on your mother.'

'Sir, I fail to see where all this is leading,' Nathan said.

'Oh, getting uppity now, are we? I always wondered why a young whippersnapper like you should come here playing farms. Well, now we know. You had no choice.'

'You overstep yourself, sir,' Nathan countered. 'I admit to being new to farming but I'm willing and able to learn. You must agree I've not made too bad a fist of it so far.'

'Aye, because you've had knowledgeable men behind you to keep you on the right track. My men! Without Merridew and the others you filched from my workforce, you wouldn't have lasted the winter.'

'Oh, come. Isn't this all rather unnecessary?'

'Think so?' Hayles growled, visibly angry. 'Drummond, I've known for some while of your history and so far I've said nothing. I'm not a hard man. I know what scandal can do and I wouldn't want to be the one to bring it down on the heads of your womenfolk, particularly your mother. But there are limits. My Verity will be ill if she goes on the way she is. As far as I can see there's only one remedy.' He paused. 'You do the decent thing and marry her.'

'Sir! I object!' Nathan cried, his eyes dark and angry in his shocked face. 'You go too far. If you truly believe this to be the way to gain your daughter's happiness then you are sadly mistaken.'

'Mistaken — poppycock!' Hayles made a dismissive gesture. 'I know my girl. It's what she wants. Of course it would make her happy.'

'But this is preposterous. What you say is blackmail and I'll have none of it.'

'Blackmail? I hardly think so. You led Verity to believe you were interested in her. As her father I'm under an obligation to support her in these matters.'

'Oh, really?' His mind working rapidly, Nathan steepled his fingers and gazed at Hayles. 'And what of your obligation as a gentleman?' he said quietly.

'I'd say that was one and the same thing.'

'Would you? Really?' Nathan took a long breath. 'Would the Fellowship of Rechabites agree? A worthy cause, I'm led to understand. I hardly think this conduct befits one of its members.'

Silence. A bluebottle buzzed irritably against the window-pane, seeking escape. Hayles, his blunt face screwed up in concentration, took out his kerchief and mopped his brow uncomfortably.

He cleared his throat.

'You've not heard the last of this, Drummond. I'll make sure of that.'

'I think you are bluffing. And now, sir, if you will excuse me, I have things to do.'

He went to open the door and watched as Hayles pulled heavily to his feet.

'One more thing,' Nathan said. 'Might I enquire the name of your informant?'

Hayles sent him a smile devoid of any humour.

'Well, since you ask . . . Know a little lady by the name of Miss Isobel Macnair? Of course you do. You seem to delight in playing fast and loose with the fairer sex, Drummond.

'This young lady was none too pleased at being cast aside, or I doubt she'd have gone so far as to contact me. Still, she did, and what she had to say was illuminating. Mind, I shouldn't think we'll be seeing her again in these parts. She must still harbour some feelings for you — I was left with the impression she'd have taken her words back if she could. A bit late for that!'

His expression thunderous, Hayles pushed past and without so much as a nod of farewell clumped away down the steps.

Nathan discovered that his palms were sweating. Isobel! What was that about hell having no fury like a woman scorned? He had thought they had parted, if not amicably, at least with some sort of understanding and mutual regard. Clearly he had been under a misapprehension.

The family would have to be told. Squaring his shoulders, Nathan went to look for his mother.

★　★　★

'Merciful heavens! Whatever next?' Florence sat down abruptly on the settle. The parlour was quiet, the door closed against listening ears.

'Calm yourself, Mama. Reflect: Hayles has known of this ever since Isobel's visit and there's not been a hint of talk.'

'Not yet. But there could be. The wicked, wicked girl! How could she?'

He looked into his mother's anguished face and felt his heart soften.

'Oh, Mama, you must hold up. I'm truly sorry to have brought trouble on us like this.'

'What do you mean?'

'It wouldn't have worked, you know. A pampered creature like Verity Hayles would no more have made a farmer's wife than a social butterfly like Isobel.'

Florence looked at him.

'What are we going to do?'

'We carry on as normal. Hayles won't talk. Not if he knows what's good for him. He's too committed to the Chapel and the Rechabite movement to resort to low tricks.' Nathan paused, running his hand through his hair. 'The girls and Finbar will have to know.'

'And my sister?'

'Oh, Aunt Dorcas never had much time for Hayles, anyway.' Florence smiled wanly.

'Dear Dorcas. She's been such a rock. What would we do without her?'

'Don't even think about it, Mama.'

'Ah, me, what a day for surprises. You won't have heard Finbar's news.'

'News?'

'There was a letter for him in the midday post. It appears there's a vacancy at a kirk in Paisley. Finbar's been invited to apply to minister there.'

'That is good news,' Nathan said warmly.

'There are other applicants, mind,' Florence added. 'He doesn't hold out much hope of being chosen, but that's typical of Finbar's modesty.'

'He's right to be cautious. When does he leave?'

'At once. He'll be staying with his parents for a while. Davina's in a state, trying to get his bags packed in time for him to catch the early morning train. She and the children are to stay here for now. If Finbar does get selected he will send for them.

'Oh, dear.' Florence heaved a sigh. 'I shall miss them dreadfully. And now this trouble with Stanton, and just when I thought he had come round. I thought him rather a nice man, too. That Verity needs a good talking to!'

*   *   *

'I'm missing Finbar dreadfully,' Davina said as she entered the kitchen with a basket of strong-smelling greenery on her arm. 'I know it's been over a week since he left, but I can't get used to him not being here.'

Aileen shrugged. Privately she considered men something of a liability, and was rather relieved that the cooling of relations between Farmer Hayles and Nathan had brought a halt to their neighbour's attentions towards herself. Still, she was fond of her sister and didn't like to see her melancholy.

'Has there been no word yet?' she said.

'Not yet,' Davina replied. She was wrestling to untie the strings of her bonnet, when she gave a little gasp and sank suddenly down on the nearest chair. She pulled off the bonnet and fanned herself with it.

'My, how close it is. I vow it is as hot as

Africa. Is it ever going to rain, I wonder?'

'It will have to some time.' Aileen, leaving off measuring flour for the bread, peered concernedly into her sister's face. 'Davvy, are you all right?'

'What? Yes, of course. It's just the heat. I should have waited until evening to go out, but I needed the eyebright to make a tincture for tomorrow's market. The goodwife with the cataracts, you know.' She paused, biting her lip. 'Aileen, don't say anything to Mama, but I think I'm increasing again.'

'Oh.' Aileen's expression said all. 'When are you due?'

'Not for a good while yet. Please, please keep quiet about it. I haven't said anything to Finbar yet.'

'I won't say a word. Perhaps you should take things a little more easily. You must have walked miles today.'

'Oh, fie! Walking does no harm. It's just the early stages, these bouts of nausea. It will pass. Wait till it's your turn. You'll see what I mean.'

'Tsk! I don't know that I want to.'

Davina looked at her strangely.

'Don't you want children? You're very good with Annabel and Catherine. They're better behaved when you're there.'

'Only because they know I won't stand any

nonsense. I treat them like people. Billing and cooing over children is silly.'

'You wait. You'll change your tune once you have one of your own.'

'I won't. Give me a horse any day — ' Aileen broke off. 'Davvy, you do look pale. Can I get you anything?'

'A cup of water would be nice. Oh, and inside the stillroom door on the left there's a phial of rosemary oil. It's excellent for faintness.'

'Is it?' Aileen poured water from a jug on the dresser, handing it to her sister. 'Fancy you knowing all this. Do you remember when we were little, how we used to make perfume out of the roses on the front of the house? It went all slimy and foul-smelling.'

Davina managed a laugh.

'Yes, I remember. There is a way of making rose water, actually. One of the women at Barotse showed me how it's done. I could make some for the stall. The bush on the porch has a good scent. It should be ideal.'

Aileen fetched the rosemary oil and watched as her sister removed the stopper and wafted the bottle under her nose, inhaling lightly.

'Ah, better.'

'That's good,' Aileen said, relieved.

* * *

'It's the Goose Fayre next Saturday, Christina,' Daniel said from his stall next to hers at the busy Saturday market.

Chrissie frowned.

'Goose Fayre?'

'You know, where the hiring is done. There's one every autumn. It's well worth a visit. There's a livestock sale and booths and entertainments —

'Yes, madam, can I help you?'

He broke off to attend to a customer. Chrissie's mind raced.

Autumn. How the time had flown. Such a lot had happened since she had made the decision to leave the Glebe. She felt older now and a good deal wiser.

She wondered how things were at Hadnall. She swallowed hard. Even now she could not think of Glebe Farm without a pang. Sometimes in the night she would wake and think she was still there, with Master Nathan sleeping under the same roof. And then cold realisation would come and her heart would twist painfully.

'Penny for 'em?'

Daniel was back, his face full of the engaging frankness that won him so many friends.

'They're not worth it. Go on with what you were saying about the Goose Fayre.'

'I'll do better than that,' Daniel said. 'What do you say to closing up at around three and going?' He hesitated, unaccountably shy. 'I've never asked a girl before. Will you come, Christina?'

Chrissie considered. All she had done since coming here was work — though that was nothing new. She'd like to see the fayre, and it would be good to have a few hours' leisure.

'Thank you, Daniel,' she said. 'I'd like to come very much.'

The wary look on Daniel's face fled. 'I'll be the envy of the other fellows, having the best-looking girl in town on my arm.'

'Away with you! You're flattering me.'

'Not a bit of it. Mind you put on your best things. Folks dress up for the fayre.'

This was unexpected, but Chrissie was not to be deterred. She could always trim her old Sunday bonnet with fresh ribbons and wear the pretty shawl Miss Aileen had passed down to her. But what was to be done about a dress? Her best gown was so threadbare it was hardly worth setting about with a needle.

Chrissie's gaze strayed to the haberdasher's across the aisle. A flocked muslin caught her eye, a beautiful white and pale blue. It wasn't the most practical of colours, but, oh, how pretty it was.

There and then, she left her stall and spent

two whole shillings of the morning's takings on a length of cloth and some dainty buttons.

Her hand shook as she counted out the money. This was the first time she had ever bought her own dress material, her previous outfits of serviceable homespun having come with the job. Before that, at the croft, they had spun and woven their own plain cloth. Chrissie's heart sang as she tucked her purchases under her arm. Tonight she would make a start.

★ ★ ★

Moist October air touched with mid-morning sunshine bathed the slopes of the hillside as Nathan climbed the stony track, Jamie's dog bounding round him in gleeful circles. There was an autumn tang of woodsmoke today: a hint of the winter to come.

Reaching the crest of the hill, Nathan stood contemplating his land, while Bess scampered about investigating interesting scents. He looked out over the farm. The grain harvest, such as it was after the worst drought the district had known in living memory, was now in, the corn gathered, too.

His eye caught movement. Davina was hurrying up towards him from the house. She looked excited.

'Nathan, what do you think?' She gasped, brandishing a letter in her hand. 'This has just arrived from Finbar. The board of session of the Paisley kirk have invited him to attend a meeting.'

'Really? It's looking hopeful, then'

'Oh, I do hope he gets it.' Davina was practically jumping up and down in excitement. 'There's a good-sized house, he says, and a garden for the children to play in.'

'Dearest Davvy!' He smiled at her. 'I'm pleased things are going well for you now.'

'What about you, Nathan? Shall you make your peace and wed Verity?'

'Most definitely not! I'm sorry about what's happened, and especially for Mama. She had developed a liking for Hayles — heaven knows how — and she's put in a lot of effort getting us accepted here . . . '

'But nothing has come of his threats. Everyone is still speaking to us. It's only the Twelve Trees people that aren't. And sales on the stall haven't been affected one bit.'

'That's good to hear. I did wonder.'

'You're as bad as Aileen. She was worried about that, too.' Davina smiled. 'She's a funny one, our little sister. She says she wants to build up a grocery business, like Papa. She's no desire to marry, doesn't care for children.'

'What's brought all this on?'

'We were talking and I happened to mention the new little one — oh!' Davina clapped her hand across her mouth. 'You didn't hear that.'

Nathan grinned.

'Are you saying there's to be another new Lennox?'

'Promise you won't say anything — not yet. I don't want Mama to have anything else to concern her at present.'

'My lips are sealed. Mind you take care, that's all. No more running up hills.'

'Oh, stuff! You should have seen me in Africa. I never stopped and it did me no harm at all. Nathan . . . when I do tell her, you will remember to be surprised, won't you? I'd hate Mama to think everyone knew but her. She'd be so hurt.'

'Don't worry, Davvy, I'll be the soul of discretion.'

★ ★ ★

Nathan watched his sister walk back to the house, past the fields below, now stubble under the wide blue sky. Next to the house the orchard stood out, stripped and bare. In the skeps by the hedge Edward Turner's bees were still working, but soon the busy droning would become drowsy and cease as the inmates settled down for their winter rest. Alongside the multitude of chutneys, pickles and jams in the farmhouse larder was a shelf of golden honey in brown crocks; a good harvest, Edward said.

On the whole, he reflected, it had not been a bad year. They had doubled their numbers with the flock thanks to Turner's skilled shepherding. The swine flourished, as did the cattle. Apart from the lead poisoning incident with Contessa, now mercifully cured, the hardy little Red Polls had been trouble free and, between them, had produced eight leggy heifer calves for them to grow on.

Nathan, feeling he had much to be thankful for, was seized with a desperate longing for Chrissie Ross to be by his side to share his gladness. Not for the first time, he wondered how she fared. Life could be hard for a woman alone and this was Chrissie — one of their own.

He made to shrug off his thoughts — he was yearning for what was now far out of reach — but he could not. Chrissie's wide smile and sea-green gaze invaded his every waking moment and haunted his dreams at night. He needed the distraction of hard physical labour to lay this ghost. Calling to the dog, he left his eyrie and headed off again down the track.

Arriving at the farmyard, Nathan found the men at the entrance to the barn, taking their midday meal. Dust motes floated in the shafts of sunlight behind them, but the far corners of the building were shadowed and cool. Turner's dogs sprawled there, dozing.

'Afternoon, gaffer,' Merridew said. 'Can I offer you aught? A slice of pasty?'

'Thank you, no. I apologise for butting in on your break. I was thinking of getting back to repairing those fences now that the harvesting is over. What about this afternoon?'

There was a murmur of assent.

'Them drains on Springfield Dip need attention, an' all,' Merridew said. 'The land's gone marshy, being so low lying and having all that water underground.'

'Natural springs, you mean? That's interesting. If we could tap the source we might be able to use it on the land.'

'An irrigation system? It wunna be a bad idea, gaffer,' Hutch said. 'Not if we get another summer like the one we've just had.'

'If it can be done,' Turner put in. 'Irrigation's a job for a land engineer.'

'I'll take a look and see what we need to do,' Nathan said. 'Meanwhile, which fences shall we tackle first?'

'Home Paddock,' Merridew said at once.

'The cows use the wall as a scratching post and it's got weakened. We dunna want the Red Polls getting through into the turnips.'

That settled the matter, and shortly afterwards they gathered to see to the repairs.

When they'd finished, Hutch said he'd get on with ploughing up the stubble while the weather held, and went to harness his horses. Edward went to fetch the cows for milking. Turner returned to the flock with his dogs, and Nathan and Jim Merridew went to inspect Springfield Dip.

The ground where the land drains had fallen in was choked with nettles and ragged spikes of reed. Merridew rummaged about in the undergrowth to see how the land drains ran, and then he and Nathan set about clearing the clogged ditches.

It was punishing work, designed to relieve Nathan of punishing thoughts, and he bent his back to the labour with a will.

Much later, aching in every joint, but less troubled in spirit, he joined the family in the farmhouse kitchen for the evening meal.

Florence served from the dish of casseroled mutton and dumplings that had been simmering fragrantly on the range for the best part of the day.

'I was only saying to Edna,' Florence said, passing laden plates to her hungry family, 'how quiet the union men have gone. Do you think they've given up?'

'I shouldn't imagine so,' Nathan replied, helping himself from the vast dish of buttered potatoes. 'Turner was out late last night, presumably at a meeting. I saw him coming in when I went to check on the cows.'

He looked across the expanse of scrubbed table at his mother.

'I don't want to worry you, but I think we should still be on our guard. These people are fanatics; they never give up.'

Florence put down her knife and fork with a sigh.

'And here I was thinking it had all blown over. I know Dorcas still has her concerns. It's not like her to worry.'

'It is funny how quiet it is,' Aileen said. 'I put it down to the harvest and people being so busy.'

'Not to mention tired,' Davina added, using her napkin to mop gravy from her youngest's chin. 'There, Catherine. Eat nicely or I shall take your supper away.'

Catherine, who lived to eat, dug her spoon into the mashed-up supper and shovelled it into her mouth in case her mother meant it. Jamie held out his plate for a second helping.

'Don't get rattled, Mama,' he said cheerfully. 'If those men come here I'll set Bess on them.

'I'll get 'em with my catapult.'

His mother looked pained.

'Where do you get these expressions, Jamie? 'Rattled', indeed.'

'Andy Fox says it all the time. Andy showed me how to use the catapult, an' all. He said I had a real good aim. I took a pot at ol' Moleface when he wasn't looking. It got him square in the — '

'Jamie, please! Remember your manners and get on with your meal.'

Chastened, Jamie turned his attention to his food. Annabel, at his side, slid him a look of mute sympathy.

'Of course,' Nathan went on, 'once winter sets in things might settle down. Let's hope so, anyway.'

As usual, the working day had been long and arduous and nobody was late retiring after supper. By the time the moon rose round and golden over Cleg's Wood, the household was slumbering peacefully.

The quiet was shattered by a violent hammering on the back door. Nathan, roused from dreams in which Chrissie Ross had made a welcome return to the Glebe, flung back the covers. Hardly daring to hope, he loped down the stairs to answer the summons.

Aileen emerged from her room, yawning and hastily throwing a shawl over her bed gown. On the landing, she bumped into her mother, a wrap over her nightclothes and hair in a long bedtime plait, her face white and strained.

Davina was the last to arrive. She had the baby in her arms and was anxiously shushing his wails of protest at being so rudely awoken. Behind closed doors, the other children slept on.

The hammering came again. Nathan shot back the bolts and wrenched open the door to find Merridew more agitated than he'd ever seen him.

'Gaffer, see over yonder!' he said, pointing.

Across the fields at Twelve Trees, the night sky was lit by a lurid red glow. They all stared in bewilderment, unable at first to grasp what it was.

'Dear Lord!' Florence whispered. 'Union trouble, it has to be!'

'My window was open,' Merridew said. 'The wind's blowing this way. It must have been the smell of burning that woke me. I got into my togs and came straight here.'

'Good man,' Nathan said. This was no time for feuds. A neighbour was in trouble and needed help.

'You'd best wake the Turners. Aileen, ride to the village for Hutch. Tell him to rustle up as many men as possible and get over to Twelve Trees at once.' He turned to his mother and elder sister. 'See that there's water heated. You might look out some bandages. There could be casualties.'

Everyone sprang to do as he said. Nathan bounded up the stairs and was soon back, dressed in more practical clothes. He was pulling on his boots when Merridew came back with Turner. The shepherd looked disconcerted. Edward, limping up out of the darkness, stopped to calm Bess, who was straining on her chain and barking wildly.

'Put her in the house with the women,' Nathan said. He seized some capes from their hooks by the door and thrust them at the men. 'Take these. You'll need something to put over your faces. Is there a well close to the house?'

'Aye, gaffer,' Merridew said.

'Thank God for that. Right then, men. Let's go.'

★ ★ ★

The distress calls from animals enveloped by heat and fumes met the party as they approached Twelve Trees at a run.

'Edward, get over there and let those beasts out,' Nathan commanded. 'Better to stray than burn.'

'Right, gaffer.'

The young man obeyed as fast as his bad leg would allow. The others hastened up the long cart-track to the farm, their breath coming in laboured gasps.

On the lawns in front of the square redbrick farmhouse, Verity was in hysterics and the housekeeper, a stout woman with a pelisse over her nightwear, was doing her best to pacify her. Nathan gestured the men on into the farmyard.

Here was mayhem. Hayricks and corn-stacks blazed fiercely and an open-sided Dutch barn, stuffed to the roof with straw, exploded into a ball of flame before their eyes. A band of farm workers were making a panicked attempt to quench the flames by flinging random buckets of water to no effect.

Nathan sprang back as the milking herd, newly released from a burning shippon, lumbered past in a great stream, fear lending them wings. Half a dozen goats, bleating in terror, made off in another direction and a cloud of birds went clapping upwards from the dovecote. Geese and ducks ran amok, and someone hollered to get down to the pigsties and turn the swine out in case the fire spread.

Coughs and hawking from men with smoke in their lungs punctuated the hysterical barking from the dogs. A small battalion of yard cats, caught ratting in the granary, shot in a lithe flow across Nathan's feet. Everywhere was the acrid stench of burning and the roar of fire racing out of control.

In all the confusion it was impossible to discern Hayles, although his voice could be heard above the rest, shouting commands that not one man in his panic obeyed.

Flames were engulfing one end of the stable block. He and his men were the farm's last hope, Nathan realised. He barked out his orders.

'Jim, start pumping up water. Turner, get the men to form a line. Aim the flow towards the middle of the stable block. We don't want that to go up, as well. One of you others, come with me. There are horses in there. We've got to get them out.'

Terrified whinnies issued from the doomed stable. A figure detached itself from the rest. It was Hayles.

'That's my Ebony!' He gasped, his voice choked and raw. 'I'm going in.'

Nathan reached out and gripped his arm.

'Not that way, man. The fire's taken hold. You'll never make it.'

'Leave off, will you! I'm getting Ebony out!'

Wrenching himself free, Hayles blundered forward and vanished into the maw of fire and smoke. By now the men were getting into a rhythm; pails of water moved along the chain rapidly to fight the blaze.

Nathan shook off his coat, dunked it in one of the pails of water and, flinging the sodden garment over his head, dived into the burning stables after Hayles.

Inside, a searing heat met him. The stalls clamoured to the tramping and shrieking of the horses straining to escape their tethers. The fire, Nathan saw, was contained in the roof timbers for now. They had a minute or two yet.

Forcing himself to stay calm, he plunged into the first of the stalls and made a start on releasing the horses. Ebony was stabled in the iron-railed stallion box at the end of the aisle. Plunging and rearing in terror, the horse was in danger of injuring himself, and Hayles was struggling desperately with the hot metal of the door.

'Let me!' Nathan shouted.

He yanked the wet coat from his head and used it to get a grip. Within seconds the animal was free. Nathan delivered a thwack on the horse's rump to send him in the right direction and had to dodge a scything kick for his pains.

A sinister creaking sound from overhead caused him to look up. Flames were licking further along the massive rafters — now like tinder from the long, dry summer. As he watched, the main beam burst into a sheet of flame and sparks showered down.

'Let's get out of here,' he yelled above the crackle of splintering timber and masonry.

Hayles had turned his attention to a box across the aisle where, unbeknown to Nathan, the lawn-pony lived. Nathan dived to assist. The tether was released and the animal pounded out to safety.

Hayles, uncomprehending and shocked, turned a smoke-grimed face to Nathan.

'My stables!' He choked. 'My farm!'

Pity stabbed Nathan, but this was no time for emotion.

Overhead, the now blazing rafters shifted with a menacing groan and further bursts of amber and crimson sparks. Gripping Hayles by the shoulders, Nathan yanked him round to face the exit.

'Go on, man. Move!'

He gave a shove that sent the farmer stumbling off through the swirling banks of smoke. Nathan sprang after him, but in that instant the roof gave.

There was an ear-splitting crash and a flaring rafter came hurtling down. Something fetched Nathan a violent blow across the shoulders, felling him.

Dimly he was aware of voices shouting his name. Clawing uselessly at the stone floor with his hands, he tried to respond, but everything was spinning and rocking around him. A fateful ringing sounded in his ears; he was sinking, sinking, and then even the flames faded to black.

11

'How is he?' Davina asked, coming softly into the sickroom. Florence glanced up from her vigil beside the still figure in the bed. Her face was pale, her eyes shadowed and strained.

'The fever has gone. We must be thankful for that.'

'Indeed,' Davina said.

They spoke in muted tones, though it struck Florence that were they to stamp and shout their loudest it would have little effect on the patient.

Following the first tortuous days of tossing and writhing, grimacing at the agony of scorched flesh and babbling in delirium, there had come a calm that was almost worse. Nathan now lay lost in some dim world of his own, hanging stoically on to life with every rasping breath.

Florence's hands hovered helplessly, smoothing the bedcovers over the son she had so very nearly lost.

'Doctor Merrick called earlier,' she said. 'He put this comatose state down to delayed shock. He couldn't praise that skin salve of yours highly enough. He called it a miracle.'

'Really?' A smile touched Davina's lips. 'One of the Barotse women showed me how to make it. It has honey as a base. We were lucky, having some to hand.'

The extent of Nathan's burns was not as bad as they had at first feared. Nor, remarkably, were there any broken bones.

Silas Turner had been the first to reach him. With no thought for his own safety, the shepherd had plunged in and dragged his master clear before the flames could do their worst.

'I've just been to the cottage,' Davina continued. 'I took them some of Edna's broth and a wedge of plum cake. Turner's partial to that.'

'Poor man. How are his hands?' Florence thought of those hands and their extraordinary deftness at shearing time, and shuddered.

'There's no infection. I changed the dressings while I was there. Edward says he had a better night. Of course, it will take time.'

'What a blessing Edward is there to look after things.' Florence paused. 'What of the men? Have they called to see him?'

'No, they haven't,' Davina said tightly.

To their dismay the shepherd's workmates had turned against him after the firing of Twelve Trees. Though it later became clear from village gossip that Turner had spoken out against the move at the last union meeting — winning him no favours with fellow members — the Glebe hands stayed away from the thatched dwelling beyond the stackyard.

Dissent at Glebe Farm was hitherto unknown. Florence frowned. As if they hadn't troubles enough without this.

'Mama, you are exhausted,' Davina said. 'The children are asleep. Let me sit with Nathan for a while.'

'I think I will. Dear Davina, you've been such a rock. I don't know how we would have coped without you.'

Rising, Florence pressed a kiss on her daughter's cheek, and with yet another troubled glance at the motionless figure in the bed, she left the room.

* * *

In the kitchen Edna Hutch was tackling a pile of ironing and the air was full of the wholesome smell of hot linen.

'There you are, ma'am,' Edna said. 'Come and sit here and I'll make a brew. How is the master now?'

'No different, Edna. I didn't like the look of him at all.'

'There, then. Happen it's a matter of

getting his strength back.

'You know, this may not be only thing that ails him. He's had a lot on his plate since coming here. It's not as if he's grown up with farming. He could be plain worn out.'

'I suppose so,' Florence said.

Edna's words touched on a growing dread in Florence. Once recovered — and the doctor had given her every hope — might Nathan resist the shackles that bound him and seek to follow his dreams of the life in engineering he had so craved? She did not doubt his loyalty, but after this, was she asking too much of him to stay?

Edna fetched the tray from the dresser.

'Miss Aileen's in the parlour. I'll set two places, shall I?'

'Yes, do,' Florence said. 'Oh, shortbread. Lovely. Thank you, Edna.'

In the parlour, Aileen sat before a crackling fire, frowning over the market stall accounts. She looked up expectantly.

'Mama? Is there any change?'

'None. Davina's with him at the moment. Edna made tea.'

'Wonderful. My figures are all to pot today.' Aileen put aside the ledger and drew up a low table. 'Shall I pour?'

'No, it's all right, my love. It will give me something to do.'

'I can't stop thinking about how Nathan kept talking about Chrissie,' Aileen mused, taking the proffered cup from Florence. 'Granted, he was rambling at the time, but, oh, I don't know . . . Nathan liked Chrissie a lot.'

'It's true. If your aunt Dorcas is right, Nathan is in love with Chrissie and has been for some while,' Florence said. 'She once approached him about it, but he shrugged it off. She thought he wasn't aware of his own feelings at the time.'

'Well, I never suspected a thing. It would explain why he tore off to find her in such a rush when she left.'

'It could be why she went. She'd guessed which way the wind was blowing and feared our reaction.'

'Oh, I don't know. Aunt Dorcas always said that Chrissie was wasted in service. She could simply have wanted to better herself.'

Aileen tilted her head mischievously.

'How would you have felt, Mama, about Nathan taking up with a member of staff? It's hardly the sort of match you had in mind for him.'

'Taking up?' Florence tutted. 'What an expression! No, it isn't what I would have hoped for, although I do see your aunt's point. Chrissie Ross had a great deal about her. Given a different background, the right education and so on . . . '

Florence sipped her tea thoughtfully.

'I'd go to any lengths to help restore your brother to health. Perhaps we should renew our efforts to find Chrissie.'

'It won't be easy. She could be anywhere by now. Aunt Dorcas was in Chrissie's confidence. Have you asked her if she knows where Chrissie might be?'

'I have, actually. She has no idea, either.'

Florence stood up.

'I had better go. The children will be awake soon, wanting their mama.'

Aileen watched her mother leave the room. An idea was forming in her mind.

She knew she would have to broach the subject with care and gave a little grimace; tact and diplomacy had never been her strongest points. Then again, anything was worth a try.

Aileen chose her moment carefully. Waiting until Edward and Rose had finished the evening milking and gone their separate ways, and Hutch had bedded down his horses for the night and left for home with Edna, she went in search of Jim Merridew.

She tracked him down at the pigsties, scratching the back of a favourite Old Spot sow affectionately with a stick.

'Miss Aileen?' He straightened, bushy eyebrows lifting. 'The gaffer, he's not — '

'No change, Jim. No worse, thank goodness. Jim — I wanted to catch you before you went. It's about Chrissie Ross.'

'Yes?' He looked guarded.

'Have you any idea where she might be? My brother . . . he thought a lot of Chrissie. We all did. She had a rare skill with healing herbs. There's a chance she may be able to help.'

'Aye, that's true,' Merridew said neutrally. 'The gaffer did question us all pretty thoroughly when she left so sudden, like. None of us could come up with any answers then.'

'Oh?' Aileen caught her breath. 'You've heard something since?'

'I could have.'

Aileen prayed for patience.

'The other night at the Dog,' Merridew continued in his measured country voice, 'I got talking to one of those traveller fellows.'

'Go on,' Aileen pressed.

'He happened to mention having supped on the best meat pie he'd ever tasted. Nantwich it was, a market stall run by a young woman with a smile to die for. Bonnie, too, he said she was. She spoke different, as well.'

279

'Chrissie?'

'It could have been. There's not many would fit that description. And her baking was something apart.'

'It has to be her.' Aileen's heart skipped a beat. 'Nantwich, you say? I don't know it at all. How do I get there?'

'You're best going by rail. I should go first thing, that'll give you time to find her . . . if it is Chrissie Ross, that is. Take the milk train and change at Whitchurch. They run pretty regular.'

'Do you know when the market is held?'

'Thursdays and Saturdays. I made sure and asked.'

'I'll go tomorrow. And, Jim — not a word to anyone. Not even Mama. I'd hate to get her hopes up.'

'Never fear, miss. My lips are sealed,' Merridew said.

★　★　★

Excitement was in the air as Chrissie and Daniel joined the flow of people bound for the Goose Fayre.

Apple-cheeked countrywomen with babies in their arms gossiped together as they ambled along. Farmers jogged past with laden traps and sweethearts sauntered hand-in hand, oblivious to all but each other.

Chrissie, in her new muslin and lacy shawl, her hair gleaming from last night's rinsing in rosemary water, presented a very different picture from usual.

'Why, you're beautiful!' Daniel had gasped when he'd seen her.

Chrissie had laughed it off.

'Tsk! My granny had a saying about fine feathers.' Nonetheless she was pleased and her heart was light as she tripped along at Daniel's side.

The hiring, where workers plied their services for the next twelve months, had started at dawn and was all but over by the time they arrived. Horses, cattle, sheep and fowl were now being sold, and the auctioneer's voice rang out above the bewildered calls of the animals and the shouts and laughter of the crowd.

Stalls and booths selling everything from local produce to pottery and fairings were set up around the perimeter. Amusements were there for the taking. Chrissie and Daniel listened to the hurdy-gurdy where a tiny monkey in a scarlet jacket collected the pennies in a tin box, and they laughed at the antics of a band of travelling players masquerading as clowns.

In a corner of the grounds a clog-dancing

competition was in progress.

'Oh, do let's watch,' Chrissie cried.

Daniel found them a front seat.

'Do you like toffee apples? I'll get us some.'

Munching the sticky treats, they watched the competition to the end.

'Wasn't it good?' Chrissie said after applauding the winner till her palms smarted.

'There's dancing here later on. We'll stay, if you like.'

'But I couldn't. I don't know how.'

'Just follow my steps. The music will do the rest,' Daniel said.

They moved on to the roll-a-penny and then to the hoopla, where Daniel's remarkably steady hand won a fairing. It was a brooch in the shape of a spray of flowers, a cheap thing of glass and tin.

'One day I'll buy you better,' Daniel said, pinning it on her shawl.

His hands brushing her shoulder made Chrissie's flesh tingle. She drew back, startled.

'Oh, but I'm happy with this one. It'll remind me of the lovely time I've had.'

'We'll do it again. There'll be other events, you'll see,' he assured her.

★ ★ ★

A chill breeze swept through the beech trees where they stood, bringing a shower of leaves floating down. It set the bunting fluttering and ruffled the thin fabric of Chrissie's gown. She shivered, drawing her shawl tighter about her. Daniel was all concern.

'Come on, you need some hot food inside you. We can watch the Punch and Judy while we eat.'

On their way to find a vendor they came across a booth with a fortune teller in a crimson shawl and gold hoops in her ears. Her black eyes glittered.

'Tell your future, missy? The palm never lies.'

'Oh, I don't think — '

'Go on,' Daniel said. Slipping the woman a coin, he gently pushed Chrissie forward.

Inside the booth there was a smell of herbs and sweet oils. The gypsy woman bade Chrissie be seated and took her palm, studying it closely.

'Two loves I see. 'Tis a long road you're travelling, missy. Full of twists and turns.'

'I'm done with travelling,' Chrissie said. 'Tell me about children.'

'I see a full nursery, though not yet awhile. You've set foot on the road, but 'tis winding and dark.'

'You talk in riddles, mother!' She snatched

her hand away. 'My granny had the Sight. She spoke in riddles, too.'

'Not riddles, missy. Wise words,' the gypsy said.

She started muttering and mumbling, rocking to and fro in her seat. All at once the pungency of burning oils and herbs and the old crone's incomprehensible patter was too much for Chrissie. She sprang up and ran out to stand in the aisle and take reviving gulps of air.

Daniel appeared at her side.

'What did she say — a fine husband and a full cradle?' He sent her a grin. 'They all play the same old tune!'

The tantalising whiff of frying wafted towards them. Daniel pointed.

'The vendor's over there.'

As the sun sank, they watched the Punch and Judy and feasted on sausages, piping hot from the brazier, washed down with local cider that went straight to Chrissie's head.

Gradually the day thickened to dusk. The stars appeared, hidden now and again by threads of wind-blown cloud. A band of musicians gathered on a rough-made podium; a fiddler and a flute player, a boy on a fife, an old man with a jaunty accordion. They struck up a phrase of notes, drawing the dancers into a ring.

'Come on,' Daniel said, taking Chrissie's hand.

It was country dancing, fast and furious, and she was soon joining in. Twirling, dipping, changing hands ... the foot-tapping, palm-slapping whirl of movement was infectious and not at all hard to follow. She felt as if she had been dancing for ever. She wanted the night to go on and on.

At length, laughing and breathless, they were forced to call a halt. Daniel bought thirst-quenching cups of small ale, and they stood watching the throng, while in the branches of the trees lanterns were lit and, high above, the clouds thickened.

Afterwards they took to the floor again. The music was slower now. The night had taken on a dreamlike quality and Chrissie was filled with a strange restiveness. Daniel, drawing her aside, dropped a kiss on her lips.

'Thank you for a real good day.'

'I've enjoyed it, too,' Chrissie whispered.

Daniel hesitated.

'Christina,' he said. 'I allow we haven't known each other long, but I think the world of you and we get on a treat. Could we make a go of it, d'you reckon? Will you wed me?'

The words thundered in Chrissie's ears. She hadn't expected this. She didn't know how to respond.

Daniel, seeing her dilemma, placed a finger across her mouth.

'Don't answer now. Think about it, eh?' She saw the flash of his smile in the darkness. 'It's been a long day. I'd best get you home.'

They did not talk much as they walked through the deserted streets, the noise of the fair growing fainter with every step. Chrissie, trailing her bonnet by its ribbons in one hand, the other clasped in Daniel's warm grip, was aware of a change between them. But her limbs felt leaden and her mind swam with tiredness, and she could only give in to the lassitude that crept over her and save more complex thoughts for another time.

Reaching her door, Daniel bid her a quiet, 'Sweet dreams.'

Chrissie, watching him go, let herself into her lodgings and closed the door with a soft click.

★   ★   ★

The autumn weather turned squally, giving a foretaste of how it would be at the market during the weeks ahead.

'Oh, this rain!' Chrissie wailed, powerless to keep her goods from being ruined.

'I'll make you an awning like mine,' Daniel said. 'For now, we'll rig up this bit of tarpaulin. It'll keep the worst off.'

It wasn't the first time Daniel had come to her rescue and Chrissie was touched. She had done a lot of thinking about Daniel's offer of marriage. In her heart she knew her feelings for him were not those she had for Nathan Drummond. But he was a good man, industrious and trustworthy, a man of her own standing who would treat her well. She liked him very much and that mattered, didn't it? Love could grow out of liking. She truly believed that in the fullness of time she could learn to love Daniel.

All morning the rain pelted down. At midday, her stall cleared, and she was scooping the day's takings into the old tea-tin kept for that purpose, anxious to get back to her lodgings and dry her clothes before a bright fire, when a voice stopped her in her tracks.

'Chrissie? Thank goodness I've found you!'

A trim figure in a dark-blue pelisse and bonnet stood before her. Chrissie looked up in startled disbelief into the face of Aileen Drummond.

'Why . . . what brings you here?' she stammered.

'I had hoped to catch the early train, but Nathan took a turn for the worse and we had to call Doctor Merrick out to him again.'

'A turn for the worse?' Chrissie's throat went dry. 'What's happened?'

Aileen gave a tired smile. Chrissie noticed the hollows in cheeks that had been rounded and firm, and the shadows beneath the grey-blue eyes. The wind gusted, showering rain, and Aileen put up a hand to keep her bonnet in place.

'Twelve Trees was targeted by the unionists. The stables were set on fire. Nathan went in to rescue the horses and got hit by a falling beam.'

'Dear God! Is it bad?'

'Not as bad as it might have been. Turner dragged him clear. Nathan was unconscious for ages. He had bruising and burns and his breathing is bad. I suppose it's the smoke. He took a fever and last night it returned. Chrissie — he's asking for you.'

'Me?' Chrissie stared at her through the slanting rain.

'Nathan needs you. You have to come back with me.'

'What, now? But I can't!' Chrissie's thoughts whirled chaotically. 'I'm soaked through. I'd need to change my clothes at the very least.'

'There's no time. The train leaves in — ' Aileen consulted her fob watch ' — just under thirty minutes. Oh, come on, Chrissie. We'll fix you up with something to wear.'

Chrissie looked wildly about her, seeking help. Daniel, occupied with customers and plainly aware that something was amiss, shot a wary glance in her direction.

'Chrissie, please.' Aileen's voice throbbed. 'This is serious. Mama wants you there.'

'You were sent by the mistress?' Chrissie cried.

She bit her lip. In that moment she felt herself slipping back again into the role of servant and her whole being rose in protest. Now that she had tasted freedom she felt she could never return to her former life.

Yet she was filled with an overwhelming urge to rush to Nathan Drummond's side. He was injured, perhaps dying. He was asking for her.

And yet there was her stall, her livelihood in Nantwich to consider. She tried to sift a way through the dilemma, collecting her thoughts, meeting the other young woman's gaze levelly.

'What you ask is out of the question. I'd have to make arrangements before I could leave.'

Disappointment clouded Aileen's face.

'Chrissie, won't you reconsider? Is it money? Your fare? Don't worry — I have enough for both of us.'

'It isn't that.'

'Then what? My brother needs you. We all do. We miss you, Chrissie. Why did you run off like that without a word to anyone?'

'I left word,' Chrissie said sharply.

She drew herself up. She was taller than the other girl and had developed a confidence and pride of bearing that made the visitor falter.

'Forgive me,' Aileen said, contrite. 'I didn't mean to offend. Mama doesn't know I've come. I came to find you on a hunch of Jim Merridew's. I wasn't sure it would come off, but I had to try.

'It's . . . it's Nathan. Doctor Merrick doesn't think his condition is fatal, but it looks that way to me. It's as if he were giving up. If Nathan knew you were there tending to him, I'm sure he'd make more of an effort.'

'There, then,' Chrissie said more gently, torn, yet clinging to her resolve. 'You have to understand that I have ties here now. I can't just drop everything and go. Perhaps in a few days . . .

'That is your last word?'

The slightest hesitation.

'For now, yes. I'm sorry.'

'So am I,' Aileen said, and with a wan little smile, she turned on her heel and walked away through the still-driving rain.

'What was all that about?' Daniel was at her side, concern on his plain, honest face.

'It was the daughter from Glebe Farm. There's been an accident.'

Rain streamed down Chrissie's face as she related what she had been told. Her hair was plastered to her head and her clothes clung, sodden and chilly.

'Daniel, they want me there. I don't know what to do.'

'Look,' Daniel said, 'you're in no fit state for decisions. Go home and get dry and we'll talk tomorrow. You've had a shock; you need to sleep on it.'

It seemed the best solution. Scooping up her baskets, Chrissie shot him a look of gratitude and left.

During the course of the night the rain stopped, and the next day a watery sun glimmered as they strolled beyond the town, following the muddy flow of the Weaver that raced, charged with floodwater, between high banks.

'What I don't see,' Daniel said, squelching along at Chrissie's side, 'is why they want you there. From what you've said they worked you pretty hard. This wouldn't be a ruse to get you back?'

'It had crossed my mind, but no, I don't think so. They relied on me during those first weeks at the Glebe. It follows that the master should be asking for me. I was the one who showed him how to milk . . . and other things.' The memory prompted a smile, sweet and sad. 'In return he taught me to read and write.'

'You'd never learned?' Daniel, brought up in the town with the benefit of moderate schooling, looked totally flabbergasted.

'How could I?' Chrissie snapped, irritated after a sleepless night. 'Where I grew up was remote. How to spin and tend the animals was all I knew. When I left for Hadnall with the Drummonds it was on the understanding that I would be given some learning.'

Chrissie heard the passion in her voice and tried to curb it, but it was hard. The more she considered the situation the greater was her concern for the man she had called master. She felt torn. Her head demanded one thing; her heart another.

Daniel, taken aback at her outburst, said nothing, and for a while they walked in silence along the soggy river path. For Chrissie, Aileen Drummond's arrival had opened a door she had imagined closed for good. Her thoughts returned to Glebe Farm and she wondered how things had changed during her absence.

Haymaking had been in full swing when

she left; the grain harvest yet to come. She had never experienced a Glebe harvest and yet she seemed to see the wheat fields golden under the sun, waiting for the scythe. The air sizzled with heat and larks soared, fluting, high above. Striding across the lush swathes of land went a tall figure, bareheaded, his eyes reflecting the blue of the autumn skies.

Dimly, Chrissie caught the wild sweet singing of the place she had called home, calling to her. Her heart twisted and she faltered.

Daniel's arm was there instantly, steadying her.

'Christina, what is it?'

Confused, she peered into the pale blur of his face until her vision cleared and his features came back into focus. Her head ached dully. She put up her hand and rubbed her temple, frowning.

'I . . . I'm not sure. I saw something. My granny was fey. Maybe I am, too, a bit.'

Daniel stared at her. This sort of thing was way beyond his understanding. But the girl he adored was troubled. He wanted more than anything to console her if he could.

'Let's get wed,' he blurted out. 'That'll solve it. You don't owe the Drummonds anything. They've no right to come ordering you back.

'Go on, Christina. Mam won't mind having us with them till we can get a place for ourselves. A tidy little cottage, eh?'

Chrissie's mind swam. She was, oh, so tempted. Daniel would look after her. She'd have a home of her own, children. The promised future enticed.

'Two loves I see. A long, lonely road you travel.' The gypsy's telling came back to her.

'Daniel, please. Rushing into marriage isn't the way.'

Daniel's face tightened. 'This Drummond fellow means a lot to you, doesn't he?'

'He was my master after the old master passed on. 'Tis natural to feel concerned,' Chrissie said with care.

'Then there's nothing more to be said.' His face seemed to grow stern. 'If you do go you'll need to pay a retainer on the stall or you'll lose it.'

'I know,' Chrissie said woodenly.

'We've walked far enough,' Daniel said more gently. 'Remember, whatever you decide is fine by me. I love you, Christina.'

'I know,' she said again.

She pressed his hand in a gesture that begged forgiveness. To her dismay the move served only to act as a spur.

'Promise me you'll give our getting wed

some thought,' Daniel urged, his eyes blazing. 'Promise me!'

'I promise,' Chrissie had no choice but to reply.

There, it was as good as done.

They turned and retraced their steps towards the town, Daniel seemingly pacified, Chrissie still wrestling with indecision, while at their feet the swollen heart of the river continued on its relentless course.

On Chrissie's return, a letter awaited her at her landlady's house.

'Lovely hand,' Dora Huxley observed, her eyes fairly popping with curiosity. 'Scented paper, too. A lady of quality, I'll be bound.'

Chrissie looked at the elegantly directed envelope. The writing was familiar. She had seen it many times, when she had collected the mail from the Glebe post box. It was from Isobel Macnair.

Puzzled and aware of her landlady's eyes following her, she hurried to her room to see what it contained.

To Chrissie Ross, the missive began.

I expect you will be surprised to receive a letter from me, and that I should know where to find you. My father's business contacts in the area have helped me in this, and I would not trouble you now if I did not believe it was important.

I have learned that Nathan Drummond, through a courageous act, has met with a serious accident and lies gravely ill. I once did him a great wrong and it is my dearest wish to make amends if I can.

I saw during my visit to Hadnall how it was between the two of you. I doubt if Nathan knew it himself yet to me it was clear where his heart lay.

He loves you. I beg of you, go to him. If there is anything that will help him during this difficult time it is your presence and faith in his recovery.

Yours respectfully,
Isobel Macnair.

Chrissie sank down on to the hard wooden chair. She made to read through the letter again, but the words blurred before her eyes. He loved her! Isobel Macnair had seen it . . . the whole world may have seen it. How could she have been so blinkered?

On the heels of one thought came another; the sobering prospect that it could all be a terrible mistake. Nathan Drummond of Glebe Farm, in love with a little nobody from the Highlands: a scrap of a girl taken on by his mother as maid of-all-work? Impossible.

Chrissie pressed her hands to her hot face and wondered afresh what to do.

12

'Dear lady,' Stanton Hayles said. 'May I trouble you for a few moments of your time?'

Florence looked up coldly at the figure on the tall black cob. But for this man her son would be hale and hearty instead of still worryingly bed-bound.

'Please,' the farmer added quietly. 'I fully appreciate how you must be feeling. I can only say how regretful I am over what has happened. I am in your debt. If it hadn't been for your lad I might not be here now — Ebony certainly would not be.'

He delivered his horse's neck a couple of hearty claps. The cob flicked his ears, chomping thoughtfully on his bit with a rattle of metal bit-rings.

Florence flushed. He might almost have read her mind. She steeled herself and, good manners prevailing, found a smile.

'Do come inside, sir. Jamie will attend to your horse.'

Hayles dismounted. The little girls had come to the door with Florence and were peeping out from behind her skirts. Florence bade Annabel to fetch her young uncle, which the child promptly did, running across the farmyard, pinafore strings and auburn curls flying. Her sister looked on solemnly, thumb straying to her mouth.

'Bonnie pair of maids,' Hayles commented.

'Indeed,' Florence agreed, reaching out to caress her younger grandchild's cheek.

In no time, Annabel returned with Jamie. Favoured with a bow for her pains, she gave Hayles a smile of extraordinary sweetness, whilst fixing her gaze on the caller's impressive side-whiskers and beard.

'Didn't you get your whiskers singed in the fire?' she enquired loudly. 'Only I heard my mama telling Edna Hutch about what happened and Edna said 'That'll have singed his whiskers for him!''

Vivid colour again swept Florence's face. She darted her guest a glance of mute apology, but Hayles was beaming broadly at the child.

'Indeed you are right, little miss. My whiskers received a proper scorching, but whiskers do grow again, I'm relieved to say.' He handed the reins of his horse to Jamie. 'Here, lad, take Ebony and tie him up for me, will you?'

'Yes, sir,' Jamie said.

They clattered off and Hayles followed Florence into the house. She took him to the parlour and settled herself opposite him with a rustle of skirts, her back rigid.

'May I enquire how the young master is?' Hayles began cautiously. 'On the mend, I trust?'

'Sadly, no. My son's recovery is distressingly slow. He took a fever after the accident and seems unable to throw it off. It goes and then returns. It is very weakening.'

'I'm sorry to hear that, deeply sorry. I'd hoped for a word with him. Would he be up to receiving a visitor?'

'I think not,' Florence said.

'Ah. Perhaps you would convey my wishes for a speedy return to health. Words can't express how indebted I am to your boy. When he and his men appeared that night I was beyond reason. Bedlam, it was. Pure bedlam. 'Twas his prompt action brought matters under control. As to the rest . . . his courage is beyond praise. If there is anything I can do in return — anything — you only have to say.'

His manner was so humble and sincere that Florence unbent a little.

'Thank you,' she murmured. 'What of yourself? Your property . . . was the damage very great?'

'Aye, I'm afraid it was. All repairable — at a cost. This year's yield is gone, of course. Hay, grains, the lot. I shall have to buy in for the winter. The barns and granaries suffered the most, and the stables. Still, I've seen the architect at Shrewsbury; he's drawing up some plans for me.' Hayles paused. 'I hear Turner was injured. Bad business, eh?'

'His hands, yes. Though I'm glad to say he's making progress. Farmer Hayles — '

'Oh, come, ma'am. Can we not forgo the formalities? You and I were on more familiar terms once and I'd like to think we could be so again.'

Florence suppressed a smile. Her visitor was doing his best to charm. She was surprised and not a little discomfited to find herself yielding to it. She tried again.

'It appears that Turner had no involvement in the fire-setting at Twelve Trees. In fact, he'd argued against it, to his own detriment.'

'Aye, I'd heard as much. I never thought for one moment I'd get trouble from that quarter. Turner was in my employ at one time. The man's got his failings, but he knows about loyalty. He'd never have been party to what went on that night.'

'Have you any idea who the miscreants were?'

'Aye, a band of drunken young hotheads, by all accounts. They'd meant to stop at firing the haycocks and got carried away. They've gone to ground, but we'll find 'em. By thunder we will!' He broke off, eyes narrowing. 'I believe you've trouble in the ranks.'

'Yes, I'm afraid we have. How did you know?'

'Bless you, Florence, you know how gossip spreads. It's said Hutch and Merridew have taken against Turner on account of what happened. Want me to have a word with them? Happen they'd listen to me.'

'You think so?' She looked at him, hesitant. 'I'm not sure. Frankly, I'm surprised at them. Merridew in particular.'

'Merridew's a proud man. Things get said in haste and then there are regrets. It's never easy to back down. Let me speak to them, eh?'

'Very well,' Florence agreed with some relief. 'Thank you . . . Stanton.'

'No problem, m'dear. Rest assured, I shall be the soul of tact.' He beamed at her, well pleased.

'Have you heard about Verity? She's courting a lad from Ellesmere way. Good family, solid background, decent young fellow. My girl's got stars in her eyes. And here I was thinking her heart was broken. Says much for the resilience of youth, eh?'

'Indeed,' Florence said.

Later, Florence reflected on the afternoon.

There was room for caution yet, but Hayles's visit had shown a side of the man she had known and come to like, and for that she was thankful.

★　★　★

'Morning, everyone!' Dorcas strode into the kitchen where Florence and Edna Hutch were preparing the meal for later and Aileen was elbow-deep in the market bake. Dorcas's face was glowing, her eyes bright beneath the jaunty black bowler. 'What weather, eh? I swear this wind comes straight from Siberia!'

She was greeted warmly and Bess, sprawled in front of the range, waved her tail in welcome though did not leave her comfortable spot.

'How lovely to see you,' Florence said. 'It isn't the best of days to be out and about. We weren't expecting anyone.'

'Oh, Gemini needed a gallop. So did I, to be honest.' Dorcas deposited the package she carried on the dresser, then peeled off her gloves and went to spread her chilled hands before the blaze at the range. 'Cooped indoors day after day, first the accountant, then Trigg — he's the new manager of works, you remember. How men do love the sound of their own voices.'

Florence's lips twitched. 'Was this a debate over the new design?'

'The Royal Violet, yes. Named in honour of Her Majesty. You know how fond she is of the flowers — violets on everything at the palace, if gossip is to be believed. Trigg was all for having it called Victoria. I ask you! There must be more knick-knacks dubbed that than he's had hot dinners. He saw sense eventually.'

Dorcas peered across at Aileen.

'Busy, niece? How's the mare?'

'Firefly is well, thank you, Aunt. I took her out first thing. The wind wasn't so fierce then. We went across the common and came back through the wood.'

'Glad to hear it. All work and no play bodes no good to anyone.' Dorcas broke off.

'What of my nephew?' she said soberly. 'Is there any improvement?'

'Only moderate,' Florence said. 'The bouts of fever seem to have run their course, though his breathing is still bad. Doctor Merrick has tried everything he knows, but nothing seems to ease it.'

'Hmph! This weather won't help. Filthy wind. Gets under Gemini's tail, makes her skittish.' Dorcas slapped her hands together and swung her arms. 'That's better. There's nothing like a good fire on a day like this. Shall I go up?'

'Yes, do. Nathan will be glad of a change of face. Gifts, too, I see.' Florence nodded towards the package on the dresser.

'Oh, he mentioned how Aileen was reading to him of an evening. I promised him another Mr Dickens. And Cook sends some grapes from the cool-house. We had a good crop this time. Amazing how long they keep, given the right conditions.'

She swept up her offerings and stomped out of the kitchen, letting in a gush of cold air from the passage.

Through the window, the men could be seen getting in the last of the turnips. To Florence, the lifting of the final rills signified the onset of winter, a bleak time, not much doing on the land, everywhere leached of colour but for the cold red sun overhead. An involuntary shiver touched her.

'What is it, Mama?' Aileen said.

'Oh, nothing. Gloomy thoughts. I never did care for this time of year.'

'I love it,' Aileen said candidly. 'There's skating and sledging to look forward to, not to mention Christmas. Though it does get chilly standing about in the market in the cold and the wet. Proper premises, now, like we had up north. That would be more the thing.'

'Oh, Aileen!'

'Oh, Aileen, what?' The girl looked amused. 'Oh, Aileen, watch your language? Or is it the thought of me running a store like Papa?'

She mocked a comically horrified face and Florence chuckled.

'Dreadful child! What's to be done with you?'

'Not a thing, ma'am,' Edna Hutch put in. 'I'd say Miss Aileen is fine as she is, beggin' your pardon, ma'am.'

'Thank you, Edna,' Aileen said. 'Mama knows there's no hope for me, really. Never mind, Mama. Look on the bright side. We have enough winter fodder for the animals, and the men are speaking again.'

'Thanks to our neighbour.' Florence scooped the last of the chopped vegetables into the pot and reached for a piece of linen to dry her hands. 'There, that's done. Is the meat ready, Edna?'

'It is. There's nothing like a mutton stew on a day like this. Happen it'll tempt the master's appetite.'

'Let us hope so,' Florence said, and moved to join her daughter in mixing the ingredients for the currant loaves.

Upstairs, Dorcas had refreshed the fire and pulled up a chair to Nathan's bed. Mouth pursed, she studied him closely.

'Hmph! If I were to say you were looking better I'd be fibbing.'

Nathan's gaunt face twisted in a semblance of a smile.

'That comes as no surprise. You, on the other hand, are blooming,' he said, wheezing.

'Flatterer! I've brought that Mr Dickens I promised you. 'Christmas Stories'. Do you think Aileen will enjoy dipping into them?'

'She might, under sufferance. Bedside reading isn't really her thing. All credit to her for persevering. Ah, grapes. You spoil me, Aunt.'

'Fudge! Least I can do.' Dorcas paused. 'I believe you had a caller a few days back.'

'Hayles, you mean? How did you know?'

'News travels. Did you get to talk with him?'

'You're not serious! Mama guards me like the very devil. She's afraid lest the slightest provocation brings on a relapse. I wouldn't have minded a word with the fellow. She tells me he's rebuilding.'

'So it appears. I've no great liking for Hayles, but he has my sympathy over this. It was a bad business. Talking of which, how's the shepherd coming along?'

'Splendidly, by all accounts. Can't wait to get back to his flock. Davina's been treating his injuries with some hocuspokery she picked up in Africa. There'll be scarring and his hands won't work as well as they did, but it looks as if he'll be able to use them again and that's the main thing.

'I believe I was given the same treatment. All I remember is the stink of the stuff. It did the trick, though. My burns are completely healed. The doctor is astounded.'

'Just shows there's more than one way to climb a mountain. Does talking tire you?'

'A little. Confound it, Aunt! I'm an encumbrance, lying here weak as a kitten. The farm's a worry, too. I want to know what's going on out there.'

'I think you can safely leave that in Merridew's hands for now. It's a slack time of year anyway. As to the other, if it's a nurse you want . . .'

'Thank you, but no. You've done more than enough already.'

'Oh, fiddle! You're family. I'm glad to have you all here.'

A sudden paroxysm of coughing left Nathan gasping for breath. Dorcas poured water from the carafe on the bedside table, and with amazing tenderness held the cup to his lips for him to drink, before easing him back on to the bolsters and straightening the covers.

'I'd best let you rest, boy. I shall look in

again before I leave.'

His eyes were already closing in sleep. Checking that the fire was still drawing well, Dorcas slipped from the room and made her way thoughtfully down the stairs.

* * *

In the kitchen Davina had joined the others with the children. John was being cooed over in his grandmother's arms.

'I've left Nathan sleeping,' Dorcas said. 'As you say, not much progress.'

'No.' Florence caught her lip as a figure went past the window. 'Here's Rose with the mail. Bless her for fetching it up.'

Davina hurried to the door. Leafing through the bundle of mail the dairymaid handed her, she gave a little cry. Among the bills and farming circulars was a letter directed in a well-loved hand. She ripped it open and scanned the pages.

'He's done it!' She looked up, joy flooding her face. 'Finbar's been appointed minister at the Paisley kirk! He wants us to join him immediately.'

'Oh, my dear girl!' Florence bundled the baby on to Edna Hutch, enfolded her daughter in her arms and kissed her. 'I'm so happy for you both.'

'Great stuff, Davvy,' Aileen said.

'Very pleased for you, m'dear,' Dorcas added. 'Changes ahead, eh? The place will seem quiet without the little tribe.'

Everyone started talking at once. Bess began woofing and the little girls looked on in astonishment at the unaccustomed excitement. Davina went suddenly still.

'What am I thinking of? I can't possibly leave just yet, not with Nathan as he is. I'm surprised at Finbar for suggesting it.' Her elation faded.

'Dearest . . . ' Florence began.

'No, Mama. No argument, please. I shall write and explain. Finbar will understand.' Davina bit her lip, thoughts chasing across her clear grey eyes. 'There's something else.'

Florence ventured a smile.

'Would you be meaning a certain event?'

'Mama! You've guessed! Well!'

'Little goose, of course we did. Edna and I have been on tenterhooks waiting for you to confirm the news.'

Dorcas looked mystified.

'Am I being singularly stupid, or have I missed something?' She looked from one smiling face to the next, brightening suddenly. 'Ah, I think I have it. There's to be another little Lennox!'

'Well,' Aileen said, 'we really shouldn't let

the news go uncelebrated. Davvy, shall we open one of your specials? The elderflower, I think.'

'By all means,' Davina said.

The wine was fetched, goblets found. Glasses had just been raised when there was a rap on the door. The front door.

'Who can that be?' Florence said, frowning.

'There's one way to find out, sister.'

The front entrance was rarely used and the air was charged with apprehension as Dorcas went to answer the summons. A murmured interchange was heard from the hallway.

Dorcas reappeared.

'What a day for surprises. You'll never guess who's here.'

She stepped aside, revealing the slim figure behind her.

'Well, bless me!' Edna cried. 'If it isn't our Chrissie!'

★   ★   ★

Nathan sat by the bedroom fire, a rug over his knees, smiling as he relived the events of the past three weeks.

It had been his aunt he had expected to see when the door had opened that blustery mid-November day, but the quip he had prepared had died on his lips. It hadn't been

Dorcas standing there — it had been Chrissie.

She had entered the room, shutting the door behind her with a well-remembered 'Tsk!' at the cloud of smoke that billowed from the chimney in the ensuing draught.

'Master Nathan,' she'd said, coming closer. 'What have you been up to?'

'Had a bit of an argument with a blazing roof timber, Chrissie. Nothing a little wholesome chivvying won't put right!'

In her everyday cloak and high-crowned bonnet she had seemed somehow older, and had a new poise about her.

He'd barely had time to utter those first words when emotion had choked his throat and to his chagrin he was gripped by one of the violent coughing attacks that left him gasping and enfeebled.

Chrissie had been there at once, offering water, murmuring encouragement, easing him back against the bolsters. Her touch was calm and she'd smelled deliciously of rose geranium.

Giving him time to recover his breath, she'd picked up the volume of Dickens on the bedside table.

''Christmas Stories'? I don't know this one.'

'Good,' he managed to wheeze. 'We can enjoy it together.'

Then the door burst open and Jamie had rocketed into the room, the dog gambolling crazily around him with excited little woofs.

'Chrissie! Chrissie! You're back! Come and see my pet lamb. Jim got these Clun Forests from Shrewsbury. Late lambers, he said they were. An' one of the ewes went an' died an' Jim said we'd have to hand-rear the lamb 'cause none of the others would do the fostering. It's grown up fine . . . '

He paused for breath, gazing at the visitor as if birthday and Christmas had happened at once.

'Chrissie, you are staying?'

'Until the wind changes,' Chrissie said briskly. She looked him up and down. 'Look at your boots, thick with mud! Why didn't you take them off before you came up?'

'Bess, be still! Good dog.'

'Master Jamie, have the sense to shut the door. Do it gently, it makes the chimney smoke.'

'You will come and see my lamb, Chrissie?'

'Afterwards,' she replied firmly.

Nathan laughed gently now. It seemed to him that Chrissie Ross had some special magic about her, for the moment she'd stepped over the threshold the place had seemed to stir, as if being woken up from a long sleep.

The women went about with smiles on their faces whilst the children clung mercilessly, lest she vanish again. The men made a point of overcoming the mistress's sickroom ban and took turns to come up and pass the time of day with him. It was partly their talk and cheerful banter that gave Nathan the incentive to get back on his feet. But there was no doubt in his mind that the driving force behind his recovery was Chrissie herself.

Nathan had come to realise what an inner voice had been telling him for so long. He was in love, deeply and irrevocably, with the housemaid they had brought with them on their flight from the north. He could not let her go again. He must not.

The clop of hoofs on the yard below heralded a visitor. A moment later, the door opened to admit his mother.

'Farmer Hayles is here. He wants to speak with you. Are you feeling up to it?'

'Of course I am. Show him up, Mama. Is Chrissie not back?'

'Not yet. She and Aileen have gone shopping to the village. Are you sure you're not in a draught?'

'Quite sure. Stop fussing, Mama, and tell Hayles to come on up. He'll freeze to death standing there in the hallway, poor fellow.'

Florence found a smile. 'Very well. I'd better tell Edna to make coffee.'

The footsteps up the stairs were heavy and measured. The farmer appeared, red of face, bringing a whiff of the wintry outdoors, laced with leather and horse. Snowflakes melted damply in his hair and beard. He offered a big, wind-chapped hand.

'Drummond. Good to see you, man.'

'And you, sir. Draw up a chair, make yourself comfortable. Sorry to have to drag you up here. I was hoping to make the stairs by now, but my legs tell me otherwise.'

'All in good time, eh?'

The farmer pulled a chair to the fire and sat down, stretching his booted feet towards the blaze. His clothes began to steam pungently in the heat.

This was their first encounter since the night Nathan had almost lost his life, and Hayles was plainly struggling to find the right words.

Nathan made his task easier.

'I understand you are rebuilding,' he said. 'How does it go?'

'Oh, slow. We've made a start, though with the weather being on the turn we may have to call a halt. The stables are going where they were originally, but the new barns and granaries are to be sited further from the house.'

'Not a bad move.'

'No. It was on the architect's advice. I've only myself to blame for how they were positioned before. I'm one of the old school: everything easily to hand. It doesn't do, you know. I could have lost my home that night and I'd have only had myself to blame. Got to learn by your mistakes, eh?'

'Quite. It's an impressive property. How long has it been up?'

'Getting on for twenty years. There was a house there before, a half-timbered dwelling something like this. Twelve Trees was my late wife's home, you understand. It had got ramshackle, the way places do. As soon as I could I had the old house pulled down and built the present one.

'Verity was born there. There was still a smell of new plaster and paint, I remember. The midwife was in a flap lest it caused the baby harm.'

The farmer paused, thinking back to happier times. Then he seemed to collect himself. He looked Nathan squarely in the face.

'Drummond,' he said. 'I want to apologise for my past behaviour. How I acted was unforgivable. I was wrapped up in my own selfish wants and there's the nub of it. I'm sorry.'

'Let's say no more about it,' Nathan said generously. 'I daresay I was at fault, too. I took the men off you. That must have grated.'

'It was their choice. It stood to reason they'd want to return to their old place of work.'

'They came for a pittance and a rat-ridden roof over their heads. It was all I could manage at the time.'

'They'd not have been on much of a wage with me. I've been wrong in that direction, too. My men pulled out all the stops the night of the fire and I'll not forget it. They had their wages upped immediately. That's the way it's going to be in future.'

There was a light tap on the door and Edna Hutch came in with a pot of coffee on a tray and a plate of gingerbread, which she set down on a small table. Pouring the coffee, she sent them a genial nod and left the room.

Hayles spooned sugar into his cup, stirring thoughtfully.

'I have to thank you for what you did that night. It was brave and you've suffered for it. If there was any justice it'd be me bound to a sickroom, and not a hale young chap like you.'

'It's as it is. Thank God I'm on the mend.'

'Amen to that.' Hayles helped himself to gingerbread.

'I saw that little maid of yours in Hadnall, the one who used to work here.'

'Chrissie Ross.'

'Aye. Bonnie wench. I should imagine she's got her wits about her and all.'

'Indeed. My return to health is due to Chrissie. She has a way with healing herbs that's quite extraordinary, even more so than my sister Davina's.'

'Some folks have the gift of knowing how to use the bounty of God's good earth.'

'You talk like my father,' Nathan said with a smile.

'Your mother's said that once or twice . . . aye, and your young sister, too. There's another with plenty about her.'

'You're right there. We've Aileen to thank for getting Chrissie over here.'

'Really? She's back for good, then?'

'Would that were so.' A shadow crossed Nathan's face. 'She's here till I'm fit again and I'm practically there. I must say it'll be good to get back on my land.'

'It'll come. Youth has a resilience all its own. My men are at your disposal, you know that. You're a man short till Turner gets back into harness. Anything you need, you have only to say.'

'Good of you, sir,' Nathan said.

'It's the least I can do. Meantime, make the

most of it. Winter isn't the most accommodating time on the land.'

'True.' Nathan's voice was rueful. 'A while ago, if anyone had told me I'd be spending my life running a farm I'd have laughed.'

'What aspirations did you have?' Hayles asked, curious. 'Following your sire into the grocery business?'

'Not exactly. I had a mind to do engineering. Either marine or the railways, there was plenty of choice where we were. I'd always tinkered with machinery. It held a fascination for me. Still does.'

'You must have found it hard, coming here.'

'It wasn't what I wanted, I admit, and then when I saw the place!' Nathan barked a laugh. 'Fields overgrown, dykes clogged up, buildings going to ruin. The house was appallingly out of repair. It was a dickens of a job knowing where to start.'

'I never for one moment expected you to stay. All credit to you for sticking at it.'

'I couldn't have coped without Merridew and the others.'

The rattle of cart wheels and slow clop of hoofs marked the return of the young women. Hayles pulled to his feet.

'I ought to make tracks. Will I call again?'

'By all means. I'll see you out.'

They were making their farewells on the

chilly confines of the landing, snow now spinning past the windows, when Chrissie came tramping up the stairs. Her face was flushed from the cold. Her green eyes glittered as she beheld her patient.

'Nathan Drummond! What are you doing in this draughty place? Inside with you this minute!'

Nathan shot the other man a glance of amused appeal.

'See what I have to put up with? Bullying, morning till night.'

'I've always found, in these circumstances, it's wise to do as you are told!' Hayles replied with a grin.

He fetched the young woman a wink and went on his way.

Smiling, Nathan returned to the welcome warmth of his fireside. Chrissie closed the door with a determined click and bustled about, building up the fire, tidying the piles of books, handing the rug for the patient's knees.

'Aren't you going to feed me one of your revolting brews? Tuck the rug around me?' Nathan enquired wryly.

'You're perfectly capable of doing that for yourself. As to the other, a dose of white nettle might be no bad thing. It tastes most vile.'

He laughed.

'Do you realise what you did just now? You dropped that 'Master' nonsense.'

Chrissie blushed.

'It's how I came to think of you. I made a resolve never to call anyone master or mistress again when I started out on my own. I only do it now because I'm not sure how else to address you.'

'You could start by calling me Nathan. Oh, stop fiddling about, woman. Come and talk to me.'

Chrissie hesitated, reluctant. Then, putting aside the newspaper she had been folding, she went to occupy the chair that Hayles had just vacated, holding her hands to the blaze.

'Did you dislike being in service so much?' Nathan asked.

'No, but I couldn't return to it. Miss Aileen turning up at the market brought home to me how much I valued my freedom. It was partly why I took so long in coming.'

'What made you change your mind and come?'

'I had a letter . . . from Isobel Macnair.'

'Isobel? Good heavens!' Nathan stared in astonishment. 'What was that in aid of?'

'It appeared she had a wrong to right. I don't know what it was. It was a very . . . persuasive letter.'

Isobel. Who would have credited it? The gesture was as commendable as it was unexpected, and Nathan couldn't help feeling more forgiving towards the girl he had once loved.

'I shall have to think about going back soon,' Chrissie said, sitting back in her chair. 'I wouldn't want to outstay my welcome.'

Nathan swallowed. It was now or never. He reached out and took her hand in his.

'Chrissie, don't go. No, wait. Let me finish — I love you. I think I always have. Please, dearest girl, tell me I'm not mistaken. I — dash it, I had a speech prepared and now it's gone clean out of my head! I shall have to come straight out with it.

'Chrissie Ross, it is my heartfelt wish to have you beside me always. Would you do me the great honour of becoming my wife?'

Chrissie gazed at him, her eyes huge in her small face.

'Oh, don't!' she whispered. Her bottom lip trembled. 'It's too late. I'm as good as promised to someone else.'

Nathan felt the room swirl about him. So that was it. He released her hand and saw how she clutched it to her, as if she never wanted to lose the warmth of his grip.

'Is he a good man?' His voice seemed to Nathan to come from a long way off.

'Very. His name is Daniel. He's kept in touch all the while I've been here. Every time he writes he expresses his trust and his feelings for me. How could I reject all that?'

'I knew you were receiving mail. Aileen thought it was from your landlady. She said you were on friendly terms.'

'We are. Dora Huxley's house has become home.'

'You're happy, then.'

It was a statement, not a question. All the same, Chrissie considered her words carefully.

'It is what I've made for myself. Daniel has become part of it.'

Nathan was silent, his mind a tumult of longing and regret. Did he have the right to come between a woman and the man she had thought to wed? His better self answered him all too readily. Besides, the die had been cast that balmy midsummer night when Chrissie Ross had quitted their roof. Her life was no longer his to command.

He saw the years stretching ahead, long, achingly solitary, and had to wonder why it seemed his lot always to be thwarted of what he held most dear.

13

'Isn't this a treat?' Aileen rolled out the pastry for the market bakes. Chrissie added cloves and a pinch of nutmeg to the apple filling she was preparing. She sniffed appreciatively. Spices were beyond her means normally, and plainer fare had to be the lot of her Nantwich customers.

'An apple tart is always the better for flavouring,' she replied.

'Goose!' Aileen darted her a look of affection. 'I meant the two of us working together. It's like old times.'

'Yes, I suppose it is ... No, sweetheart ... ' Chrissie said to Annabel, who was pulling at her skirts.

Wherever she went she seemed to be shadowed by the little girls, and Jamie always greeted her eagerly when he came in from school. The look of relief on his young face when he saw that she was still there tore Chrissie apart.

She gave Annabel a smile.

'We can't go out just now, my pet. It's snowing. Let's roll up your sleeves and you shall have some pastry to play with.'

'Ooh, yes!' Annabel said.

'Me, too?' her sister lisped, making a futile effort to unbutton the cuffs of her dress with chubby fingers.

Abandoning the apple mixture, Chrissie dealt with the children. She settled them at a corner of the table. They knelt on chairs, enthusiastically moulding the lumps of pastry they had been handed.

Returning to her task, Chrissie lined the waiting row of baking tins, trimming the edges with deft slashes of the kitchen knife.

'You should tell them to go and play,' Aileen grumbled. 'That's what I do. It works, too.'

Chrissie didn't doubt it. It had struck her before that Aileen Drummond could have been a first-class schoolmistress!

'Chrissie, may I tell you something?' Aileen said in more serious tones.

'Of course.' She wondered what was coming next.

'You know the shop on the corner in Hadnall, the one that has stood empty since old Mrs Timms passed away?'

'The sweet shop that was?'

'That's right. Well, the other day when we went shopping I slipped across for a look round.

'Chrissie, it would make a marvellous

general store. The position is perfect. It's plenty big enough, and the dues are reasonable.'

Chrissie's hands stilled over spooning apple into the pastry cases.

'Miss Aileen, you're never thinking of going into the grocery trade?'

'Why not? It's what Papa did. Besides, one has to start somewhere. Oh, don't look like that, Chrissie. I've got it all planned.

'I shall stock all the basic requirements, much the same as at Glasgow, and sell the baked goods at weekends — more often once I get going . . . Well, there are the regulars to consider. They might keep away if I left off doing the cakes and pies, and that would never do.'

Chrissie hid a smile. For a gently reared young woman, Aileen Drummond had a remarkable grasp of human nature.

'Have you thought how you'll do the baking on top of everything else? You can't be in two places at once,' she pointed out.

'I shall just have to manage until I can afford to take on some staff. I daresay Davvy won't be here for much longer, either,' Aileen added with a regretful little sigh. 'A pity. Those remedies of hers have really caught on. But there it is. What do you think, Chrissie?'

'It isn't up to me,' she said. 'You're better

putting the question to your mama.'

'I was hoping you would do that for me.'

'What, me?'

'Of course, you! Who better? Mama will listen to you, Chrissie. She always has. It's no use me doing it. Mama wants me to be like my sister, married with a brood of children.'

'There are worse things,' Chrissie said guardedly. 'And starting a business is no simple matter. Have you thought how to fund it?'

'Oh, yes. Aunt Dorcas is going to help. We've worked it all out. My aunt will put up the initial capital and take a share of the returns.' Ambition blazed on Aileen's face. 'Chrissie, I know I can do this. Please say you think it's a good idea.'

'Well, on the face of it, it is. You're fortunate to have the backing.'

'Oh, I know. Aunt Dorcas is so supportive. She'll do anything for us. I suppose it comes of having no children herself.'

'And you're right about the premises. The position is ideal: right in the centre of the village and close to the butcher and the greengrocer.'

'I knew you'd see it my way,' Aileen said. 'You will speak for me?'

The children continued to roll and thump, their faces rapt, modelling the dough into magical shapes before abandoning each idea for a better one.

'Miss Aileen, I couldn't. It's not my place.'

'Not your place?' Aileen echoed. 'Since when did that bother Chrissie Ross? You've been ordering us around for ages!'

'I have not. You shouldn't speak so.'

'Dearest Chrissie, please don't be offended. It was meant kindly. You've every right to order us around. Why, you're practically one of us.'

'Of course she is.'

A voice from the doorway made them look up. Dorcas Webb stood on the step, stamping snow from her boots and shaking the flakes from her cape.

'Aunt Dorcas!' Aileen cried. 'Do come in and close the door. You're letting in the cold.'

'Just a flying visit, my dears. The weather, you know. Can't have Gemini foundering in the snow.' Dorcas went to the range and stood with her back to it, warming herself. She peered across at the industry at the end of the table.

'Hey ho, moppets. Helping with the baking?'

'Yes, we are,' Annabel replied. 'We're finished now. Please may we see Gemini, Auntie Dorcas? May we give her some sugar?'

'Yes, yes, in a moment. You'll need to wrap

up, mind. Run along and find your grandmama; ask her to get you into your outdoor things.'

Slapping the sticky pastry bits from their hands, the children clambered down from the table and ran obediently off, their faces glowing in anticipation at the treat in store. Dorcas turned to Aileen and Chrissie.

'You two were looking serious when I came in. Is something amiss?'

'Not really, Aunt,' Aileen said. 'I needed an ally over the question of the shop. I wanted Chrissie to speak to Mama for me.'

'Oh, I'll do that. Chances are Florence will need a little nudge in the right direction.' Dorcas glanced round. 'Where's Nathan?'

'He's in the parlour, looking over the farm accounts. It's warmer for him than the office. Why don't you go through?'

'I shall in a moment. I wouldn't mind a word first with Chrissie, if it's convenient.'

Aileen went to the washstand under the window to deal with her hands.

'I'll go and tell Nathan you're here.'

When she had gone, Dorcas turned to Chrissie.

'Tell me to mind my own business if you wish, but I wondered what your plans were now. From what I see, you seem well settled in once more. Have you had second thoughts about leaving?'

Chrissie stared.

'My decision to go still stands. Why should it be otherwise?'

'If you take off now, my girl, you'll leave behind desolation and despair, particularly in one quarter. You do know that, don't you?'

'I . . . I . . . ' Chrissie stammered to a stop. She knew all about the agony of a broken heart. Her own ached unbearably, ever since the moment when the one she had thought never to call her own had laid bare his soul to her. What should she say to this shrewd woman who stood looking at her with such concern? What *could* she say?

'I have to go back,' she said, hearing the tremble in her voice. 'If it wasn't for the snow and the difficulties in travelling I would be gone by now. The master is making a good recovery. I have no choice but to leave.'

Dorcas gave a snort.

'Fudge! Of course you have a choice. I must say, I admire your tenacity. I only hope this suitor, whoever he is, is worthy of such loyalty. Oh, don't pout, Chrissie. I wasn't born yesterday. Only a young man could have this sort of pull on a girl.'

'I was making my way,' Chrissie cried. 'Even if I choose not to accept Dan — even if I remain single, I know now I can fend for myself. There's satisfaction in that.'

'Maybe, but don't throw away the chance of happiness for the sake of an ideal. I'm speaking from experience now.' Dorcas's rather severe features softened, and Chrissie caught a glimpse of the attractive young woman she had once been.

'I've never told anyone this before, but I was in love once. I'd just started taking an active interest in the family firm. He was an officer in the cavalry. Tall, debonair, handsome — the girls flocked around him like butterflies. We loved each other desperately. He wanted us to marry. It would have meant leaving all I held dear; my parents, the manor, the business . . . I couldn't do it.'

'You have regrets?'

'Oh, child, there are always regrets. I've not been unhappy with my lot. It could be that this way suited me best.

'You are different. You are made for wifehood. It's plain where your rightful place is. If you can find it in you to stay, I for one would be proud to call you mistress of Glebe Farm.'

Tears were now coursing down Chrissie's cheeks. Dorcas reached out and patted her hand.

'There, now, I'll say no more, clumsy oaf that I am for upsetting you. You must do what you think is right.' Her lips moved towards a smile. 'I can hear those imps coming back. I'd best have a quick word with my nephew.'

She left the room. Chrissie mopped up her tears with a corner of her pinafore and shook her head wordlessly at the sheer unfairness of life.

★   ★   ★

'Confounded stink!' Silas Turner muttered. Davina was making her daily call to the shepherd's cottage to change his dressings, and the now familiar reek of strong wayside herbs wafted through the room, making his eyes smart. He blinked rapidly, sniffing.

'I wunna be sorry to see an end to this. All wrapped up like an Egyptian mummy, reeking of an apothecary shop! Even the dogs refuse to keep me company nowadays!

'Not that I'm complaining — it's a rare job you've done, Mrs Lennox. But for you there's no telling how I'd have ended up. I'm more grateful than I can say.'

'Thank you, Silas.'

Over the weeks a rapport had grown between the taciturn shepherd and the young woman from the farmhouse. Davina looked forward to the visits. She'd been gratified to watch the healing brought about by the salve she had been shown in the steamy heat of a

Barotse compound. She had recorded the recipe meticulously in the small leather-backed book she carried with her always.

This salve had required some diligent scrutiny of the hedgerows, and an urgent trip to the apothecary at Shrewsbury for the lesser-known ingredients that grew only in warmer climes. Pounded with honey from the Glebe skeps, and with a worshipful wish on her lips, it had emerged as strong-smelling and potent as that made by a dark-skinned native on that sweltering African day.

Davina secured the wrappings in a neat bow.

'There. You're coming along nicely. We should soon be able to leave off the binding. You'll still need to use the treatment for the time being. After that you must make sure and always keep the skin lubricated. I'll give you a light salve for that. Marigold should do it.'

'You should have been born a boy, Mrs Lennox. You'd have made a fine doctor.'

'Think so? There's a new college of medicine for ladies opened up in London and not before time. If I was free I might have been tempted to follow that path. Bit late now, I fear. Perhaps one of my girls will show an interest. You never know, in days to come a woman physician might stand a better chance of becoming accepted than now.'

Turner looked at her. Mostly, he had a healthy regard for what the young woman had to say, though on this matter, he remained sceptical.

'How's the parson getting on?' he asked, changing tack.

'He's well, thank you. Missing us, naturally,'

'Aye, he must be. You'll want to join him before long, I dunna wonder, a new little'n on the way an' all.'

Davina shot him a sharp look.

'How did you know?'

She had sworn the family to secrecy and had taken to wearing loose-fitting gowns.

'Females get a certain look about them when they're breeding.' The shepherd's eyes twinkled in what passed for a grin in his stern face.

'Go on,' Davina said, smiling despite herself. 'You'll be telling me next your ewes are the same.'

'I wunna argue to the contrary. An addition to the family will be no bad thing, Mrs Lennox. Three's a crowd, they say, but four's a good round number. Parson'll be pleased.'

'Indeed.'

She was saved any more discussion by a round of barking from the dogs in the shed. A moment later Ploughman Hutch's bewhiskered face appeared round the door.

'Ah. Didn't know you were here, Mrs Lennox. I'll call back.'

'No need, Hutch. I was just going. Come inside, do.'

'I've been sawing up that old apple tree that came down in the storm,' Hutch said to Turner. 'I've brought you a load of logs. Want me to stack them in the woodshed?'

'Aye, you could do, thanks, Wilkie. You must be ready for a sup of something. Sit down a moment while I get it.'

The two men settled down by the fire and Davina, glad to see how well harmony was restored after their recent disagreements, slipped softly away.

* * *

'Florence, m'dear! Good morning to you.' Stanton Hayles brandished his hat in greeting and drew the trap to a halt on the slushy village street. 'It's not often we see you here at this hour.'

'Good morning, Stanton.' Hadnall was bustling with activity and Florence had to raise her voice to be heard above the clamour of passing vehicles, the shouts of the market goers and hammering from the blacksmith and the wheelwright shops opposite.

'I felt like some air, and since the girls were coming in anyway, I decided to join them.'

It was partly true. She had also wanted to inspect the shop premises Aileen had apparently set her heart upon. Petitioned from all sides, hopelessly outnumbered, she had at last come to accept that her younger daughter was destined for a path other than marriage . . . though, of course, one never quite knew what lay around the corner.

Despite her regrets, she had to acknowledge that her late husband would have been proud of Aileen. The small corner shop had been everything Aileen had said. Florence could see how she had been so taken with it.

'It will be some while before the girls are finished. I shall make my own way back,' she went on. 'The snow is melting and the walk will do me good.'

'Walk all that way?' The farmer looked horrified. 'I won't hear of it. If you don't mind biding a moment while I call at the saddler's, I'll be delighted to take you home in the trap.'

He climbed down and assisted her into the high seat, before hastening across the street and disappearing into the narrow alleyway where the saddler had his dark little cavern of a shop.

Florence, loosely holding the horse's reins, looked about her. A fiery sun shone from a sky of faultless blue. Smoke billowed from the chimneys of dwelling houses and other buildings. In the distance Florence could see the bonneted heads of the two girls as they served the queue of people at the Glebe Farm stall.

She caught her breath. How she wished Chrissie could be persuaded to stay on. She had been surprised at how graciously the girl had matured during her relatively short spell away. It was hard to credit that this poised young woman was the little Highland maid they had brought with them from Glasgow. That her son should want her for his wife was no longer beyond Florence's comprehension. Without doubt, the girl could now be a worthy mistress of Glebe Farm.

But Chrissie had graced their hearth a good while longer than she had intended and she needed to be on her way. Within a day or two she would be gone. Florence was seized by a terrible sadness at the thought.

They would be doubly bereft, for earlier that week Davina had received yet another plea from Finbar for her to take the train north with the children. He had pointed out, fairly enough, that with Nathan practically restored to health and Chrissie still with them, Davina's presence at the farm was no longer as crucial as it had been.

Loath though she was to lose her eldest girl, Florence had bid farewell to the little family the day before, amid tearful embraces and promises to write. She wiped away a fresh tear at the thought.

★　★　★

'Here we are.' Tossing a set of repaired harness into the back of the trap, Hayles clambered up into the driver's seat and resumed charge of the reins. Smartly he clicked his tongue to the horse, and with a lurch and a splattering of muddy snow they were on their way, bowling down the village street where dogs chased them, barking, and straying poultry ran squawking out of the way.

Once on the homeward road, the snowy fields spread out on either side, the farmer threw Florence an appraising glance.

'I see you are out of deep mourning. That colour becomes you.'

'Thank you, sir.' Florence smoothed her lavender skirts of half-mourning over her knees, and brushed a speck of straw from her winter mantle of warm grey woollen.

'Granted 'tis early days yet, but there's

something I'd like to say,' Hayles went on, tentative. 'It's . . . forgive me, I'm not good at this sort of talk, but I wonder, would you object if I were to call at Glebe Farm on a more . . . shall we say, personal basis?'

She looked at him, startled, the cold air drifting past.

'Do I take it, sir, that you still harbour an interest in my daughter?'

'Miss Aileen? Bless you, Florence, no! It's true it crossed my mind at one time. Your girl is a stylish young miss. What man wouldn't be interested?' He gave her an engaging smile, a little abashed at his own daring. 'Florence, lass, 'tis your sweet self I find claiming my thoughts these days. Has been for some while.'

It was a pretty speech for a bluff-spoken man and Florence felt the colour rush to her face.

'A fellow gets lonesome on his own,' Hayles continued, emboldened by her quiet attention. 'Verity is to be wed next spring, as you know. The place will seem empty without her. Besides, Twelve Trees has lacked a proper mistress for long enough.

'I'd not stint you, Florence. Anything you want you shall have — geegaws and fripperies, your own trap to get you about, anything. You'd have a free rein with the house. Any changes you choose to make shall be done.'

He paused for breath and Florence seized the opportunity to speak.

'Stanton, would all this be leading where I think?'

'I'll not deny it. Truth is I've grown mighty fond of you, Florence. I'd be proud to call you wife.' He slid her a sideways look. 'Have I reason to hope?'

Florence swallowed hard. She had grown to like this man beside her. He had been there from the start, a thorn in the flesh at times, true, but there: a local personage, high-ranking within his own circle and respected in the chapel. She remembered how kind and helpful he had been when Balfour had passed on, lending them a conveyance for the funeral, offering his services for whatever else they required. And there was his grateful support of Nathan during his convalescence.

Hayles's enmity, such as it was, had not been with them personally, but with their tenure of Glebe Farm. In one illuminating moment Florence saw the situation his way: a man fired with ambition and purpose, who had had the object of his plans unexpectedly snatched from him.

She took a breath.

'Sir, what you suggest is not displeasing to me, though perhaps this discussion is a little premature.' She broke off, trying to frame the right words. 'There is one matter that should be cleared between us. It concerns Glebe Farm. You are aware that the ownership is no longer in my name?'

'Aye, it had come to my notice. One of the men let it slip. There's not much happens hereabouts that doesn't reach Twelve Trees eventually. The farm now officially belongs to your boy.'

'That is correct. The change was sanctioned some while ago. Nathan has long reached his majority and he's matured greatly since coming here.'

'I know what you're saying, Florence. I've been an avaricious fool, setting my sights on what I could never have. I'd had my eye on the Glebe ever since old Reeve Webb took sickly and let the place go. I should have accepted when you came that it would never be mine.'

'Glebe Farm will never again be under my jurisdiction,' Florence pressed on, anxious to drive the point home. 'It's best that Nathan should be master in every sense of the word. As soon as the legalities were completed I told the men myself how it would be. I was touched at how readily they accepted my word.'

'I wouldn't have it any other way,' Hayles

said. 'Please believe me when I say how mortified I am at how I've behaved, fool that I was.'

'We all make mistakes,' Florence murmured.

'Aye, well.' He sent her a look of contrition. 'There then, all sorted. Let us concentrate on the future from now on, eh?'

Beaming, he slapped the reins and sent the horse forward at a spanking trot, gritty snow and mud spilling out from under the pounding hoofs. Florence, aware of a new lightness between them, held on to her bonnet and prepared to enjoy the rest of the drive home.

Nathan stood on the crest of the hill, watching the slender form of Chrissie Ross walking away. Only that morning he had begged her to stay, but Chrissie had been resolute. He had been forced to give in and make his goodbyes. She had insisted on leaving without fuss, and refused his offer to drive her to the station in the trap. He had not even been permitted to accompany her to the lane where she was to meet the carrier's cart that would take her to the train.

'At least let me take you to the gate,' Nathan had said. 'You'll have baggage to carry. It will be heavy.'

She had shaken her head, making a jest of it.

'Away with you, I'll manage. What a good thing the china is travelling separately. I might have dropped it and blackened my name for good.'

They had given her a rousing send-off the previous evening. Aileen and Edna Hutch had put their heads together and arranged a feast. Everyone came to wish Chrissie well. In the farmhouse kitchen the big scrubbed table groaned under the weight of the food. There was a whole quarter of beef, courtesy of Twelve Trees, and another of bacon. There were pickles and chutneys from the larder, butter and cream from the dairy, fresh-baked bread and one of the famous Glebe mutton pies, so large it had to take centre place.

In a corner of the room rested a barrel of strong ale from Aunt Dorcas. For Jamie and those who preferred a lighter beverage there was lemonade, sharp and sweet. Plum cake, sponges, a fruit tart ... How Edna had managed to achieve such a spread while the women were out at the market took some believing, but achieve it she had, aided by her niece, Rose.

After the feasting, Wilkie Hutch recited a comic monologue that had them weeping with laughter. Jim treated them to a rendering of the old songs and they'd all joined in with the choruses. Silas Turner and Edward had held them rapt with a tale of long ago, taking turns in the narration and proving astonishingly adept at the different voices of the characters.

As the level of ale in the barrel dropped, the atmosphere grew merrier. The table was pushed back to the wall, Edward took up a flute and the dancing began.

At first Nathan, feeling strangely detached from the jollity around him, had stood back with tankard in hand and watched. He saw Rose Hutch led on to the floor by Jim Merridew, though it was Edward Turner who received the fullness of her smile, and Edward's side she returned to when the dance was over. Wilkie and Edna Hutch kept casting each other the sort of glances typical of a couple long at harmony together. Nor had it escaped Nathan's notice how bright-eyed and girlish his mother had looked since the day Stanton Hayles had brought her home from Hadnall in the trap. Plainly something in which he had no part was abroad in the air.

Dorcas had attended, resplendent in emerald velvet, and presented Chrissie with a farewell gift of a Webb tea service in the new Royal Violet design, crated and packed in straw in readiness to be transported by rail to its new destination.

As the merrymaking drew to a close, Nathan had left off drinking to take the final dance with Chrissie. She had felt fragile in his arms, like a little hedgerow bird, and yet he knew the strength in that small frame and treasured the moment, locking it away in his mind to be taken out and reminisced over in times to come.

The sound of a robin brought Nathan back to the present moment. Chrissie had reached the end of the cart track now and was setting off for the lane end to await the carrier.

The air was clean and cold, the sky a clear eggshell blue, and on the drystone wall close by the robin piped another joyful phrase of notes. Nathan wondered how it could all be so perfect when his soul was being rent apart.

Shivering, for his former robust health was not yet fully returned, he let his glance roam around his land. He recalled the fineness of the tilth under the plough, took in the grazing meadows, patched now with snow, and home paddock, stoutly fenced thanks to the efforts of his men. He thought of the leas of good red clover they would sow come spring. His gaze travelled on to the bare black tracery of the orchard, home to the winter-quiet skeps and their slumbering bees. Lingering a while on the house, snug beneath its mended roof, he watched the tall chimneys huffing the blue smoke that spoke of warmth and comfort within.

Home. Nathan felt his throat constrict.

He heard the clop and jangle of the approaching carrier's cart. The moment was almost here. The vehicle pulled to a stop. Nathan looked on as Chrissie tossed her bundle into the back and took her place beside the driver.

The man had barely cracked the whip before the mail-boy came trudging along, hailing them down. A letter was passed over; the cart moved on once more. Nathan frowned, craning to see. Chrissie's head was bent, as if she was poring over what she had just received, but the vehicle was now passing between high hedgerows of holly and ivy and out of view.

He heard the trap stop again, caught the driver's strangled oath, and then Chrissie appeared, running wildly, her hair escaping its pins, her baggage bouncing on her shoulders.

Before he knew it, Nathan was striding, almost running, down the hillside towards her. Seeing him, she let her bundle fall and increased her pace, stumbling a little on the snowy, uneven ground. Then she was in his arms, sobbing and laughing at once.

'It's all right,' she gasped, looking up into his face as if she could never get enough of him. 'There was a letter from Daniel. It's been a while since he wrote and I was anxious. He'd been mulling things over. He says this is where I really belong.

'I know it's only what others have been telling me, but, don't you see, coming from him — it makes it right.'

The robin sang louder now; it was all Nathan could do not to join him. 'You're staying?' he said, wanting to hear it from her own lips. 'You're not going back?'

'No. Oh, no! Daniel has released me. I'd never actually promised to wed him, but it felt that way and I know he believed I would. He says it's clear where my heart lies and he wishes me well. Dear Daniel. I hope he finds happiness with someone else. He truly deserves it.'

'And you? Are you happy to be giving up all you've striven for?'

She sent him a nod.

'More than happy. Nathan, please . . . ' she whispered, almost afraid to go on. 'Tell me I'm not mistaken. You do want me to stay?'

'After what I've just heard? My darling girl, you actually called me by my name!'

He gathered her to him and held her close.

He had never before dared to dream of such a moment and he wondered what it would be like to kiss her. But she stood there so quietly in his embrace, the sweet curve of her cheek resting against the roughness of his coat, that it was enough simply to bow his head to hers and hold her, savouring the closeness. Then, of one accord, they drew apart and walked hand in hand, back to where the farm waited.

The robin watched them go, its bright black eyes knowing, and for the couple it was as if the whole world sang a benediction.

Nathan, in years to come, was to remember it clearly; the robin's song, the shimmer of wintry sun on snow, and at his side the girl he had thought lost to him, keeping step with him as they headed for home.

We do hope that you have enjoyed reading this large print book.

Did you know that all of our titles are available for purchase?

We publish a wide range of high quality large print books including:
Romances, Mysteries, Classics
General Fiction
Non Fiction and Westerns

Special interest titles available in large print are:
The Little Oxford Dictionary
Music Book
Song Book
Hymn Book
Service Book

Also available from us courtesy of Oxford University Press:
Young Readers' Dictionary
(large print edition)
Young Readers' Thesaurus
(large print edition)

For further information or a free brochure, please contact us at:
Ulverscroft Large Print Books Ltd.,
The Green, Bradgate Road, Anstey,
Leicester, LE7 7FU, England.
Tel: (00 44) 0116 236 4325
Fax: (00 44) 0116 234 0205

LOVE VIRTUALLY

Daniel Glattauer

It begins by chance: Leo receives e-mails in error from an unknown woman called Emmi. Being polite he replies, and Emmi writes back. A few brief exchanges spark a mutual interest in each other, and soon Emmi and Leo are sharing their innermost secrets and desires. The erotic tension simmers; it seems only a matter of time before they will meet in person. But they keep putting off the moment — the prospect both excites and unsettles them. And Emmi is happily married. Will their feelings for each other survive the test of a real-life commitment? And if so, what then?

ANOTHER HOME, ANOTHER LOVE

Gwen Kirkwood

Rosemary Palmer-Farr loves farming and animals — her childhood was spent mostly at Bengairney Farm with her dear friends the Carafords. Now a young woman, she wants to prove her worth in running the gardens of her father's dwindling estate. However, her mother Catherine only wants her to secure a good marriage and believes that tenant farmers like the Carafords are inferior. So when her daughter's childhood friendship deepens into love, Catherine takes action to keep the young couple apart. She throws her daughter into the company of eligible young gentlemen whom Rosemary despises, yearning only for Sam's love . . .

LADY ELEANOR'S SECRET

Fenella-Jane Miller

Lady Eleanor feels destined forever to endure the misery of living as an unpaid governess to her brother Edward's children — until she meets Alexander, Lord Bentley. Alex is seeking a suitable wife to care for his children, leaving him to live freely. Then, mistakenly believing he's compromised Eleanor, he makes her an offer, and she accepts with delight. However, on discovering his real motive, Eleanor is horrified. If she tells him the truth he will surely send her away. And while Edward, needing his sister's inheritance, plans to separate them, will Eleanor's secret also ruin everything when it is revealed?

SECOND THOUGHTS

Sandra Heath

The dashing Lord Carismont could take any girl of the *ton* for his wife, but the widower has his daughter's interests at heart. Requiring a governess, he interviews Kate Kingsley and believes he's discovered a suitable mother for his little girl. Kate, a young widow with a son to care for, is offered a marriage of convenience and security. Hesitantly, she accepts his proposal. However, when she arrives at his castle off the coast of England, someone — or something — is determined to keep them apart . . . and only the magic of true love can dispel the doubts she now feels.

DRIFTING SHADOWS

Christina Green

Life on a Dartmoor tenant farm is hard and when Becky Yeo meets Joseph, a travelling labourer and folk-singer, her desire is to change her own life. Then, disobeying her family, she refuses to marry Nat, the farm bailiff. She finds work as a kitchen maid at the Manor House, which harbours a dark mystery concerning her family. Meanwhile, Nat, seeking revenge, blackmails her. When Joseph returns, his love for Becky becomes clear and he must challenge Nat for Becky's hand. But after her secret is revealed, can Becky keep her family together and prevent Joseph from leaving once again?

THE STATISTICAL PROBABILITY OF LOVE AT FIRST SIGHT

Jennifer E. Smith

Stuck at New York's JFK airport, seventeen-year-old Hadley Sullivan faces being late for her father's second wedding in London. And she's not even met her new stepmother. Then, in the waiting area she meets the perfect boy. Oliver is British, with his own reasons for not wanting to return home to London. He's booked in seat 18C. Hadley is in 18A. On the long flight from New York to London they get on very well . . . Unfortunately, landing at Heathrow, Hadley and Oliver lose track of each other in the airport chaos — and she doesn't even know his last name . . .